WORTH THE WANT

BEA BORGES

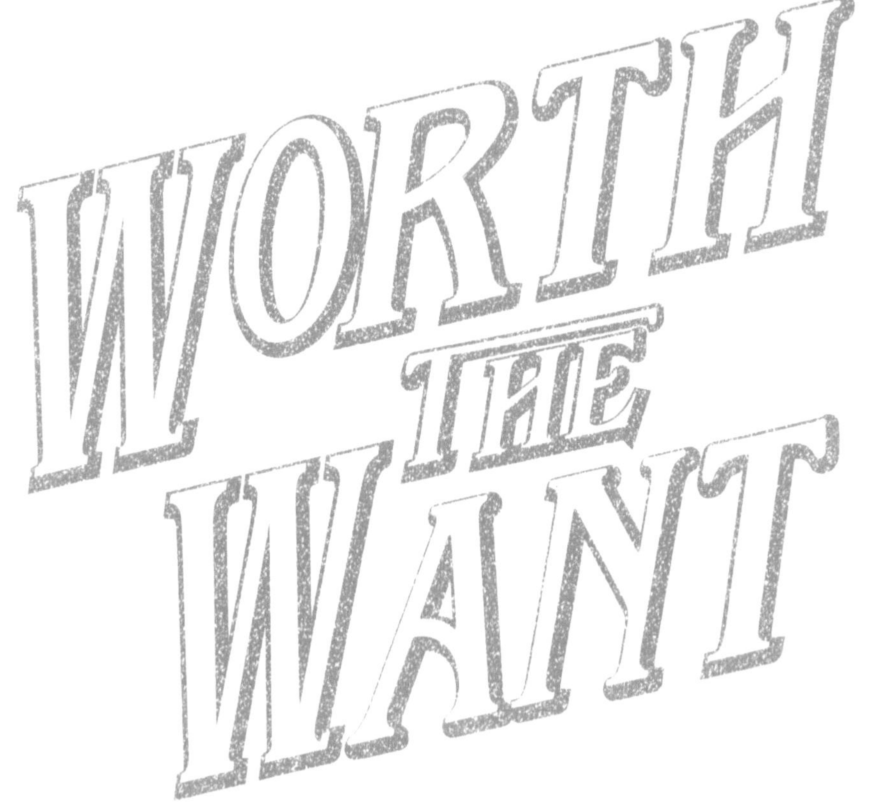

WORTH THE WANT

BEA BORGES

*This one's for the caretakers. We come in all shapes and sizes.
Some of us were born into the role, while some of us were
thrown into it.
I hope this is a gentle reminder to you that it's okay
to let someone take care of you for a change.
You deserve it.*

XO, Bea

CONTENT WARNINGS

Hello readers!

Worth The Want is a love story at its core, and while it's full of sweet and swoony, and humorous moments, it also deals with sensitive subjects that some could find distressing. Please read these content warnings before the book. Your mental health should be taken care of.

+death and loss
+health issues
+violence (on and off page)
+explicit sex

"C'mon, Knox, one little drink won't kill you." Slurring, with a shot glass clutched in each hand, Allen attempts to convince me to take one with him. Only, there won't be much of the clear liquor left in the small glasses after he's done waving them around in the air at me. Grabbing one from him, I set it on the table in front of me and watch as he downs his, then reaches for the same one he offered me just seconds ago.

"I think you've had enough for the both of us," I tell my colleague. His response is a respectable *boo* followed by flipping me the bird. "You know what? After that charming display, I think I'll go get us another round," I announce, placing my palms on the table and standing.

"Hell yeah! That's what I'm talking about. Let loose a little, Holloway." He throws his hands up in victory, tossing the rest of the shot of tequila behind him.

"Of water," I deadpan. A few of our coworkers chuckle, but I see them nod in agreement. "It's Tuesday, Allen, you'll have a new case on your desk in the morning, and you have that meeting with the partners to look forward to."

"Yeah, yeah. Always the buzzkill," he accuses, casting an arm in my direction.

I drum my hands over the tabletop. "Guilty as charged. I'll be back with the waters." More boos follow me as I walk toward the bar, contemplating pulling an Irish goodbye. Only if I order a car for them, I don't trust them to get into it, not without force. I don't get out much, but when I do, it always seems to fall to me to make sure everyone makes it home safe.

A few years ago, I might have joined in on the festivities. Hell, maybe even a few months ago I would've, but lately I've been doing my best to cut all the shit out that doesn't serve me. I guess that's what happens when you're thirty-seven, and despite making all the right career moves—making all the appropriate connections—none of them make you feel fulfilled.

In a few years, when my contract is up, I'll move back to Silverthorne to open my own law firm. Family law isn't something I've been able to practice here in the city, but it's something I'm looking forward to offering to the community back home. *Home.* I miss the mountains and everything that comes with them. Hiking in upstate New York has its charms, but it isn't Colorado. Colorado holds more for me. The peaceful evenings and the stars on a clear night. Nothing beats a quiet night in the mountains.

Staying in the city was never the plan for me, it's just where I ended up after law school. When I was offered this job, unsure if it was the best fit—it's not—I knew it would allow me to put money away while getting the experience I know will be beneficial in the long run. Being away from family and friends back home has been challenging though.

Making friends doesn't come easily for me, and when I do manage, it's a struggle to keep up with them. I've been lucky to go home for all the major holidays, except for the Christmas my whole family made the journey here. Seeing as it was my first year at the firm, I wasn't able to take the time off, but the picture I have of us all in Times Square has been a treasured memento while away from them.

Now it's been six months since I've been home—and that visit wasn't my *finest* moment. Drinking too much, I ended up doing some things I knew better than. Vague memories of a woman on my lap in the bar, an unfamiliar bedroom, and the smell of too-sweet perfume cloud my brain. Shaking off the memory, my feet carry me to the bar where I hold up a couple fingers to catch the bartender's eye.

"And who do we have here?" a sultry voice drawls at my side. Turning, I'm met with a practiced, self-assured smirk of a young woman, her eyes already grazing over my body like I'm what she ordered for dinner. She's propped against the bar, leaning on her elbow. The shirt she has on ties behind her delicate neck, which is left exposed with her hair pulled up into a ponytail. She's beautiful.

Looking into her heart-shaped face, I can see what she's trying to put off—confidence radiates from her. I can also tell by the innocence in her light-brown eyes that she's young. Really young. Too fucking young for me. Believing she's twenty-one is a stretch, and I'm not that limber.

"Not happening," I tell her before turning back to the bar.

"Hey!" She laughs. "You didn't even give me a chance."

Sighing, I turn back to her. "Nothing personal. I just don't entertain girls with daddy issues." At that, her mouth falls open, but it's only delighted shock that I find in her expression; not a hint of outrage in sight.

"You know, that would feel pretty fucking personal if I didn't happen to have a *great* relationship with my father," she tells me, placing a hand on her cocked hip. "I really think you should buy me a drink now. It only seems right after that unprovoked insult." She flutters her long lashes at me, making me grin. She's funny, but still entirely too young for me—and possibly to even be drinking. I'm preparing to say just that when I'm startled by another woman's voice shouting beside me—practically in my ear.

"What the fuck, Han?! You said you were going to the bathroom. I've now been to three different bars!" Glancing over my shoulder, I see her profile. Upturned nose adorned with a thin gold hoop, dark-brown hair just to her collarbone, scowling brown eyes, and glossy pink, pursed lips. She's staggeringly beautiful—and small. It's not uncommon for women to be shorter than me, but this one is tiny.

"I *did* go to the bathroom...I just also *left* the bathroom and ended up here. The hotel bar was so stuffy. You know that's not really *me*," the younger woman—*Hawn*—answers.

"You're eighteen years old, you don't know *who* you are," Tiny deadpans, pinching the bridge of her nose. A laugh escapes me, and I try to smother it with a cough. She sounds like me when I'm talking to my little sister. I also find the fact that *Hawn* is eighteen humorous but quickly figure out that I shouldn't.

Tiny turns the full scope of her fury on me then. I hold my hands up, ready to surrender. She may be small, but I have a feeling she makes up for it with attitude.

At the sight of her, I forget what I'm about to say, only able to take her in now that she's fully facing me. Looking into those big, brown eyes; they're dark, almost black in color, I'm momentarily stunned until I realize she's speaking *to me*, and she does not look happy. "Yeah, buddy. She's *eighteen*." She stresses the word. "So go find someone else to be your sugar baby." She casts her arms as wide as they'll go, encouraging me to leave. My lips twitch. She can't be much older than her friend.

"Oh my god! Please stop it, you are so embarrassing. I am not a child in need of mothering—*or fathering*." Eighteen-year-old—*Hawn*—throws the last word at me. This is none of my business, and I'm happy to butt out immediately, but this woman, this tiny woman has ensnared me. I can't look away.

"Then maybe don't run off—*alone*—in the murder capital of the world, trying to end up on an episode of *60 minutes*, and I'll start believing you. You never think about anyone but yourself, and you're not exactly doing a good job of that either." Her hands are like a second voice, ghosting through the air, echoing her words.

I hear a surprised gasp, looking between them. "That's not true, and you know it. I shared my lunch with Cecily Armstrong in fifth grade when her mom packed her a tuna sandwich, and she was too embarrassed to eat it," *Hawn* counters, and Tiny lets out a startled laugh before an adorable snort slips free.

"Han. Please just tell me when you want to leave somewhere, or go somewhere, I'll go with you. We're supposed to be scouting the area *together*. Mom and Dad will kill me if something happens to their baby before she moves here." *So she's her sister. Older sister.*

"You're exaggerating, and I repeat, I am *not* a child. I can handle myself."

Tiny sighs. "You wouldn't say that if it were true. Can we go now?" she asks.

The con artist faces me then.

"Any chance you're still buying me a drink?" she asks.

"None." I give it to her straight, and she makes a pouty face before answering her sister.

"Fine, let's go then. Lead the way, Girl Scout." At that, Tiny's mouth pops open, and she lets out another laugh. It's the cutest thing I've ever heard; the sound has my lips curving again in response.

"You are such a bitch! *You* were a Girl Scout too!" she tells her as they both break out into laughter. I watch them reach for each other, their laughter shaking their bodies. If I didn't just hear their conversation, I wouldn't believe they had ever argued. It's the kind of bond you can only share with a sibling. The way anger is so easily dissolved with laughter or a terrible pun.

It reminds me of when my younger brothers physically fought over Alder getting hit in the head with a baseball bat, but they ended up laughing over the way Rhett had pronounced the word accident, "Axtident" when screaming "I didn't mean to! It was an axtident!"

It's starting to feel like I'm intruding, and I go to turn, when a small hand wraps around my forearm, I note the light-pink shade of her fingernails as I'm pulled back into their conversation. "I'm s-so sorry you have to witness th-this." She barely gets the words out, laughter causing her to stutter, her high cheekbones are now flushed pink. I spot a few freckles peeking through, and those combined with her short hair brushing her bare shoulders is unexpectedly the sexiest thing I can remember seeing.

"It's fine. You ladies have a good evening." Nodding, I turn my back again, effectively disconnecting her body from mine, and *damn,* I already miss the weight of her hand on me. They laugh a few moments more before I hear the scrape of the barstools being pulled out. *So they're staying?*

"I'm just going to the bathroom. I'll be right back." Tiny must be giving her a look because there's another laugh before she assures her that she'll only be a couple of minutes. The bartender comes by, and I ask for five waters and a club soda with lime.

"Not drinking tonight?" That bright voice from earlier asks from the stool next to mine.

Twisting, unable to fight the pull, our eyes connect. "The group I'm here with has drunk enough for the whole bar," I tell her.

"But not you?"

"Designated driver."

"That tracks," she says, nodding.

"Is that so? In what way?"

She looks at me, eyes shining with humor. I'm caught up in them again, admiring their unique shade of brown. "You just look like you would be the designated driver," she tells me while taking a sip of her rum and Coke.

"And what does that look like exactly?" I ask, turning my body to fully face her now.

"Oh, don't be offended. I know what one looks like because *I'm* typically the D.D. Takes one to know one and all that," she admits.

I nod toward her drink, and she grins before whispering, "It's just a Coke, no rum." She adds a wink at me and it's so fucking cute.

"I'm Knox," I introduce myself, holding my hand out to her. She takes it, and my whole body hums.

"Nice to meet you, Knox."

She doesn't tell me her name. Just gives me a sweet smile.

"Do you live around here?" I ask, sounding a little too hopeful, but she shakes her head.

"I'm only in town for a few days with my sister. What about you?"

"I *do* live around here."

"But you're not *from* New York." She surmises. I try not to bristle at her comment.

"And what makes you say that?"

She cocks her head to the side, her short hair once again brushing against her bare shoulder where her shirt has slipped off, then she looks back toward the table I've come from. "I can just tell," she says, sipping her Coke.

I narrow my eyes. "And if I told you I was born and raised here in The Big Apple?"

She shrugs her shoulders, a small laugh escaping her lips. "You weren't, so you'd be lying." The way she's so sure of herself is as equally annoying as it is attractive.

"You seem pretty confident in your assessment. I have to know what's giving me away. What's making me stand out?"

"Besides calling it *The Big Apple*?" she teases before studying me. Openly.

Her eyes travel up and down my body. She takes her time looking at my shoulders, down to the unbuttoned collar of my dress shirt where my chest hair is peeking out to the rolled-up sleeves at my forearms. Her eyes flick back to mine, her cheeks flushing with her grin. I've been checked out before, I'm not uncomfortable with my body—but having her eyes roam over me like she can remove my clothing with her mind is making my neck hot. I *want* her to keep looking at me.

She clears her throat. "Well," she starts, turning to face me on her stool. "I'm afraid my inspection isn't all that thorough, and I don't know if I can pinpoint it for you, but I'm not sure you can help it, Knox. You just...stand out." She's giving me a shy smile that my fingers itch to reach out and trace the curve of.

"And what could I do to help you be more thorough?" I ask her before I can overthink it. *Flirting*—if that's what we're doing here—isn't something I'm well-versed in.

Her eyes spark at the question. "Hmm..." She taps her chin thoughtfully, playfully, before answering. "I can think of a few things—none of them appropriate for a hole in the wall bar, unfortunately." My mind works overtime to come up with other venues—my bed being number one on the list. *I stop the thought in its tracks.*

Tiny isn't going to ask me to take her to bed tonight, she's here after tracking down her sister, and she's not going to leave her now. Not wanting this to be the only chance I have with her, I say the only thing I can think of in the moment. "What about a pizza parlor? Tomorrow?" *Smooth, Knox.* I don't ask women out in the city. I don't ask women out, period. The last time I was on a date was in college, but there's something about her. She looks at me in a way that leaves me wanting. I want to hear all her thoughts and watch her hands dance around in the air while she tells me them.

The look on her face is hard to read. I see the shock; she wasn't expecting a date—but she also looks curious? Tempted even? That makes two of us. She turns away from me abruptly.

Okay, I guess there's my answer. This is one of the reasons I don't make a habit of approaching women.

I can't read the room. Here I thought she was intrigued. *Interested* even. Now her back is to me, and I'm disappointed to say the least. I reach for the waters that have been sitting next to me, untouched, but the feel of her hand on my arm again stops me. She's holding her phone out to me, biting her lip.

"Put your number in," she orders. My lips twitch, and I do as she says, feeling more relieved than I want to admit.

"Can I have yours?" I ask her, but she shakes her head.

"No. Tell me where this pizza place is, and when I should be there." Once again, I do as she says as she types something into her phone before her sister gets back to us. "I'll see you tomorrow." Her smile mirrors my own. I don't remember the last time I felt like this—if I ever have.

This compelling attraction and need to see someone again.

"I'll see you then. I'm looking forward to a more thorough evaluation."

"Looking forward to giving it," she quips.

Content for now with the promise of seeing her again, I grab the waters before heading back to my friends, already anticipating the pushback over me cutting them off.

Later that night, after I get everyone home safe, I feel my phone go off in my pocket as I clear the door to the lobby of my apartment building. Smiling, because I assume I know who it is. *I guess Tiny couldn't wait to talk to me either.* But when I pull my phone out, it's a contact already in my phone. A name I haven't given much thought to flashes across the screen. Fingers hovering, I contemplate answering.

After six months of no contact, I had assumed she wouldn't need closure. It was one night—one night I don't even remember that well, if I'm being honest. Scrubbing a hand down my face, waiting for the elevator doors to open, and desperate to get to bed, I hold my still-vibrating phone. Why would she be calling me now? I thought we had an understanding after our last conversation.

The elevator dings as I look at my phone again. Sighing, I step between the open doors and tap the icon to answer.

"Emily?"

"Hey, Knox. I-I need to talk to you."

THREE YEARS LATER

Papers that were neatly stacked on my desk just this morning are now strewn across the floor and chair in the corner of my home office. I'm tying my tie with my phone tucked between my shoulder and my ear while also making sure all crucial documents make it into my briefcase. Somewhere between making Hazel breakfast and going to pack her day bag, my sweet, *almost*-three-year-old decided to throw the curated files I needed for my case this morning—everywhere.

That paired with the phone conversation I'm having is making my jaw sore from how tight I'm clenching it.

"No," I say out loud, tapping the speaker on my phone, and setting it down to adjust the loop around my neck under my collar.

"Pleeease," the small voice whines.

I rub at my temple. "Like I told Florence earlier—no."

"Knox. There's nowhere else I can think to put her, and it

won't be forever! Just until we can get the plumbing fixed," my baby brother's fiancée rambles from the far side of my desk where I have my phone sitting. Win's been like a sister to me since I've known her, which means she annoys me just as much as Florence.

"You don't even know her, Winnie, and you're asking me to let her stay at my house?" I ask incredulously, hoping she sees the problem.

"It's not like she would actually be at *your* house, Knox. Just down the road." *Only a half mile.* "Out of the way. And I kind of know her! I like her. She was great on the phone. You probably won't even notice she's there," she tells me. I huff, not believing that for a second. "Come on. Just a small favor for your soon-to-be-sister." I can almost hear the fluttering lashes on the other end.

"You know I like my privacy, Win. I don't want someone coming in and out all the time, and I have Hazel to think about." The line goes quiet. "Win? Are you still there?" I ask.

"I'm here. Sorry, I'm just thinking...I'll try and come up with something. I'm sure everything will work out." She throws every ounce of guilt trip she can muster at me.

I sigh—in annoyance *and defeat*—tipping my head back. "It's not ready for someone to live there," I relent, and squealing fills the room.

"Thank you, thank you, thank you! You won't regret it!"

I scrub a hand down my face. "I already do. First sign of trouble, and she's out of there, Winnie. I mean it."

"Oh my gosh, will you stop? There isn't going to be any trouble, old man. She isn't some criminal I picked up fresh from the slammer. If your memory wasn't so bad, you'd remember I did do a basic background check on her—no priors to speak of."

Yeah, the one I suggested. "Indiana Holmes, twenty-seven, college graduate, glowing references—"

"I get it, Win."

"Anyway, Lo has a room for her tonight, so I'll drive over with her tomorrow, and we'll get the place all ready. You don't need to do anything other than be there so I can introduce you."

"Is that necessary?" I ask.

"She's new here, Knox. Just be nice," she sighs.

"Nice? I'm giving her a place to stay." *Unwillingly.* "I think that's nice enough."

"You don't fool me. I know you're a marshmallow somewhere deep inside...really, *really* deep down," she mumbles the last bit.

"Yeah, yeah. Keep thinking what you want. It's okay to be wrong, just don't come crying to me if she robs you blind."

She laughs softly. "Thank you. Really. I need this to work out, especially with the wedding coming up. I'm going to need her help, and she can't help if she doesn't have somewhere to live."

I grunt in response, and she giggles.

"Love you. Kiss Hazey for me." The mention of her affection for my daughter softens me a little.

"I will."

"Tell her sleepover soon!"

"Bye, Winnie."

"Bye! See you tomorrow!" I tap my phone and run a hand through my hair. I know this isn't a good idea, but now I've already agreed, creating unnecessary work for myself. No one's been in the guesthouse since the fall camping trip. I haven't even bothered to look at it all winter. I'll need to make sure the thermostat and water are working before Winnie brings her new manager over tomorrow. *Indiana.* She sounds like a character—literally.

Sighing, I turn my attention back to more pressing matters. Like getting me and my daughter out the door so I'm not late for this meeting.

"Hazey!" I call for my tiny tornado. "Have you finished your breakfast?"

"No!" she shouts back to me, then starts giggling like it's the funniest thing she's ever told me. Sounds about right. I take a calming breath, trying not to let the fact that my alarm didn't go off this morning, due to a random power surge, interfere with how I interact with her. My frustration is not on her little shoulders.

"Well, we may have to take it to go because I need to drop you off at Grammy and Grandpa's house this morning." *Because time is not on our side.*

"Okay, Daddy!" she happily agrees. Hazel Holloway is my personal ray of sunshine. No matter life's inconveniences, her love will always be my guidepost. Getting spoiled by my entire family—with or *without* my permission—would make a better case for her being a bit of a brat, but she's always had this sweet nature about her. I smile thinking about my siblings and their friendly competition to earn the title of Hazel's favorite. *An ice cream cone here, a stuffed animal bigger than her there.*

Grabbing the last document I need and walking from my office, I pass Hazel holding a blueberry pancake in one hand and a doll in the other, singing. I look from her little hands to the messy, soft, brown waves sticking out from on top of her head. An errant thought, one that I try to keep hidden even from myself, pops into my head. *It would be nice to have someone else here.*

"Looks like Grandma will get to do your hair at her house today, dragonfly."

"Okay!" she answers me, dancing slightly in her highchair.

"Let's get you out to the truck," I tell her, lifting her from the chair and grabbing her day bag beside my briefcase on the way out the front door.

After setting Haze into her car seat, I get in my old truck, setting my things in the passenger seat before pulling away from our house on the lake. There's still mist from the morning rising off it, catching the cresting sun's glow. The meadow between our place and the guesthouse is starting to sprout the wildflowers Hazel and I sprinkled last summer, bringing some color to the valley.

My brothers and I stumbled across this place looking for a spot to fish when I was a junior in high school. It sat vacant for years until I moved back home. The big house was bare bones, not having been taken care of over the years, and even those had to be replaced before renovations could start. The small guesthouse that sits just under a half mile down the road disappears in the rearview. Taunting me with the realization that someone will be living there by tomorrow.

It's been just the two of us out here for over two years now. Glancing back at Hazel in the rearview, I see her holding up her half-eaten pancake. It's hard to believe she'll be three soon. *Could it really have been that long?* When I answered that call years ago, it flipped all the carefully laid plans I had for my life upside down.

Hearing those two words. Two words that were only the

beginning of my life changing. Changing plans, changing jobs, and ultimately changing my address.

Now I have new plans—all revolving around the little girl singing and munching happily on a blueberry pancake in the backseat. I turn the radio up slightly, and she starts singing louder with Shania. I grin, knowing she has no clue what "No One Needs To Know" is about, but damn, she's got a set of pipes.

After kissing Hazel's chubby cheek goodbye, I take off down my parents' driveway, heading into my office in town.

I enjoy my job as a small-town lawyer, working small-town cases. It feels more fulfilling knowing the people I'm working for are deserving of the help I can provide them. It was an adjustment, but one I'm grateful I've been able to make. Smaller office, but you can't beat the mountain view.

Looking at those mountains that I never tire of, I pull onto the side street that backs up to the office building, seeing the familiar words Holloway Family Law Offices etched into the frosted glass on the door. Wishing I had time to get a coffee but knowing I only have fifteen minutes, I get out of my truck. Forgoing the caffeine, I'm ready to get my day back on track when I see the blue SUV parked across from the office, letting me know my secretary is already here.

Not having a very strenuous workload, she only works part-time for me and another office in the next town over. She's a nice woman—a bit forward every time I've seen her around town—but she's always kept it professional in the office.

She's pretty enough—*and she knows it*; funny, smart, and at one time I thought about the possibility of us going out—but then I overheard her on the phone telling someone she can't stand kids. I haven't entertained the idea of her again.

"Good morning, Knox. How was your weekend?"

"Morning, Cora. It was fine," I tell her, walking down the hall to my office. I find it best to keep my answers short and not to ask her any questions. Last time I made that mistake, I was held hostage by her long-winded answer.

"Would you like a coffee this morning?" she asks, coming to stand in front of me, blocking my escape. As much as I don't want to, I find myself taking her up on the offer, hoping it will keep her busy.

"That would be great. Thank you."

"Of course. I was thinking of staying in town tonight. Are you gonna be around?" She looks up at me from under long, dark lashes, biting the side of her red bottom lip. Cora is a beauty, but I'm not interested in starting something with her.

"I have a few things to take care of back home tonight. Winnie and my sister have roped me into something. Sorry," I tell her.

"That's too bad." She pouts. "I'll just have to be patient," she adds wistfully. I give her a tight smile, unsure of what response I could give her that wouldn't be rude. Cora and I don't have a future as anything beyond friends.

Once I make it to my office, I open my briefcase and pull out the case files. Putting my glasses on to look them over once more, I can't help thinking about how much has changed in my job.

The type of services I provide now is a stark contrast to what I was doing those years I spent in the city. Instead of corporate clients, I mostly deal with property lines. Everybody believes somebody is trying to encroach on their land.

Today is a little different. Ms. June Carter passed away last week, leaving her property, its contents, and all her holdings to the Sorel family. The Sorels had been taking care of her and her properties for her the last six years. No one in town batted an eye when this came out. It seemed only natural. The Sorels had come to live on Ms. June's property and seeing as she hadn't had a visit from any actual relatives in ten-plus years, they were more than just caretakers. Ms. June saw them as her family.

"Here's your coffee, Knox. Black right?" she asks.

"Appreciate it, Cora."

"Of course. Let me know if you need anything else," she tells me, smiling as she backs out of my office. I don't miss her emphasis on *anything*. It was about as subtle as Hazel is when she's asking for dessert before dinner.

Opening my laptop, it's still on the last web page I was on, looking up Ms. June's nephew's lawyer. The law firm representing him is a larger one based out of New York. I'm a little surprised he was able to secure their representation, seeing as they mostly work with high-profile clients who come with high-profile cases, but I have no doubt he knows someone who knows someone.

At the sound of the building's front door opening, I set my cup down before standing.

"Good morning. How can I help you?" I hear Cora say.

"I'm here to meet with Knox Holloway." I hear a man's voice tell her.

"Is he expecting you, Mr....?" Cora's voice remains polite.

"Carter. Yes, he should be expecting me."

"Oh yes, I see your name here on his schedule." *He's my only meeting today, but I do appreciate Cora's professionalism.* "Let me walk you to his office."

I hear footsteps coming toward me, and then Cora pops her

head around the corner. "There's a Mr. Carter here to see you," she announces, then she looks back to the front. "And it looks like another member of your party has just arrived as well."

"Thanks, Cora. You can send him back." I tell her. She smiles and heads back to the front.

A man comes into view. His chin is tipped slightly in the air and there's an overly cordial expression on his face. I give him a tight smile, holding out my hand to him.

"Hello. Knox Holloway," I introduce myself as another man with a suit walks in behind him, his lawyer, I presume.

"Kirk *Carter*." He emphasizes the last name. I suppose he wants me to know that he shares it with Ms. June. It does nothing to convince me he's deserving of anything of hers. Deserving and last names rarely have anything to do with each other.

"Nice to meet you, Mr. Carter."

"Alex Shepherd. I'll be representing Mr. Carter." The other man speaks up, holding his hand out.

I take it, shaking it as I speak. "Hopefully, we can get this resolved soon, and everyone can be on their way."

"Yes, there seems to be a problem with my client's late aunt's will. I'm sure once you take a better look at the facts, you'll be able to steer your client in the *right* direction." His words are dripping with condescension.

"I suppose we'll just have to look at all the facts to come to the right conclusion, won't we?" I challenge. His expression is mildly annoyed. *Me too, asshole.*

INDIANA

"Okay, Han. I need to go. I'm currently changing my clothes in a rest stop bathroom because of my flight delay, so I have no time to entertain you," I tease. "I love you. I miss you. Bye," I tell her out of reflex before quickly tapping my screen and taking a deep breath. There's still an hour drive ahead of me, and I need to mentally prepare myself to make a good first impression.

Being considered, let alone hired, to be a part-time manager for a bakery is still hard to believe. I have no experience with being a manager—or bakeries—but I *do* interview really well, and the owner seemed to like the mock-ups I did for the website. Working as a web designer for a hotel chain for the past four years was fine—until it wasn't. The job was good, and there was even a little bit of travel involved, but I was never a project manager. They were never really *my* projects.

With the encouragement of my sister, and the camera she lent me, I started going to photography classes on the weekends a year ago in an attempt to start a more freelance career, but that all seemed to fall apart just a few months later. Feeling unimportant—*like a lot of things.*

The rumbling on the sink lets me know I'm getting another call. Wrangling the zipper on my bag, I check the name.

Wyatt.

He must have heard through the grapevine—my parents— that I left the city. Wyatt isn't a bad guy, and even though my parents would like him to be, he also isn't *my* guy. I'm pretty sure, at least, I feel like I would know if he was. All our conversations started to end up the same way; he wanted to be together, and I...I didn't know if that's what I wanted.

A common thread in the tapestry of my life—I don't know what I want.

I've always had trouble sticking with things. There was painting, then the tumbling class, and before that it was dance. It seemed to get worse in my early twenties. I get restless and sometimes that comes across as flaky or impulsive—but this doesn't feel like it has in the past.

No, the urge to leave the city was there long before my breakup with Wyatt; it was there before last summer. I used to love the hustle and bustle of city streets. I loved being with my family, and the people watching from our apartment window. Now the noise makes my head ache, and the constant stimulation makes it hard for me to sleep or focus.

The vibrating stops, and I let out a sigh. It rumbles again, telling me I have a message, and I groan, looking at it.

WYATT

I heard you left. Are you okay?

I roll my eyes, biting the inside of my cheek. *Surely he*

knows I can see right through this. My fingers hover over the screen before I tap out a quick reply.

ME

I did. I'm fine, and you can tell them that.

Three dots appear immediately.

WYATT

They're just worried about you.

I rub at the ache in my shoulder. This requires a longer conversation, but I'm not ready for that. I don't know when, or *if,* I will be. I slip my phone into my bag, and close my eyes, inhaling deeply through my nose. Crossing my arms over my chest and wrapping my hands around my upper arms, I squeeze them once, then twice. After the third time, I feel more centered and able to continue my hunt for appropriate clothing.

When I've finished getting dressed, I look at myself in the dirty mirror above the sink. The dark spots under my brown eyes have lessened but are still easily visible, and I desperately need to have a moment alone with the sun.

I'll be different here. I have to be.

Closing my eyes in an attempt to fight through the swarm of bees that are trying to make a nest in my head, I take in another lungful of air.

I don't really know what I'm doing with my life—unsure if coming here is the right choice. I may be twenty-seven, but I still have so much to figure out. I'm not asking to have it all together, but having *some* of it together could be fun. Just enough to move the needle in a productive direction. I mean, I cut my own hair last week. It was just the bangs—but still.

Planning isn't really my area of expertise. Though, I'm not sure what you would expect with the upbringing I had. It was *chaotic*—in the most magical way. My parents are both artists, so eccentric and eclectic are just two of the words I would use to describe my childhood.

I like to think I'm *artsy,* but I'm definitely not an *artist.* I've learned I require a little more structure if I want my mental health out of the garbage. My sister has always been a different story. Melodic and energetic—Hana Holmes *is* music. Not in the way that she's a talented musician, but in the way that she knows the perfect song for every specific moment of your life. Not a single drop of personal musical talent in her body—but damn can she recognize it.

Hana—Han, as in Solo. I smile at the incredibly kitschy names my parents bestowed on the both of us. Han and Indiana. In the Holmes household, we consumed art in all forms: cinema, music, sculpting, dance—you name it, we tried it at least once.

Our parents are huge film buffs. We grew up hearing the intricacies of Harrison Ford movies—so much so that they would name their two daughters after two of his more famous characters. To be fair, I don't hate my namesake. In fact, I love *Raiders of the Lost Ark.* I genuinely thought I would be a history professor slash archaeologist up until the age of ten.

I fold my discarded clothes, placing them into my bag before zipping it up. I walk down the convenience store aisles, picking out a granola bar and a sparkling water from the coolers. Setting them on the counter, a rack of sunglasses and postcards grabs my attention. I pluck a pair of sunglasses for myself off their stand and a stack of postcards for Han. I've sent her a postcard from everywhere I've ever been. I'll need a few since I'm planning on being here for a while.

"Will this be all for you?" the cashier asks from behind the counter. He's older than me with salt and pepper hair, maybe in his fifties, but the kind smile on his face makes him seem younger.

"This should do it," I answer brightly.

He scans my items, putting them into a paper bag. "Receipt?"

"That's okay. Thank you. Have a good day," I tell him, grabbing my brown paper bag.

As I put on my cheap sunglasses, I give myself permission to believe this is all going to work out.

Stepping out of the automatic doors and walking back to my car, I take in my surroundings. The air is thinner already, not cool exactly, but crisp in a way that has my lips turning up and my mood lifting. It's hard to be in a bad mood when I'm surrounded by mountains as far as my eyes can see. A soft bubbling and trickling draws my attention to the creek running alongside the road.

The view makes me feel small. *Grounded.* Sometimes my issues feel so much bigger than me, like they can take on a physical form, towering over me. But looking at the stunning rock formations before me, my issues start to feel smaller too. Lifting my face to meet the light breeze that's ruffling my already messy hair, a reassuring thought comes to me. Maybe *this* is what I've yearned for.

Applying for this job may have been a spur-of-the-moment decision, but from the second I hit send on my application, I haven't been able to stop picturing what my life in Colorado could be. I bought a book titled: *Must Do Hikes In Colorado* and a backpack before I even got the call back from the bakery owner with the offer.

Accepting immediately, I started looking up rental properties. Searching online turned up no viable prospects, with the closest home being two hours outside of town. I was starting to get a little worried—only to get a call back thirty minutes later from my new boss saying she had a small cottage that was for rent, right off the town square, within walking distance to the bakery. She sent me one picture, and I was sold.

An hour later, I'm parked on the town square in Silverthorne. I study the buildings with my windows down, it's bright and there are spring flowers overflowing from decorative pots—suddenly, Colorful Colorado makes a lot of sense. An American flag waves in the breeze, and the mountains behind it give me a very patriotic feeling. I know a cover for a John Cougar Mellencamp cover when I see one.

I grab one of the postcards I bought at the gas station, wanting to document my first moments of this grand adventure I'm embarking on. I reach for the pen that's fallen out of my purse and jot down a few lines to Han.

> *It smells like pine trees and sunshine.*
> *It feels like possibilities.*
> *I love you. I miss you.*
> *Love, Indiana*

I spot the sign for Thistle and Sage bakery, quickly checking myself over again in the visor mirror—my shoulder-length hair is a bit windblown but otherwise I'm presentable. Reapplying my lip balm, I grab my briefcase containing my laptop from the passenger seat, my camera that I don't go anywhere without these days, open my door, and step into the sun—and my fresh start.

Inside the bakery I'm greeted by a small line of customers at the front counter and the most heavenly smell to ever grace my senses. The space is beautiful. Light and airy, with wood accents and a black-and-white tiled floor. I peek around the line to see a young woman behind the counter. She's smiling, chatting with customers, and getting them their orders. I'm not sure if I should wait here or knock on the door that leads into the back.

I decide to wait in line—but I'm second-guessing that choice. Waiting in line feels awkward, but so does walking up to the front and looking like I'm cutting in front of everyone. While I'm contemplating what I should do, I hear "next!" and it's already my turn.

"Hi!" I say brightly—*maybe too brightly*. "I'm the new manager-um, I'm Indiana. Hi." *Well, I botched that introduction perfectly.*

"Hi! Oh my gosh, it's so nice to meet you! I'm Winnie," she introduces herself, holding out a hand. I take it, noticing she's about my height of five foot one. Her eyes are a warm amber that's similar to the color of whiskey, and her smile reminds me of *something*, but I can't put my finger on it. She has her hair up on top of her head with a few dark curls escaping.

"It's nice to meet you too. I'm so sorry I'm later than we originally talked about."

"Oh no worries." She waves me off. "I have just a couple more orders to take and then it should be slowing down. Can I get you something while you wait? A coffee? Cinnamon roll?"

I glance in the display case, seeing a huge chocolate croissant.

"Could I have a hot tea? And maybe one of those chocolate croissants? They look too good to pass up."

"Of course. I might be biased, but they're a crowd pleaser and a personal favorite," she tells me, and turns to fill my order. "Is Earl Grey okay?"

"Yeah, that's perfect," I reply, looking over my shoulder, seeing a couple of people in line behind me. Not staring exactly, but definitely curious.

"Here you go! Pick any place you want, and I'll be over in just a few." she tells me with a smile, and I nod, grabbing my cup and pastry before walking to a table by one of the windows.

Once I sit down, I take a look out at the town. I've seen plenty of small towns—mostly on the Travel Channel—but there's something about this place. It has a very wholesome feel to it. I watch men and women walk in and out of the shops on the square, imagining what they're up to, what their story is. I've always liked telling stories.

A smile makes its way to my face, thinking about the last one I told. Han begged me for a bedtime story, and even if we're not kids anymore, she's still the baby, and I can't say no to her. The golden mermaid, whose magic scales were coveted, so she was forced to hide away so no one would discover her secret. Taking a bite of my croissant, I groan at the taste of the flaky pastry and chocolate melting on my tongue. I'm going to need five more of these immediately.

A hum comes from my mouth as I take my next bite of

buttery goodness, admiring the cascading mountains in the distance. When I stumbled across the job post, I spent a lot of time googling the area. With each new link I clicked on I was shown waterfall trails and rock climbing and mountain lakes the color of turquoise. I've been daydreaming of hiking here, of what it might be like, and if I'll enjoy it. I made a vision board and everything. I've never really been hiking—beyond the occasional walk in a park—but it's one of the things I'm most excited about. Maybe I've seen too many outdoor posters for Colorado, but being able to see the views I've been admiring in person sounds like a dream.

"Sorry about that," Winnie says at my side, stirring me from my daydreams.

"No problem at all. I'm the one who had to change things around in the first place."

"Your flight being canceled is a pretty decent excuse." She gives me a reassuring smile. "So, as we talked about before, along with working from home three days a week on the website, you'll be expected to work here two days as manager."

I nod. "Absolutely. I'm really looking forward to it. I've been checking out the website and have some ideas already. I may not know much about the inner workings of a bakery," I tell her. "But I *am* a very quick learner," I rush to add.

"I have no doubt you'll pick it up in no time," she reassures me, then her expression turns worried—nervous, maybe? "So, um...I have one small thing that I need to make you aware of."

"Okay...should I be worried? Is the bakery actually a front for illegal activity? Because I could be into that."

She laughs, but there's still an edge to it. "No. No, it's nothing like that. The job is legit, although it's good to hear you'd be down if it wasn't. It's your living arrangements."

"My living arrangements?" That wasn't something I expected her to say.

"Yes. So originally I had planned to have you rent my cottage, and that *is* still the plan long term, but, well...it flooded last night, due to a clogged pipe or something ridiculous, and we just caught it this morning."

"Oh. Okay." Well, that's disappointing. I had really been looking forward to settling into my own place tonight.

"I'm so sorry, Indiana. I don't know how this could have happened. I swear everything has been fine for months...*years* even."

"You mean you didn't *plan* to offer me a job and a place to live, and then clog a pipe and flood it as soon as I settled in?" I tease, trying to make light of a bad situation.

"Rhett, that's my fiancé, called his sister, and we have a room at the hotel in town for you tonight, but it's full after tonight for at least the next month."

"Oh. Okay. Well, I'll just get on one of my apps and see if I can find something else more long-term," I tell her. Inwardly, I want to have a little cry sesh, but the eldest daughter in me won't make Winnie feel worse than she already does.

"There isn't really anything for rent around here, but don't worry, we found you another place to stay." This conversation is starting to feel like a roller coaster.

"Hey, honeybee!" I glance up just in time to catch a bright smile and a flash of dark hair before a man bends in front of Winnie, kissing her thoroughly. *Damn.*

When he stands back up, Winnie's face is comically flustered, cheeks flushed red. She clears her throat. "Rhett, this is Indiana, my new manager. Indiana, this is Rhett, my fiancé."

"Nice to meet you, Indiana." He holds his hand out to me. *Holy fucking shit. This man can get it. Go, Winnie.*

"Nice to meet you too." I give his hand a shake.

"I was just about to tell Indiana about the place we found for her to stay," Winnie tells him.

Rhett blows out a breath. "In that case, I think I'll take off. Just wanted to say hi on my way home." He leans in to plant another kiss to her lips. "Bye, darlin'," he says against her lips. I grin. *So they're like* really *in love then.*

He nods at me. "See you around, Indiana," he tells me, then, under his breath, but also in a very distinct singsong voice adds, "if there's anything left of you." *What?*

"He's being silly. There will be plenty left of you." *Again... what?*

"I'm starting to feel like I'm missing something."

"The place we found for you is on Rhett's brother's property." That doesn't sound so bad.

"Brother, huh? Blood related?" I ask, teasing but also not.

She lets out a laugh but nods. "You know, you're not the only woman to ask me that in the last year, and the other woman ended up happily pregnant with the other brother." She sighs, staring at the opposite wall with a dreamy expression on her face. "I get it though. Those are some damn good genes."

"Hell yeah, they are. I'm looking forward to meeting this brother," I tease.

She laughs at that. "He may be as easy on the eyes as Rhett, but their personalities could not be any more different."

"Color me intrigued."

"Intriguing is actually a really good word for him. In all honesty, I'm teasing more than anything. He's a good man. The Holloways don't raise bad ones." She grins. I let that sink in.

Meeting a good man isn't really why I'm here, but it doesn't sound half bad.

We spend the next four hours working alongside each other. She shows me how to display pastries, where everything goes in the back, the office space I'll be working in from time to time, and how to work the ovens. At the end of my shift, I even try my hand at making chocolate muffins and am downright giddy over how they turned out.

"The hotel is just around the corner and down a block, The Holloway Hotel. I can walk you over if you want. Florence had to leave, but she made sure to tell the chef in the hotel to send you up dinner," Winnie tells me when we're done for the day. *I'm guessing Florence must be the sister then.*

"Thank you, I'm sure I can make it."

"Okay, I'm sorry again about all of this."

"It's really okay. Sometimes things just happen." *And you can't change them even though you wish you could.*

"I guess you're right, but I still feel bad. Go ahead, get some rest tonight. Call me if you need anything, I live just off the town square."

"Okay, I will. Are you sure you don't need me to stay?"

"I'm good. Promise. I'm sure you're exhausted from traveling all day. I'll see you in the morning." *I am exhausted.*

"Alright, if you're sure. See you tomorrow, Winnie." The bell chimes as I back out through the glass door onto the sidewalk that will lead me to my bed for the night. I look back at the mountains, breathing in the cool air coming from them. I grab my camera out of its case and snap a couple of pictures. There's an old yellow pickup parked on the street, adding the perfect pop of color. Maybe I'm off to a slightly rocky start, but hey, there's a reason they call em' the Rocky Mountains.

KNOX

BABY LO

Knox, did you get the link I sent you?

ME

Yes, Lo. I got it.

BABY LO

Annnnd? Did you order it?

ME

Yes.

ALDER

I have entertainment!

RHETT

No one wants to see you reenact a mission… again.

IVY

I do.

WINNIE

••

RHETT

WINNIE, I SWEAR TO GOD.

WINNIE

Hahahaha. KIDDING. I only have eyes for you,
babe.

ME

Entertainment? Why does this concern me?

ALDER

Because…you don't want this party to
kick ass?

RHETT

That's too bad because this Dinosaur
Princess party is going to kick some serious
ass.

ME

Perfect. That's just what Hazel wanted.

WINNIE

Btw, I have the cake design ready to go.
Flavors are strawberry with a lemon frosting
as the princess requested.

ME

Thanks, Win.

BABY LO

Perfect! I'm so excited. I can't believe my little
Hazey baby is going to be 3! Mom and Dad
will handle the food.

ALDER

Is Dad grilling?

BABY LO

Yes, he insisted.

RHETT

Looking forward to another inappropriate apron.

IVY

I definitely am. The apron at Christmas is why I'm with Alder.

ALDER

I thought it was because I'm irresistible and unimaginably charming, but okay. 😈

IVY

No. It's because of your dad's apron. Sorry, Search and Rescue.

ME

That tracks.

ALDER

Chuckling, I set my phone down before turning my attention back to my laptop. I've been trying to narrow down the enormous document of Kirk's phone records. I'll need to have it all highlighted before I meet with Ms. June's nephew and his lawyer tomorrow afternoon. After our first meeting, we discovered that Kirk hadn't spoken to his aunt in over six years. No contact at all, even though he tried to claim phone calls and emails. Ms. June didn't even own a computer, so I knew that was a lie the moment it came out of his mouth. Which leads me to believe most everything else will be too.

The Sorel family moved into town a few months after Mr. Carter passed. The ranching job that Mr. Sorel moved his family here for was sold within months of them settling in, leaving him needing work. Ms. June caught wind of their predicament, and things fell into place quickly.

It's shitty that they even have to worry themselves with this right now. Ms. June was clear about what she wanted after she passed. Having your wishes respected is all you have left when you pass. Speaking of respecting someone's wishes, I'm going to need to have a talk with my family about respecting mine. The blatant display of emotional manipulation from Winnie and Lo this morning isn't a foreign concept. They've teamed up on more than one occasion over the years to get me to agree to their various escapades.

Shopping trips, letting them paint my nails, and of course, the time I drove them to Wyoming for fireworks because they *had* to have the big ones.

I'm really rethinking this tenant thing they've sprung on me. *At least it's temporary.* I prefer being alone on my property. There's a peace that comes with having the lake to myself whenever I need the exercise and quiet. My walks around the lake with Hazel, teaching her to fish without an audience, are special.

She'll be gone in a couple of weeks max. What's the worst that could happen?

An hour later, I'm slipping my laptop into my briefcase and walking out of the office. Time to go get my girl from Mom and Dad's. Thankful again for family being so close by, I scroll through the pictures Ivy and my mom have sent me today. In one, she's wearing a chef hat while helping my mom bake cookies, and it looks like Ivy taught her a new hand gesture. *Great.*

I make it out to my truck, and as I'm opening my door, I notice a woman holding up her camera toward the mountains. Her sunglasses and the shadow of downtown hide her face from my view. I glance at where she's looking. Having grown up here, sometimes I forget how amazing it is to be surrounded by these mountains.

When I turn my head back to the tourist, I see that she's already walking away. Making her way down the sidewalk with a bag under her arm, turning her head, looking around as she goes, taking everything in. I'm not sure why, but I smile before hopping into the driver's seat, tossing my things onto the bench seat beside me.

My engine revs loudly, and I pull away from the sidewalk. The drive to my parents isn't long, maybe twenty minutes. Shifting gears when I make it onto the two-lane highway that leads deeper into the mountains, I use the crank handle on the door to roll the window down and let in some fresh air.

This truck is my longest relationship. It's been there through all the stages of my life. My dad bought it to use as a farm truck, but after teaching me to drive it, I developed an attachment to it. With a little coaxing, he decided to let me keep it. I picked my first date up in it, had my first kiss in it, and I even brought Hazel home from the hospital in it.

Downshifting, I slow my speed to make the turn onto their tree-lined driveway. I drive the familiar side road without giving it much thought until the trees break and their house comes into view. With it, I see that my brother has joined the party out here today. He has Hazel on his back, and he's bucking around like a bronc at the rodeo.

Coming to a stop, I park my truck beside Alder's old Bronco. When I open my door, I'm greeted by the sound of Hazel's giggling. She's laughing so hard she can barely breathe. Ivy's laughter echoes my daughters from where she's sitting on the porch, enjoying the show her fiancé is putting on in the yard, holding her growing belly. Mom and Dad step out to see what's going on, my mom snorting as she takes in the scene before her. Seeing Alder act like a circus clown to make Hazel happy isn't new, but seeing Ivy watch him with undeniable affection is a welcome change.

"Alder, be careful with your niece!" Mom shouts, but she can't hide the laughter in her voice.

"Oh, she's tough though. So tough I can't even buck her off. Isn't that right, Hazey?"

"Yes! I'm tough!" she yells, grabbing two fistfuls of Alder's hair, holding on for dear life. He rears back, making a god-awful noise that I think is supposed to be a horse, before starting to buck again.

"Woo! Let's go, Hazey! Eight seconds!" Ivy shouts, and the whole porch starts counting.

"One, two, three, four, five, six, seven, eight!"

Cheers erupt, and Alder lies flat on the ground catching his breath. Hazel dismounts and takes an adorable bow. The sight of her proud face—I'm not sure how, but I find new ways to love her more every day.

I let out a whistle, and her head snaps in my direction.

"Daddy!" she shouts, seeing me across the yard from her. "Did you see me?"

"I saw, baby! You're a real rodeo champ," I call across the yard.

"I am! I am!" she yells, running toward me, full tilt. I worry she may trip, so I start running for her—arms open. I crouch, and when she hits my chest, it's like the other part of my heart is there again, making me whole.

"Hi, Hazel," I say, breathing in the smell of her tiny toddler head. "I missed you, dragonfly."

"I missed you too."

"Did you have so much fun with Andy Ivy, and Grammy today?"

"Yes, yes, yes!!" she chants at me, and I grin at my happy girl.

"That's good to hear." I tell her, standing with her in my arms, and walking over to the rest of the family.

"Hey, Knox. Busy day at the office?" my dad asks.

"Still working on the case for the Sorels."

He shakes his head. "It's really a shame someone would question how well that family took care of Ms. June."

"I don't think anyone is questioning that exactly, but they are questioning the validity of her will. I'm doing my best to ensure it holds up without having to go to court. And if all goes well, that should be the case."

He nods. "Good. I'm sure they're really thankful you're willing to do that."

"The Sorels are good people, and I like to help where I can."

"And that's very admirable, son." He claps me on the back and then goes to ask my mom a question.

"Hey, buckin' bronco, how's your back?" I greet my brother, who's standing by his girlfriend as she tries to tame his wild hair.

"Better than yours, old man." He shoots the taunt at me.

"Not too old to kick your—" I cut myself off, looking at Hazel smiling at me. "Tush," I finish. Ivy and Alder start laughing.

"Daddy said tush!" Hazel says, covering her mouth with her little hands, eyes comically wide.

"Such a potty mouth, Knox. Please be more selective with

your words," Ivy chides, unable to hide her grin. I look up at the sky, catching sight of the shiny silver SUV pulling up beside my truck. Florence gets out and comes to meet us on the porch.

"Hi, Hazey baby!" she greets Hazel first.

"Hi, Andy Lo." She smiles sweetly at my sister, then slowly leans her way, letting us know she wants Andy Lo to hold her now. Florence takes her, squeezing her tightly.

"Oh, Andy Lo missed you, sweet girl," she whispers, then to me says, "So how's Silverthorne's newest landlord?"

I roll my eyes. "Reluctant," I tell her, and she laughs a little at me.

"Oh, it'll be fine, and it's only for a few weeks—probably."

"What's this? Are you renting out a property?" my mom asks, my dad looking to me for an answer as well.

"I'm letting Winnie's new manager stay in the guesthouse down the road from me until she and Rhett can get her cottage's plumbing fixed. It's not a big deal," I tell them. Because to someone else, it probably wouldn't be that big of a deal. To me? Huge deal. Huge inconvenience. I'm already annoyed just thinking about someone else being out there.

"Winnie stopped by the hotel to bring some croissants for tomorrow morning and caught me up this afternoon. Apparently, she's great. A fast learner, funny...gorgeous," Florence informs us.

Gorgeous, huh? "Great, just what I need. More people who think they're funny," I muse.

"Honestly, it wouldn't hurt you to broaden your sense of humor, ya grouch. Isn't Daddy a silly grouch?" she asks Hazel.

"No! Daddy is not a grouch," she tells my sister with a very grouchy face of her own. I grin.

"See? I'm not a grouch at all, am I, babygirl?" My daughter looks at me, smiling.

"Nope." She pops the p loudly, and I grab her from Florence, spinning her in a circle, making her giggle.

"Alright, Hazel and I are gonna head out. I won't be heading into the office until noon tomorrow since I'm meeting my new tenant in the morning. Can I drop Hazel off around eleven thirty?"

"That will be just fine. Are you gonna help Grandpa feed some cows?" my dad asks Hazel.

"Yes, yes!" she says, clapping her hands.

"Oh good, I don't think I could do it without my best partner," he tells her.

"We'll see you tomorrow, sweet Hazel. I love you more," my mom says, kissing her cheeks.

"Bye, Hazey," Ivy calls from beside Alder. "I had so much fun with you today."

"Bye, Andy Ivy," she says to her, yawning. Both Ivy and Alder step forward to give her a hug and a kiss. If I do everything else wrong in this life, at least I've given Hazel this family. She'll always know how loved she is.

"You'll be ready for a bull in no time, Haze," Alder tells her, tapping his knuckles to her tiny closed fist. I stifle my eye roll.

"Night, everyone!" I call over my shoulder, carrying Hazel out to the truck. I get her buckled in, tucking her blanket and the shark stuffy she's obsessed with at the moment next to her. Pressing my lips to her head, and smoothing the wild hair from her face, I breathe her in before starting the truck. Our drive home is peaceful. The sun is starting to set, casting neon orange across the sky, painting the clouds with it, and reflecting off the lake's surface below.

When we pull up to our house, I check the rearview and see that Hazel has fallen asleep on the drive. I cut the engine and just sit there for a moment, listening to the distant sounds of an owl hooting and the frogs by the water. My mind wanders back to my brothers and how happy they are, how genuinely happy I am for them that they've found that.

Looking out over the water, I see the lone chair sitting on the dock, and just for a moment, I think seeing two wouldn't be so bad.

INDIANA

"Okay." The tiny woman claps her hands together. "Let's get you moved into your new place. Knox is probably waiting for us." *Knox.* The name plucks on a string tethered to an embarrassing memory. I quickly dismiss it, swinging my camera strap over my head. Winnie's here to take me over to my temporary home until the cottage is fixed, and the nervous energy in me is most likely just a side effect of having only tea in my system this morning.

"Sounds good, I just need to grab my bags over by the door."

"Need any help?"

"Nah, it's only two small bags. Should I just follow you?"

"Yeah, it's only about a thirty-minute drive or so, and it's a pretty one."

"Great. Everything I've seen so far has been beautiful. I can't wait to see more."

"I saw you had a camera. Do you take all the photos for the websites you work on?" she asks, pointing to my side where Han's camera hangs from the worn leather strap.

"I actually need to get a new one eventually. This is my sister's I'm borrowing. I haven't been the main photographer for the projects I've worked on, but I took all the photos for the mock-ups I showed you."

"Those were great. I'm chomping at the bit to see what you do with the site."

"Everything here makes me want to take a picture of it—Thistle and Sage is no exception. You did something special there."

"Ah, thanks. Well, you'll have plenty of sights at the lake. Knox's property is one of the most beautiful I've seen," she tells me before holding the door for me.

With every new snippet of information she gives me, it just makes me more excited to see this place. I let my mind wander as we walk out of the hotel and down the sidewalk to my car. I stow my bags in the trunk before getting into the driver's seat. Winnie pulls away from the curb, and I do the same, following close behind her as we clear downtown and make it to the main road.

As soon as we hit the two-lane highway, I roll my windows down, letting the wind whip my short hair around in front of my sunglasses. Being out on this road is surprisingly thrilling. I watch the mountains in the distance become bigger the further we travel into them. I'm daydreaming about exploring them when I see Winnie's right blinker ticking. Slowing, I turn onto a side road that takes us deeper into the forest.

If I didn't have a good sense about people, I might think Winnie was taking me to a secluded lake to murder me—or maybe I've just listened to one too many true crime podcasts on my runs.

We drive along a river for another ten minutes before we

turn again onto a winding dirt road, marked only by a mailbox that looks like a cuckoo clock. My chest aches at the sight. Making me homesick for a tiny apartment that's filled with laughter and eccentric art. I blink, and the trees start to thin.

When they do, I have to remind myself to also watch the road. This view is—indescribable. Stunning, unreal, movie set material. The smile on my face physically hurts because I'm grinning so hard. *Are you kidding me?* This is where I get to live?

A large, green, two-story house catches my eye, sitting just up the way a little farther. There's a familiar-looking yellow and tan truck parked beside it. It could be a coincidence, but it looks just like the one I took a picture of yesterday in town. We slow even more, coming to a stop in front of the big house. From here, I can see a smaller white one, similar to the big house, about half a mile down the dirt road from this one. It's so cute I can't stand it. I squeal. *Inwardly.* On the outside, I keep it together like an adult.

When I get out of my car, I'm drawn toward the sparkling lake. I push my sunglasses up onto my head, breathing in the fresh air. My vision begins to blur, emotion climbing up my throat as tears threaten. *Oh god, how embarrassing.* I wipe at my eyes and put on a bright smile, turning just as Winnie gets out of her car.

"Come on!" She waves me over, and I jog to her side as we approach the house.

"Winnie. It's gorgeous out here. I've never been anywhere like this before," I tell her, and then she does something that has my throat threatening to tighten again. Linking her arm into mine like we've been friends for years, she falls into step with me, sighing contently.

"I know. It's like a little secret hideaway. We love coming out here in the spring and summers, occasionally in the fall for a bonfire or camping trip." Her casual familiarity takes me by surprise but is absolutely welcomed. I squeeze her arm in mine once more before we take the final step up to the porch. Winnie knocks on the door before she rings the doorbell. I take another moment to peek behind us, admiring the view once more.

"You're late," I hear a deep, gravelly voice huff out behind me. I turn to meet the owner of that voice, who I presume will be my new landlord. Our gazes collide, a rush of recognition there. His navy-blue eyes widen slightly, confusion swirling in them. They widen further when Winnie stumbles backward, tripping over her own feet and into me, causing me to tumble off the porch into perfectly manicured hedges. *Shit.*

It's first time in years that I've seen the man who left me a little heart sick at a pizza place in Brooklyn, and I just showed up at his house without warning before falling off his porch.

"Indiana! Oh my gosh, are you alright?" I hear Winnie ask nervously. *I want to die.* Please just leave me here and tell my family that I had a great last few moments. I went peacefully, sinking into the ground—gracefully.

No such luck. As soon as I ask the universe to swallow me, the sunny day is eclipsed by *him. A god.* A god I would happily wor—

"Are you alright?" His deep voice scatters my thoughts as he reaches out to offer me his large hand. I gulp but take it. Electricity hums beneath my skin at the contact.

Upright again, I dust myself off. Maybe it didn't look as bad as I think it did—as bad as my ass feels. *That's gonna leave a mark.* "I'm fine. Happens all the time." *Okay, wait. What the hell am I saying? No, it doesn't.*

"Have you fallen off that many porches?" he asks, disbelief coloring the rich tone of his voice. My hands rub at my lower back where the hedges dug in.

"Well, actually no. I've stood on plenty, but this would be the first I've actually taken a tumble off of," I ramble, wiping my hands on my shorts. *Why am I so fucking nervous?*

"I wouldn't judge you if there had been more. I've fallen off plenty of them," Winnie tells me reassuringly. I can't help the laugh that escapes at her confession.

Looking back at Knox, my stomach does a little flip at his smirk. *Oh holy shit, he looks good.* Better than I remember. There's some crinkling happening around his ocean-blue eyes, and the specs of gray hair at his temples have me biting my lip. Don't get me started on the brawny-man build and the way his shirt fits snug across his chest. He's the most gorgeous man I have ever laid eyes on, and I've seen him before—been *stood up* by him before. *Fuck.* I have to look away to keep myself from staring. *Down, girl.*

"That's putting it lightly. How many times have you fallen on flat ground?" he asks her, his voice teasing now.

"Aaand we're done talking about me," she says in a singsong voice. "Knox, this is Indiana. Indiana, Knox." She waves her arm in our direction.

"It's nice to see you," I tell him, holding out my hand. *Again.* I add in my head. He's gigantic. I remember him being a big guy, but somehow, he seems even bigger. The family resemblance between him and Rhett is easy enough to see. Dark hair, dark brows, built like a lumberjack, but those eyes. Holy fucking shit, *those eyes.*

Knox's brows are furrowed, but he doesn't say anything,

only holds out his hand to me. I take it, his engulfing mine, and he moves our hands up and down once before releasing me. It's brief, a barely there connection, but I *feel* it. In more places than my hand. It's like it was before, what made me say yes to a date with him in the first place—*a date he stood you up for, Indie. Please play this a little cooler.*

My face heats when I realize he's just staring at me, so intently that I think he can see into my head. Is he reading my mind right now? *If I told you that you had a great body, would you hold it against me?* He arches his brow at me. *Gasp! Can you read my mind?*

His inspection moves from my face to the top of my head. Reaching out, his hand slips into my hair, and I have to stop myself from nuzzling into it. Thank God I do because when he pulls it back, he's holding a twig. *Oh. Okay, so no to the mind reading.*

"Did you hit your head?" he asks me, eyes full of concern.

"No, I-I'm fine. Really. My b-back may be s-sore later, but I'm okay," I stutter out, nerves suddenly running rampant. I turn my attention to Winnie. She's grinning at me like a lunatic. I widen my eyes at her. Classic signal for *help me.* She snickers but speaks up.

"Alright. Well, now that you've been introduced, we should probably head down to the house so you can get settled," she says.

"Right," I agree, then look back at Knox. He's still looking at me like I'm some kind of puzzle to work out but he hasn't acknowledged any previous meeting. "Thank you again for letting me stay in your guesthouse. It's beautiful out here." I wave my hand in the air in a sweeping motion.

"Not really much of a choice," he mumbles. *Ouch.* I open my mouth to say something—anything—because he's being so fucking rude for someone who blew me off all those years ago. Then it hits me. *He doesn't remember me.* That night was obviously a much bigger deal to me than it was for him.

How mortifying.

Out of the corner of my eye I see motion and flinch, letting out a small yelp before realizing it's a dog. A pretty one. It jumps up on me but it's gentle, not demanding.

"Well, hello there," I say.

"Sally!" I hear from the stairs. The dog immediately sits back. Whining beside me, begging me to pet her. I do, reaching over to run my hand through her soft fur.

"I need to get Hazel to Mom and Dad's before heading into town, so I'll leave you ladies to it," Knox announces.

"I thought the dog's name was Sally," I question.

"It is," he answers plainly.

I don't understand. It must show on my face because he clarifies.

"Hazel is my daughter." *He has a daughter?*

"Daughter?" I ask, my voice betraying my attempt at casual, sounding shocked and going up an octave.

"Yes," he confirms, handing me a key. "Here's your key, electric and water are turned on." He turns then pauses next to Winnie. "See you at dinner tomorrow, Win," he says on his way up the stairs.

"Sure, thanks again, Knox," I call. He nods, his squinting eyes widening slightly before he disappears into the house, muttering something about my size, while the dog—*Sally*—happily pants beside me.

I'm not sure what I expected of my first full day here, but moving in next door to the only man who's ever left me wondering what might have been wasn't on the agenda. Him not remembering me leaves a bitter taste in my mouth and a lump in my throat.

KNOX

The sound of my name coming out of her mouth causes my stomach to tighten. A response I'm unfamiliar with—and unwilling to examine too closely right now. I give her a once-over, looking from her short, dark hair down her toned, tan legs. Dropping the key into her hand, I notice her nails. They're pink, almost the same shade as her pouty lips. The color is so familiar to me, like a song or a scent takes you back to a moment in time. Standing next to her, I realize I'm practically towering over her. She's so small. Tiny. That word flashes in my mind like an answer that's on the tip of my tongue.

I nod, not sure what to say to her. Turning to head back into my house, I give Winnie a side hug, telling her I'll see her at dinner on the way. *Wait, Tiny?*

Those big, brown eyes. Those pink, puffy lips curving into a smile. Walking to the window, I watch her walk back to her car, playing with Sally and laughing with Winnie. That laugh —that loud, confident sound—knocks loose an image of her head thrown back in a dimly lit bar. *Is that really her? Is she really here?* Why would she be here?

I haven't seen her in years, only thinking of her every so often on long nights that leave me lonely. Turning from the window, I grab Hazel's bag and my briefcase inside, setting them by the door before placing our breakfast dishes from earlier into the sink. I don't have time right now to piece this out. I've got a long day ahead of me, and my head is already spinning with what this could mean—if it means anything at all.

Pushing the growing thought out of my head, I rinse out Hazel's sippy cup and put some juice in it before getting her up from her morning nap. She doesn't always take one these days, but this morning, she was up so early that it only made sense for her to take one before we left.

Gently pushing open the door to her room, I take in her sleeping form. She clutches her blanket in one hand, and the other is tossed over her head. "Hey, Hazey, time to get up and go to Grammy's," I say quietly. She rolls over, opening one eye to look at me, then the other before giving me a big smile. "Hi, happy girl."

She opens her arms wide, letting me know she wants me to pick her up. I melt. There's a part of me that never wants her to stop being this little. Scooping her up, my arms memorize the weight of her while walking into the living room where I have her clothes laid out for the day. Handing Hazel her sippy cup and setting her on the couch, the sleepy look she gives me puts a smile on my face.

"Thank you, Daddy," she says as she sits back into a throw pillow, drinking her juice.

"You're welcome, baby. After your drink let's get you

ready," I tell her. She nods with the cup in her mouth. Movement from outside the window catches my eye. Looking closer, I see Winnie and Indiana carrying boxes and bags into the guesthouse. *Indiana.* That's her name.

Having never given it to me, I always just thought of her as Tiny. The older but smaller sister from that night out all those years ago. The woman who had me breaking my rules of not asking out women in bars. Then life changed, and I—well, I still wonder about her. If she went to the pizza place, or if she even bothered to show.

I watch a few more minutes as the two women down the road go back and forth from the house to the black car, and back just a couple more times. Sally is down there, hovering, walking up and down the front steps with them. Already finding a new friend in our new neighbor. No one has lived in the old lake house since before it was mine, but as odd as it sounds, I can almost picture her there. In the kitchen, having coffee in the mornings, on the brown leather sofa, relaxing, in the bedroom...*and that's where I decide to stop the picturing.*

I get Hazel dressed; luckily, we have just moved out of the phase where she pretends to be a saltwater crocodile that I'm trying to wrestle into tiny clothes. I brush her wavy, dark hair into a bun on her head. One of the few hairstyles I can manage. I learned how to do her hair from the internet—with some help from my mom and Florence. When Hazel's hair really started growing, I couldn't get away with just brushing it and putting a bow in like I had before.

After a few hair tutorials, I can now do a ponytail, a bun, *space buns* as Florence calls them, and a loose braid—so loose that it falls out almost immediately. It's a work in progress. I look at her soft baby hairs curling around her face. I never want that to change. I can't believe this tiny human will be three in a matter of weeks. *Where has time gone, and how do I get it back?*

I carry Hazel's day bag and my briefcase to the truck, holding her hand, letting her jump off the bottom step before getting her buckled into her car seat. I give her the blanky and sippy cup filled with water this time, and we're off. My thoughts are already wandering back to the delicate beauty who was at my front door this morning. I had barely had the time to take in her appearance when she fell backward off my porch.

It's just attraction. I'm attracted to her.

She's gorgeous—of course I'm attracted to her. You'd have to be blind or a fucking idiot not to be.

There's no point in exploring it though. I heard the change in her voice at my mention of Hazel. She'll only be my tenant for a couple of weeks then she'll be back on the other side of town. Easy to avoid. Maybe I'll see her around town since she'll be working at Winnie's bakery—those two look like they're already as thick as thieves—but it's not like she'll be at family dinners. Unless she *is* going to be at family dinners.

That thought is a little worrisome, but it's the next one that has me scrubbing my hand down my face. Thinking of her deep-brown eyes and her legs in those tiny denim shorts. *I wouldn't mind her being there.*

Fuck. My head's a mess. Shaking it, I pull into the driveway of my childhood home, seeing my dad loading up the side by side with a small cooler and a bag that I'm sure contains multiple snacks for Hazel and him. Mom is on the porch in the rocking chair, waving to us. I put my truck in park and quickly unclip Hazel from her seat, setting her on the ground. She immediately runs to my mom, who picks her up, spinning in a circle.

Careful not to forget anything, I grab her bag, sippy, and blanky, walking them over to the porch. Making sure everything she needs has become a mental checklist over the years. When it's just you, the remembering is your responsibility alone.

"Hey, Mom," I call.

"Hi Knox, how's your morning been, hun?" she asks me while swaying Hazel on her hip.

I mull the question over before answering. "Mmm...interesting could be a word for it, I guess."

"Oh yeah? What was so interesting about it?"

I lean against the porch railing, crossing one leg over the other. "Winnie brought by her new manager this morning—my new tenant." *One I'm having conflicting feelings about.*

"Ah, yes. I forgot you offered up your guesthouse for her."

"*Offered up* would be a bit of an overstatement," I grumble under my breath. My mom laughs but doesn't comment.

"Well, hello there! Is that my help for the day?" Dad calls from the bottom of the steps.

"Yes!" Hazel yells and claps her little hands. "I'm help! I'm help!" she chants.

"Thank goodness. I don't know how I get anything done around here without you, babygirl."

"You don't," Mom teases him.

He grabs at his chest. "You wound me, woman."

Her answering smile is the same one she's given him my whole life. Indulgent, thoroughly amused. If I'm ever lucky enough to find someone to spend my life with, I'd like us to balance each other out the way they do.

"Alright, I'm off to work for a while. It's only a meeting, so I shouldn't be late. I'll see you in a bit, dragonfly. Be good for Grammy, and try to keep Grandpa in line," I tell her with a wink.

She grins at me, her freckles and her sweet dimple visible in the sun. "Okay. Bye, Daddy! I'll be good."

"I'm not worried." I kiss her cheek, waving to my parents before making my way into town.

On the drive to the office, thoughts of having someone on my property now while I'm away, and how uncomfortable it makes me, start to creep in. I'm not sure whether Winnie is there or not, and I'm not used to having to wonder what someone else is doing around my house. *Should I get security cameras?* That seems extreme, doesn't it? But what if she has people over? A *man* over.

Fuck, no. That's not happening.

It does remind me that I don't really know her, though, do I? *Do I want to?* No, there's no point. The words feel hollow, but if I keep repeating them, maybe they'll feel more true. I'm contemplating this as I park my truck on the street across from the old office building. Walking in, I flip on the lights as I go. Cora's at her other office job since I only have the one meeting, so it'll just be me here today.

In my office, I turn on my computer and open the document I was looking at yesterday afternoon. I grab the papers from my briefcase to cross-reference the phone records I've already combed through. The ones I received from Kirk were not what I received from Ms. June's service provider. I knew I had a gut instinct about him. I'll be able to present this to him and his lawyer today, and that should be the end of it.

I check the clock on my wall; there's about twenty

minutes until they arrive. I make a list of points to go over and then make a list of things I need to get done at home. *That* list is never-ending, and I'm always adding to it, but I try to make it a point to get on top of it at least once a week. It's hard to find time to get anything done these days as a one-man band. With Hazel staying the night with Rhett and Winnie tomorrow night, I'll hopefully be able to get a head start.

I hear the door open, alerting me to Kirk Carter and his rep's arrival. I stand and grab a few papers, tucking them under my arm, before walking to the entrance to my office.

"Mr. Carter. Mr. Shepherd,"

"Mr. Holloway. I hope you're well," Shepherd says, holding out his hand. I shake it, then extend my hand to Kirk. After the niceties, I direct them to the room across from my office so we can talk in a larger space. I've found it helps to put someone at ease, feeling more like neutral territory than someone's personal office.

"If you gentlemen will head through here, we can get started." I hold my arm out across the hall.

"Sounds great, this shouldn't take too long," Kirk says. *He's right, but probably not in the way he thinks he is.*

"Okay, Mr. Holloway. I'll cut right to the chase. It seems like this is a classic case of an elderly soul being taken advantage of," Shepherd starts. I did a little research on him last night as well, finding out he was drafted onto this case. A favor for a friend of a friend of the firm he works for. He isn't even the lawyer listed on the original document.

I narrow my eyes on him. "I can see how it may seem that way to someone on the outside looking in," I say conversationally. "But seeing as you're representing someone involved, I would assume you could glean the actual problem here," I add pointedly.

"I'm not sure what you mean." He says it with a tight smile, remaining cordial, but he's annoyed with my subtle jab.

I take my glasses out of my shirt pocket and slip them on, pretending to look over the documents that I now know backward and forward. "Would you mind if I asked your client a couple of clarifying questions? I think that may help the situation."

He looks puzzled but nods. "Of course."

Turning my attention to the lying piece of shit, I put my most compassionate foot forward. "First of all, I would like to extend my deepest sympathies over the passing of your aunt. Ms. June was a shining light in our community and will be missed," I tell Kirk. It's a truth he will never know, but the truth nonetheless.

"Thank you, I appreciate that." His faux solemn expression pisses me off.

"So the records I received from you stating your communication and interactions with Ms. June tell a little bit of a different story than the records I was able to obtain from her service provider. Maybe you sent the wrong documents?" I question. I can see his throat work and the fidgeting starts.

He sniffs, and his eyes look up and to the right. "That's strange. Those should have been the correct records." *Lie.*

"Well, I've verified that they couldn't possibly be correct. Did you perhaps communicate with your aunt in another way, or possibly from a different phone number?" I ask him these questions, knowing that it isn't true, but I don't mind him and his lawyer coming to the same conclusion: they have no leg to stand on.

"Uh-yeah. Actually, I may have called from another number a couple of times, and I, uh. I have some letters," he says, pulling at the collar of his dress shirt, swallowing.

"Excellent. Could you give me that number then? I'll go ahead and check it against my records so there's no false information presented." I click my pen and look at him expectantly. He glances at Shepherd. *He can't help you, you little shit. He has nothing. Got you, fucker.*

"You know, I may have to get back to you on that. I've had a couple of different phones, and I wouldn't want to give you the wrong number again." He's lying through his teeth again—and not very well.

"Sure. That's very considerate. In the meantime, I'll take a look at those letters from Ms. June. We were unable to locate any from you to her." I relay the information. Shepherd sighs. He knows this isn't going anywhere. "The small window of time for you to present any evidence that Ms. June's will is inaccurate is closing, so I would be swift in getting all necessary information back to me."

"Thank you for your time, Mr. Holloway. I'm not sure when you'll be hearing from us again, but I'll try to set up a date to meet soon," Shepherd tells me while pushing his chair back to stand. I stand with him, and he extends his hand again before swiftly making his exit. Kirk follows like a sad puppy. I doubt I'll hear from them again at all.

Since my day has opened up, I decide to hit the grocery store before getting Hazel. She's most likely out in the field with my dad anyway, having the time of her life, singing to the cows, and I don't want to rain on her parade. I leave the office ready to check one thing off my list for the next couple of days, and maybe get my mind back on track and off my new tenant.

INDIANA

"Thank you for all your help this morning," I tell Winnie from the front steps of my temporary home. She's walking out to her car to leave after helping me carry my boxes and totes from my car into the house. Now all that's left is to put things away—which she volunteered to help with—but I know she needs to get to the bakery so Anna can leave for the afternoon.

"Anytime, Indie!" Her use of my nickname takes me by surprise while simultaneously bringing a smile to my face. I watch some dust gather behind her car as she disappears down the dirt road. When it dissipates, it's just me here—alone.

Turning to look back at the house, I see Sally lying on the porch on her side. *So not completely alone.* I've decided I like having her around. Her coloring reminds me of a Mountain Bernese—black ears and back with some caramel-colored fur mixed in, and a fluffy white chest. She's not quite as big, though, leading me to believe she must be a mix of some kind. Whatever she is—I think I love her.

Walking into the small house, I take myself on a small tour

of the place. I say small because this place is *cozy* in the way that only two people could fit in the kitchen at one time. It's beautiful though. If the hotel room was light and airy, this is the perfect contrast.

It's like I'm being pulled further into an enchanted forest. Dark and moody with earthy greens and rich wood. The curtains are a sheer material that lets light in but are colored a deep-sage green. The floors look like original wood with tapestry-style rugs decorating them. Rust and burnt orange weaves seamlessly in with the warm beige and greens. It's bohemian in the middle of the forest. I love it. I grin and spin in a circle. I'm not sure how I'm lucking out, but you shouldn't gift a horse a...you shouldn't give a gift in front of a horse? You shouldn't look...whatever that saying is.

I grab two bags and head into the bedroom to unpack some clothes. It's small with a queen bed pushed snug against the wall across from a big window. The bedframe is a beautiful wrought iron, bent and shaped in arches. The floorboards creak as I walk toward the closet to hang a few of my things. Most should fit in the dresser on the opposite wall.

Over the dresser hangs a large rectangular mirror with a metal scrolled frame. It's stunning. The glass looks old, and I wonder if it's an antique, what its story is. As a kid, we used to go to the flea markets and give items backstories. What would Han tell me about this one? *It was used in an old burlesque dressing room. The woman who used it was the star of the show, and everyone was jealous of her.* Maybe I should call her again. I know I did a couple of days ago, but I really want to tell her about this place.

I grab my phone out of my back pocket. I have a few missed calls and texts, but I swipe the notifications away and click on

Han's name. It rings five times before her voicemail picks up, and I hear Princess Leia tell Han Solo she loves him for the first time followed by his reply of "I Know" before it beeps, and I chuckle.

"Hey, sis. It's been a crazy couple of days. It's a long story, but the condensed version is that my first residence in Silverthorne turned into a waterpark, so I had to stay at the hotel in town, and now? I am now staying at my boss's fiancé's brother's guesthouse. What a mouthful. Who is *he,* you might ask? *The guy.* The hot guy from the bar in New York who never showed up for pizza! Knox Holloway. God, even his name is sexy. I don't even think he remembers me. He's still hot—he may even be hotter. Ugh, I couldn't make this up if I tried. It sounds like a lot, I know, but get this: the guesthouse is by a lake—in the mountains! Ugh, you would love it here. I'll call again in a couple of days. I love you—so much. I miss you. Bye, Han."

I tap my phone, setting it down on the dresser, ready to dive into unpacking my clothes and washing my laundry from the last couple of days. The rest of my things are already en route to Winnie's cottage, so I'll have to make sure I check for any deliveries. I'll ask Winnie to keep an eye out for me when I see her tomorrow.

In what feels like no time at all, all my clothes are put away, and a load of laundry is washing in the machine. I'm a little sweaty, so I decide to take a quick shower, but am disappointed when I can't get the hot water to work. *Am I turning it the wrong way?* A quick turn of the handle the opposite way brings an arctic blast, eliciting a yelp. *Nope. Not turning it the wrong way then.* I'll have to ask about it next time I see Knox, unfortunately. I hate having to bother him with something already, but I will have to take a hot shower at some point.

My stomach grumbles as I put a fresh, oversized T-shirt on, reminding me I have no food here, so a grocery store run is necessary. I'm hoping there's one in town, so I don't have to go any further to find one. A quick check of the apps on my phone tells me there are zero delivery services in the area. *Sigh, I'll miss that convenience.*

While getting ready to go into town, the scenery outside the window catches my attention, my eyes snagging on a dock. The lake is so pretty here, surrounded by nature, nestled in the mountains. I grab my borrowed camera and slip the carrying strap over my head. Maybe I'll explore a little before making the trip. Taking in the terrain as I go, I notice you can't see another house around—well, except Knox's.

Knox. I cringe. He didn't really say much before when I said it was nice to see him. Most likely because he has no idea who I am. *What do you mean thirty minutes of undeniable attraction in a bar isn't enough to go on?* I, on the other hand, don't know how I could forget him. He's the most ruggedly handsome man I've ever encountered in my life. It may have been years ago, but that doesn't change the imprint he left on my brain...and then I fell off his porch.

My hand massages at my forehead. I'm actually not a clumsy person. I even played a couple of sports in high school; volleyball, a little tennis, and I love to dance. Unfortunately, Knox Holloway may never know how coordinated I am. If standing me up wasn't him writing me off, he might've when he had to help me out of the bushes in front of his house.

Looking down the road, I study the big, green house for a moment. The yard is meticulously kept, not a leaf on the lawn or a stray blade of grass on the path that leads into the beautiful wildflower field between our houses. It reminds me of the photos you see in a home and gardening magazine.

While admiring the property, I spot a parting in the tall grass on the lake side of the road and make my way toward it from the main road. The trail down to the water is marked and easy to stay on. There are wildflowers growing all around me. Reaching out, I run my hand over them as I pass by. Stepping onto the dock, I leisurely walk the length of the wooden slats, taking photos as I go. There's a metal canoe, a paddleboard, and a kayak tied to dock cleats, and one lone Adirondack sitting at the end. It's all so solitary, a setup just for one.

Considering the boats, I realize I've never been in or on any of them. I stop next to the paddleboard and picture myself out on the lake. My balance is relatively good, and I've seen people stand on them before, so I'm sure I could figure it out. Bending to set my camera in the middle of the dock, ensuring that in no way it could be knocked into the water. Then I glance around to double-check that I'm still alone. Although there are only two houses on Knox's property, I'm not sure if anyone else lives on the lake. I slip my tennis shoes off and set them next to the camera.

Sitting next to the floating paddleboard, I slowly lower my feet onto it. Looking over my shoulder to check the area again for anyone and finding I'm still alone, I try to stand. First attempt—unsuccessful. My ass hits the dock when the board slides out from under me. Maybe this is a commit-to-it thing. I can do that. I'm a very commit-to-the-bit person. It could be that I'm just going too slow. I stand quickly, and—I'm up! *Now what?* There wasn't a paddle out here, and I'm still tethered to the dock. But at least I know I can balance on it, and maybe I'll be able to convince its stony—but incredibly handsome—owner to let me try it out. Motion to the right of me gets my attention. I flinch, only to see it's Sally coming down the dock.

I catch myself and huff a laugh at my jumpiness, sitting back down as she nuzzles into me while I stroke her soft fur. Reaching behind me to slip my camera back on, I watch Sally trot to the end of the dock to lie in the sun next to the chair. My camera makes a quick shutter sound when I snap a picture before walking out to sit with her.

Choosing to forgo the chair and sit on the dock, I dangle my feet off the edge. Once I'm settled, Sally lays her head in my lap. The birds fly over the lake and back to the trees while wildlife makes various sounds in the thick forest surrounding me. Chipmunks and squirrels are scurrying. This is the most submerged in nature I've ever been.

Lying back against the sun-warmed boards, I bend my knees, bringing my feet to rest on the edge of the dock. I close my eyes and let the sun's rays warm my face as well. It's so peaceful out here. I've never seen any place like it that wasn't on a postcard or in a movie. Listening to the sounds around me and feeling Sally next to me, I relax into the moment. Not sleeping well at night is starting to catch up to me. Trying to focus only on the things that surround me, I start to drift off. While I feel consciousness slip away, a question runs through my mind on repeat—had Knox Holloway completely forgotten me?

I don't know how long I lie there asleep. All I know is that I'm woken up by my sense of awareness returning, the sun disappearing, and in its place is a very large man. Groggy and disoriented, I don't think—I just react. My leg shoots out on instinct, kicking sideways at the figure. I hear my foot make contact with a very solid stomach, or rather the other person's painful grunt, and then they're gone.

A splash echoes off the water as Sally starts barking, and I remember where I am. Out over the lake, on the dock. *Knox's dock. Shit. The large man.* Scrambling to the edge of the dock, I let out a gasp when a head breaks the surface, my eyes locking with a pair of sapphire blues. A whimper escapes me.

"Oh, fuck."

KNOX

She's been here less than a day, and she's already trying to claim my dog and my place out on the end of *my* dock.

I examine her—face untroubled in sleep. One of her slender arms is up over her head, the other over her lower stomach, covering part of the design on her shirt. A bat? It reads: Even Batties Get Saddies. Good lord. I scrub a hand down my face. I know Winnie said she was twenty-seven, but she looks young—a lot younger than me. Her lips slightly parted; a light flush on her skin. I briefly let myself wonder what all her skin would look like in the sun. That only makes this situation more frustrating for me.

I look up at the sky, attempting to get a hold of myself—of my imagination. When I look back down, she slowly opens her eyes. At the sight of me, she lets out a blood-curdling scream that has me rearing back and off balance. Before I can regain it, she kicks her toned legs out, successfully making contact with my gut and knocking me off the end of the dock—into the freezing lake below.

I break the surface after being completely submerged and reach up to grip the end of the dock, gaze locking with Indiana's. At the sight of her big, brown eyes, a memory floods my brain. *A teasing taunt sparks in them as she looks me up and down.* There's no mistaking it now.

Espresso-brown eyes that have haunted my dreams for years stare back at me.

"Oh fuck," she whimpers from above me. "Oh my god, I'm so sorry. You scared me! I must have fallen asleep, and then you were just standing there—over me—like some psycho—" she rambles as I pull half my body up onto the dock, out of the water. She's kneeling right in front of me. I look at her face to—I don't know, scold her? Say something mean? But looking up at her now, the sun lighting her from behind like she has a fucking halo, sitting back on her knees, her top teeth worrying her lip, the only words that come to mind range from sticky sweet to undeniably filthy.

"Hi, Knox." She breathes. That soft, breathy voice saying my name is—more than it should be. I haul myself onto the dock fully, catching my breath and standing. "I'm so sorry," she says again.

I don't say anything back, my brain not wanting to register how charming she looks. How to reconcile the idea I've had of her over the years with her sitting in front of me right now. How incredibly tempting her pink, pouty lips are, so instead, I just walk by her and off the dock, straight to my porch, where I strip off my shirt and boots.

"Hey, I said I was sorry. I know this is an inconvenience, but you could at least acknowledge my apology—acknowledge *me*," a soft voice calls, trailing behind me.

I groan. I assumed that my leaving without speaking would

tip her off to the fact that I don't feel like speaking right now—or anytime soon. I need to get a handle on the unfamiliar feelings this woman stirs up in me.

"If you're expecting me to say it's okay, then you should really manage your expectations," I snap. *Shit. That's not—I don't—fuck, she's got me out of sorts.*

"Excuse me?" she asks, sounding indignant.

I turn to her then. Her eyes widen, sweeping down my face to my chest and finally stopping when they get to my stomach. I'm annoyed at how having her eyes on me puts fire in my veins, making it hard to form coherent thoughts, and at the same time, making me want to say more than I should. Her mouth opens, then shuts. She blinks before raising her eyes back up to my face, where they flare with heat, seeing the smirk on it. "Get a good look?" I ask.

"Oh my god. Stop it. N-no. That's not what I—" she stutters out. She places her hands on her hips, blowing air out of her nose, eyes shut. "You scared me back there. I *am* sorry I pushed, er, well, *kicked* you off the dock, but I'm not sure how you expected me to respond to a man standing over me. How long *had* you been standing there?" I turn her words over, and when looking at it from that point of view, see how waking up to someone—a stranger—might have been jarring. I also have to admit that her kick had a lot more power behind it than I expected out of her tiny frame.

"I didn't mean to startle you—on *my* dock, mind you. I'm not used to anyone being out there. You shouldn't have been—and definitely not asleep." That sounded nothing like an apology—which is what I had intended when I started talking.

She tenses, then awkwardly cocks her hip to the side, showcasing the toned muscles of her thighs before crossing her arms over her chest. Her shirt rides up with the action, giving me a peek of more of her skin, driving me crazy thinking about what her soft skin might feel like under my fingers.

"Why? Are there bears out here or something?" she asks quietly. Curiously. I want to laugh. *This woman.*

"No, Indiana." I have to force my thoughts away from the way her name feels on my tongue. The taste of it. "It's not bears I'm worried about," I tell her. The breeze coming off the surrounding mountains chills my skin that's been heated by her gaze, and with it, my sense returns. "You just shouldn't have been out there. It's not your dock."

Her beautiful, brown eyes go wide at my harsh tone. *Shit. I can't seem to pick a lane.* She swallows, face tinged pink. *Fuck, I'm an asshole.* "I won't go out there again," she tells me before all but fleeing back down the road. I stand on the porch a few moments longer, my jeans dripping onto the wood.

Well, you got exactly what you wanted, Knox. So why do you feel like shit over it?

Possibly because she's done nothing to provoke me other than exist. I scratch the back of my neck. *Damn it.* As much as I hate to admit it, I think her being here is starting to bring out some long-buried feelings. Feelings I'm not sure I can—or want to—explore anymore.

I also don't like admitting I'm wrong because nine and a half times out of ten, I'm not. But she's been here one day, and I already have to say I'm sorry?

Looking over at the guesthouse, I see she's getting in her car, muttering to herself. I contemplate waving her down when she comes by. Say my piece and move on—only when she drives by, she doesn't even glance at me. Her head is firmly facing forward, ignoring me. *Guess I won't be apologizing tonight after all.* I head inside, not bothering to close the door behind me. Kicking off my wet jeans and underwear, I throw them in the wash.

Walking through the house naked isn't something I make a habit of, seeing as I have Hazel. But she's with my parents, there aren't any other houses around for miles, and I just watched the only person who would have been here drive away. So while I'm walking toward the hall bathroom, I tell myself I must be imagining the feeling of eyes on me.

Still unable to shake the feeling, I turn to look back through the house, and standing in my doorway is none other than my five-foot-nothing tenant, looking almost comically scandalized.

"Oh my god. Oh my god. I'm s-so sorry," she says as she stares at my body. Specifically, my lower half. I'm frozen, making no move to cover up. Having her eyes on me does something to me. Something I'm not sure how to name. It leaves me wanting. What, I'm not sure. Slapping a hand over her eyes, she spins around to face the lake. "I d-didn't mean—how am I managing to make a worse impression every time I see you today?" she whines.

Grabbing a blanket from the back of the couch, I cover myself. "Was there something you needed, Indiana?" I ask.

"Indie. Y-you can call me Indie," she stutters.

"Yeah, now that we've gotten to know each other so well, it only seems right," I mutter under my breath.

"I was just going to ask you about something in the house, but I-er-I will talk to you about it another time—maybe when you're less naked," she jokes.

I don't know where it comes from, but the overwhelming urge to tease her, even though I know she's already embarrassed, bubbles up inside me. "Just *less* naked? Not completely clothed?" I'm rewarded with her surprised laugh.

"So he does have a sense of humor," she muses.

"Occasionally," I confirm.

"Good to know."

"Yeah?"

She clears her throat. "Okay, well. I'm sorry I saw you naked," she says and then shakes her head.

"Are you?" The question is out of my mouth before I can stop it. I'm finding it difficult to keep my head around this woman.

"I'm sorry if it made you uncomfortable." I don't miss the distinction.

"I'm comfortable, Indie. And covered now," I tell her, watching the blush on her cheeks spread to her neck. I'm sure if I could see it, her chest would be the same color. "Are you alright?"

"I-I'm fine," she breathes out, trying her best to keep her gaze fixed on the lake.

"Good." *Is it good?* I have no idea, but something in me *wants* her to be comfortable with me.

She swallows, nodding. "Great. Right. Thank you. I'll get out of your way now, I'm sure you have things to do and clothes to put on. I should leave. So, bye!" she rushes out, hopping down the stairs like a scared rabbit, making a beeline for her car, looking more athletic than I'd given her credit for. Her windows are down, and I can't help my grin, hearing her fit of laughter, seeing her shoulders shake as I watch her car take off again, leaving a little cloud of dust in her wake and an odd feeling in my chest.

I go through the motions of drying off and getting dressed in a daze. Only able to think of Indiana—*Indie*—her mouth hanging open, what other T-shirts she may have, and how she might look in one of mine.

INDIANA

"Can I get a manager to checkout, please?" I hear a bored voice announce over the intercom at the small grocery store in Silverthorne. I glance around, surmising that the cashier could have just yelled it, and the manager would have heard it. I've been walking the aisles for the past fifteen minutes. My brain refuses to focus on anything but the memory of a very grumpy—very naked—Knox Holloway.

His rippling abs, his chest hair—*oh god the chest hair*—the way his damp hair curled on the ends, his eyes...on me, that flash of ink on his thigh, and the *V* pointing directly to his—

"Excuse me," a woman's voice calls at my side. I jump, shrugging off the memory that's playing out like a cinematic masterpiece on repeat. "Are you planning on buying that?" Her tone would suggest that I had better.

Looking down at my hands, I see that I am holding a vegetable. A zucchini, to be more specific. I don't *love* how my hands are positioned on it. To be honest, I don't even remember picking it up. "I'm sorry...y-yes. I am," I say, putting it in my shopping basket and escaping down the cereal aisle. *What the fuck am I going to make with zucchini?* I have no idea, but I couldn't put it back after the look that lady gave me.

"Oh my god, Indie. You're going to get labeled as the town weirdo already." I can hear what my sister would tell me if she were here. I smile; she would be right. *Okay, Indiana. Focus! You need meals for the week and snacks. A lot of snacks.*

While I throw things into my cart, I already know future me is going to be pissed that there was no planning put into this grocery haul. My stomach grumbles again, fueling the chaotic energy this trip is giving. I look into my basket. Cookies, crackers, bacon, cereal, bread, cheese, one lone zucchini, a bottle of wine, tea bags, and frozen fries. *Dinner of champions.*

I'm thinking tonight is going to be a recovery night. I need junk food and TV.

Except, it occurs to me now that I forgot to ask about the Wi-Fi situation and if I'll be able to sign into my Netflix account. I don't think I could bring myself to ask Knox a question today—to face him at all. I can't even think about him without clenching my thighs together. Looks like it could be a night to catch up on reading then. I have a good romantic thriller that I've been switching back and forth between the audio and my Kindle.

I had just gotten to the part where the struggling writer hears about the first murder that happened in her new town years prior, and she starts piecing together a pattern of other murders in the neighboring towns. I already have a few theories about who the killer may be—it's the same person I also think she's going to fall for. I grin just thinking about it.

I fall into the category of true-crime enthusiast—I have a shirt that says as much. I think it's a misunderstood genre. I'm obviously not a fan of the horrific acts. It's more about the justice served. It's when we catch the bad guy. It's the feeling of human camaraderie that comes with a survivor's story being told. I celebrate the cold cases that get solved with the new platform it's given.

I look down, seeing the shirt I threw on today, and my cheeks flush thinking about seeing my landlord, *stark naked,* in all his delicious glory while I was standing there with a big T-shirt that has a bad pun on it. It's not that I'm ashamed of my shirt collection—I am obsessed with them—but I also recognize that Knox doesn't know me very well. *I don't think he wants to know me very well.*

But I'm working on a plan to change that because I kind of like this new place on the lake, and the idea of potentially *not* having to move my things again is appealing.

The first phase of the plan: don't see him naked again. This one is solely for him. I could see that every day of my life, and *oh god,* it would be a really good life. Personal space is important to most people. I didn't get that gene. I'm overly affectionate, and the lines between friendly and friendship are often blurred for me. That would be all thanks to my trusty SPD.

Sensory Processing Disorder.

I wasn't diagnosed until I was in my early twenties, when a basic college course load was causing me to feel overwhelmed constantly. It was a daily occurrence for me to feel out of place or need to find a calming environment. Everything was over-stimulating. I was isolating myself more and more. My friends started to worry about me, thinking I was depressed—and to be honest, I think I was.

I wasn't sure where it had come from—seemingly out of nowhere. I had always been loud and outgoing. Getting in trouble in school a lot for talking, but I always had good grades, so no one thought there was cause for concern. I had friends, I played sports, I graduated with honors. It wasn't until the chronic exhaustion and never-ending headaches that my parents stepped in and made sure I got some support.

Meditation and other various exercises were suggested, but nothing stuck. One day, a girl in my dorm was going for a run with her track team. Impulsively, I joined. I went for a run almost every day after. Running gave me the time to decompress, to reflect on all the things I had done and wanted to get done in a way that felt less overwhelming. It made my life feel manageable.

My behavioral specialist said this was because my brain was tricked into thinking I was checking items off my to-do list, making things I needed to get done feel more achievable. Coping and putting systems into place when I start feeling like things are too much has been a lifesaver. I think one of the reasons I was looking forward to being here is that my job will be slower paced for the most part. The city feels like too much these days. Too many people and too many memories.

My hand finds its way up to my left shoulder, where I know a faint scar sits. Flashes hit me without permission, threatening to overtake me here in the middle of the grocery store. *It's dark, and the humidity is smothering me.* That familiar high-pitched keening rings in my ears. *Refocus, distract until it's manageable.*

I start reading the back of the first cereal box I can grab. One hundred-seventy calories, four grams of fat, thirty-three carbohydrates, twelve sugars, vitamin D, calcium, iron, potassium…I take a deep breath and focus on the steady beeping coming from the checkout at the front of the store. Old ladies chatter about their grandkids in the produce section, and I hear a kid asking their mom to get them a candy bar, *please, please, please.*

I'm here. I am *here.* I close my eyes tightly, then open them, feeling triumphant. *Hell yes, Indie!* I hear the cheer echo in my ears, and with renewed confidence, I take my items to the front, helping the checker bag them before walking out to my car. A few months ago, I probably would have been curled up into a ball on the sticky grocery store floor. I've come a long way. Smiling and feeling a little proud of myself, I stow my brown paper bag in the backseat.

Main Street is quiet. Stores are starting to close for the evening, and there are fewer cars parked on the street. The sun dips lower in the sky, casting shadows over the town. I'm not sure what I thought moving across the country would look like, but I didn't expect to feel so much peace already. Silverthorne is quickly becoming a comforting balm to my soul. I'll write that one down on a postcard for Han later. She'll appreciate the poetic nature of it.

The drive back to Knox's guesthouse—my house for the foreseeable future—is calming. I turn my music up and roll my windows down, enjoying the evening air. The sunset is reflecting off the clouds over the mountain, making them look like orange and raspberry sherbet. *I should have gotten some of that.* I hit the long, forest-lined drive, and the view when I reach the lake is otherworldly. The lake looks lit up by the fading glow of the sun, reflecting the sky on the calm water. I slowly pass the faded old truck in front of the big house and park my car, grabbing my camera and running down to the water.

Making sure not to step one foot onto Knox Holloway's dock, I walk to the water's edge, squatting down to get the angle of the water and the sky above just right. I snap a few before adjusting my settings, and the next few photos look like they belong on a postcard. *Maybe I'll make my own.* I can hear the sounds of the forest around me, and closing my eyes to hear them better, I let myself sink into this moment until a high-pitched giggle has my head snapping to the side. When my eyes refocus, I see the most adorable little girl I've ever seen in my life.

Beside her is the man I kicked into the lake earlier—then saw naked.

KNOX

Nestled into the tall grass near the edge of the lake, I'm watching my daughter enjoy the rest of her already exciting day. We came outside to watch the fading sunset, and after an adorable *pretty please,* we both ended up with a bowl of ice cream. Rocky road for me and chocolate for her. We relax on an old blanket; Hazel sits beside me, licking her spoon, melting ice cream dribbling down her chin while she's at it. She has questions about the car that drove by a couple of minutes ago.

"Who's that?"

"That's Indiana. She's going to be staying there for a little bit."

"Why?"

"Because she needed somewhere to stay."

"Why?"

"Well, the place she was staying before had a problem."

"Why?"

"Because Muncle Rhett didn't fix some pipes." She giggles.

"Muncle Rhett's funny," she says, taking another lick off her spoon.

"Yeah, he's funny," I agree, giving her little side a tickle.

I've just answered to her satisfaction when the object of her questions comes racing out of the small white guesthouse down the dirt road, running down the path to the water. Where is she going in such a hurry? She makes a show of avoiding the dock, making me feel a little like an ass for how hard I came down on her this afternoon. I do need to know she can swim, but maybe telling her she wasn't *allowed* on it wasn't called for.

I watch her kneel by the edge of the water, hold her camera up, and mess with something on it before smiling. It's a big, beautiful smile, full of awe for the scene in front of her. It generally annoys me when people bring their cameras everywhere. Like they can't live in the moment without documenting every little detail for their social media pages. But watching her right now, the orange light of sunset on her face tells me that's not what this is. I will myself to look away, setting my bowl next to me and leaning back onto my hands, crossing one foot over the other.

Hazel looks back at me, so I bare my teeth and give her a growl, causing her to giggle. She twirls in a circle, holding tight to her bowl, the sugary contents making their way through her bloodstream. Smiling, I watch her dance back and forth, catching the sun going down behind her as it casts vibrant light into the sky and paints the clouds. It's one of our favorite things to do out here, together, just me and her.

"Hi," a voice like honey calls from just below us at the water.

"Hi!" Hazel yells back. Her sweet voice is so pure and

friendly. I guess I should be talking to her about stranger danger soon.

"Evening," I say, sitting up as she walks over.

"Sorry if I'm intruding." *She is.* "I just had to get out here and see this sunset." *But I'm glad.*

"It's so pretty! Orange and pink!" Hazel yells at her, already hopped up on sugar and spooning another mouthful of chocolate into her mouth.

"It is. It might be the prettiest sunset I've ever seen," she tells Hazey. "I'm Indiana. It's really nice to meet you."

"I'm Hazel Emilia Holloway," she introduces herself, like she's older than her three years. It's adorable.

"What a beautiful name." Indiana fawns over her, then shifts her feet, like she's unsure if she should still be standing here. I suppose I'll need to say something then.

"Thank you," Hazel says politely. Well, at least some things I'm teaching her are sticking—maybe I should try being a bit more polite.

"You're welcome," Indiana replies, before looking over at me. "I wanted to say sorry again for earlier. I'll stay off your dock, and I'll—she clears her throat—"call before just showing up on your doorstep. I didn't mean to catch you at a bad time," she tells me. Her sincerity is clear. I feel worse for my over-reaction.

"Indiana—"

"Indie," she interrupts. "Call me Indie, please. You know, since we know each other so well," she adds, reusing my muttered words from earlier.

Indie. It suits her. "Indie, can you swim?"

"Y-yes. Why? Are you going to throw me in the lake?" she asks. At the ridiculous question, I feel my lips twitch. She's really trying to extend that olive branch, even though I think it falls on me.

"Because if you're going to be on the dock, then you need to know how to swim," I tell her. She pinches her lips together in an attempt to hide her smile, tucking one side of her short, chestnut hair behind an ear.

"I can swim," she confirms.

"I can swim!" Hazels chirps.

"Not alone, and not without a life vest," I remind her.

"Okay," she agrees. One of the first things I did when we moved to the lake house was get Hazel into baby swim lessons. She's still taking them at the town community center and making her way up the levels.

"What kind of ice cream are you having?" Indie asks my daughter, whose face is covered in chocolate streaks.

"Chocolate!"

"Ohh, that's a good choice," Indie tells her.

"What's your favorite?" Hazel asks.

Indie taps her chin, looking up as she does. "I would have to go with cherry."

"Cherry?" I ask. Why cherry when there are so many other flavors?

"Yep. Cherry. It's my favorite flavor. Pies, candy, danishes, and ice cream," she says, hands fluttering out from her.

"Chocolate is better," Hazel states, making Indie laugh. Her laugh hits me right in the chest. I feel too warm—at odds with the cooler spring evening we're standing out in.

"Hazel, remember to be nice," I remind her, and she nods.

"That's okay." Indie waves it off. "My sister has always been about chocolate in any form."

My mind flashes with the memory of Indie's feisty sister. "I remember the sister," I say, smiling over her boldness. I don't think my comment is out of line or rude. But something about it has Indie looking nervous.

Her smile is a little off-kilter when she replies with a soft hum. "Mhm. Well, I've taken up enough of your evening. I'll see you around," she says to me, then looks at Hazel. "It was so lovely to meet you, Hazel Emilia Holloway." She gives us both one more smile before turning on her heel to head for the guesthouse. With the last of the sunlight fading, I can barely make out her small form walking away. I fold the blanket we were sitting on and pick up my discarded bowl.

I wait until I hear her door shut and see a light turn on before picking Hazel up into my arms. She's still holding her ice cream bowl and licking at her spoon, only now, instead of dribbling down her face, it's dripping onto me.

"Okay, Hazey. I think that's enough sugar for tonight. I know you had a cookie at Grammy and Grandpa's house too." Along with who knows what else.

"I did and I had a peanut butter cup," she says, and I laugh at her honesty, hugging her close to kiss the crown of her head. This little girl has changed my life in unimaginable ways and brought more love into it than I ever expected. She's always going to come first for me. Her head makes its way under my chin as we climb the stairs of the front porch.

I sit her on the kitchen counter inside, and take her bowl to put our dishes in the sink, and wet a rag with warm water to wipe her face down.

"Now, I know Hazel is around here somewhere," I say before swiping the rag over her mouth and cheeks.

"I'm here!" she yells.

"She was right here just a second ago," I tease.

"Daddy, it's me!" I give her chin a couple more wipes.

"There's my girl. Gosh, you're pretty. Has anyone ever told you that?" I ask her, looking into her soft, brown eyes.

Her smile is sweet, almost shy. "Yes. I know that."

"And you're so smart too."

"Yep," she agrees.

"Okay, smarty pants. Let's get you into some jammies and ready for bed."

"I'm not tired," she says, but then she yawns almost immediately after the words leave her mouth.

"You're not even a little tired?"

"Uh-uh." She shakes her head at me.

I hum. "What if we read a book together? Would that help?" She nods at my suggestion. "Okay, babygirl. Which PJ's tonight? Princess gown or sharks?"

"Sharks!" she yells.

"Sharks it is," I say, picking her up and walking into her bedroom. The pink bow stencils on the walls were Florence's doing. Hazel loves them. Her bedspread is light pink with small satin bows on the edges. There's a canopy netting above that gives it a very princess feel. I set her on the bed and open the drawer to her old, cream dresser to get her shark pajamas. It's one I picked up at a flea market and put new hardware on.

"Alright, Hazey. Let's get you changed."

After we're changed, teeth and hair brushed, I sit down on the couch in the living room, letting Hazel crawl up into my lap. We've picked *Guess How Much I Love You* as our book tonight. I feel her yawn, snuggling into me.

"I love you, Hazey," I whisper over the top of her head.

"I love you bigger than the moon, Daddy."

"I love you more than that," I say before reading the story.

It's not a long book, but I think Hazel has fallen asleep before I get to the third page. I keep reading, though, feeling her arm go limp against my chest. After I finish the book, I stay there for a few minutes, soaking up the moment. She's getting so big.

With my daughter in my arms, I carry her to her room, laying her on her princess bed, covering her up, and tucking in her blanky and stuffies. I kiss her sweet curls once more and then head to change for bed as well. Later in the living room, while I look over a case for a potential client, I see that the light is still on at the guesthouse. Sliding my reading glasses off my nose and setting them on the table beside me, I don't want to, but I wonder what she's doing over there tonight and if she may be thinking about me too.

Indiana

It's been three days since I talked with Knox and Hazel down by the lake. One week of life at the lake house. I've tried my best to keep to myself, but I can't help the pull I'm feeling. I slept so hard last night, only getting up once in the night to guzzle a glass of water before stumbling back to bed. I had planned on reading more last night, but instead, I called Han while I went through a box, and after that, I felt so tired I just wanted to sleep.

I make myself a tea and a piece of toast, thankful to see that there was already a toaster here. Walking around the small kitchen, I see the various pots and pans, cooking utensils, and even a waffle maker. I'm not really big on cooking meals, but I know how to make a few things. Grilled cheese. Macaroni and cheese. Cheese quesadilla. *Okay, so I know that I like cheese.*

I've been itching to run and have learned over the years that I have to fuel myself if I want to feel good about it afterward. I look out my windows while sipping the rest of my tea. The birds call to one another, and the trees sway in the breeze.

I hear the delicate windchime on the porch and see dragonflies flitting about the edge of the lake over the tops of colorful wild-flowers.

Getting dressed, I check my weather app. It hasn't warmed up yet today, so a sweatshirt over my sports bra is necessary. I pull on some bike shorts, socks, and running shoes, making sure to lace them fairly tight. This will be a little different terrain than I'm used to, but I've been doing a lot of research on trail running, and I think we're going to get along just fine.

My hair is causing problems for me. It's so short, and my little side quest with the scissors leaves strands falling into my face as soon as I secure my hair tie. I need some clips. While looking for my stash of bobby pins, I see a ball cap hanging on a coat rack by the front door. It's a faded blue and has Canyon-lands National Park embroidered in orange on the front. I pull it on and tighten the back, so it fits snugly. Hair contained.

I still have a few boxes to sift through, but the one I went through last night had all my notebooks and pens in it. It gave me an idea, so I grab the hot-pink sticky note after making my bed and throwing my discarded clothes into the basket by the washing machine. By the front door, I grab my running pack. I started carrying mace and a taser on my runs. My keychain has a rape whistle and a compass combo thing on it as well. I do my best to stay safe while continuing to live my life.

Stepping out onto the front porch, I start stretching. The sun is just coming up, lighting up the tops of the evergreen trees in the distance. The little, white house sits in the shadow of the mountain behind me causing the morning chill to still hang in the air around me. I take deep breaths, trying to acclimate to it. I remind myself that although I've been running for six years, completed two half marathons and one full, running at this elevation could prove a challenge.

Feeling limber enough to start, I jog over to Knox's house. Instead of knocking on his door and disrupting his life again, I stick my scribbled note asking about the water heater to his door. Three days of cold showers has to come to an end.

After clearing his front steps, I click the side of my watch that's connected to my phone app to track my run and vitals throughout it. I slide my phone into its zip pocket on the side of my shorts and take off at a light jog. Thinking it's better to warm up and see how I feel after the first ten minutes before I pick up my pace. We'll see how these mountains decide to push me today.

It turns out the mountains *did* want to push me. I'm a sweating mess when I get back to the property. Knox's truck is gone when I make it back to the main drive. A quick glance at my watch tells me that I've run five miles. It felt more like twelve. The view from up higher on the hiking trail was breathtaking—and that's not just because I was out of breath after trekking over two miles straight up to the lookout. I'll have to hike back up there with my camera another day. A picture from there will make another good postcard.

Admiring the big lake house as I pass by, I note the flower boxes under the front windows overflowing with color. It's odd, Knox doesn't strike me as the plant-pretty-flowers type of man. Then a thought occurs to me. An absolutely horrifying thought.

Is Knox with someone?

Oh my god. He is. I slap a hand over my forehead. Why had I not assumed this? Neither Winnie nor Rhett mentioned a wife, but I hadn't exactly asked about a girlfriend. Seeing him naked yesterday now has my face flaming for another reason entirely. He's told her! Of course he told her! Now she'll hate me—whoever she is. How will I come back from this? Do I need to apologize to her? *I don't want to move just yet.*

While I'm walking to cool down from my run—and my racing thoughts—I pass by the dock. I *am* allowed on it now, so I decide to take advantage. Once on the wooden dock, I feel the sun warming me further. The temperature has risen, so I shrug off my sweatshirt, tying it around my waist while walking out. I hear a noise behind me and spin around to see Sally.

"Hey, Sally. What are you up to today, girl?" I ask as she trots out onto the dock after me. Crouching down, Sally runs at me, almost knocking me backward. "Such a sweet girl," I tell her, sitting back as she nuzzles further into me. I stay there only a few minutes, knowing I need to clean up and get dressed. I'm heading into work for a few hours to shadow Anna in the front of the bakery.

"I'll be back later, and maybe you can come on a hike with me." Sally gives me a small bark as an answer, and I smile while walking back to my house. She goes the opposite direction, back toward her place, wagging her tail as she goes. I've never had a dog. We always lived in an apartment, and that doesn't necessarily mean you *can't* have a pet, but my parents weren't interested in having one. They also were not swayed by mine or my sister's attempts to convince them it would be a good idea.

I'm still thinking about the cat we stole from one of our

neighbors in the building when I notice a neon-yellow sticky note on the front door. Wiping my forehead with the back of my arm, I hop up the steps.

Hot water is fixed.

That's all it says. The handwriting is masculine and clear. Reaching out, I peel it from the door, looking at the big lake house down the road as I do. He must have come while I was out running. I'm thankful, seeing as a hot shower is needed before I head into work. One can only wash her hair in the sink for so long, and boiling some water for a bath had been so time-consuming. But I *am* a little disappointed I didn't get to see him.

Opening the door I hang my borrowed ball cap back on the hook I found it on, and I untie my sweatshirt from my waist, tossing it into the laundry basket on my way to the bathroom.

The bathroom is small, but everything in it is beautiful. There's a white clawfoot tub that sits underneath a big skylight in the ceiling. A wrought iron, curved curtain rod that a white shower curtain hangs from wraps around the outside of the tub. The faucet, and shower head that's detachable, are an antique gold. The sink is free-standing white porcelain with the same style faucets, and the floor is a stunning jade stone tile.

I check the water to see it's warming up, feeling my whole body relax, knowing I'll be getting a hot shower soon. Taking my phone out of my pocket, I set it on a wooden stool in the corner of the bathroom, then peel my sweaty clothes off, tossing them into the laundry with the rest of my clothes. I look at my reflection. Hair a mess and face still flushed, my neck is splotchy. I stop at the mark on my shoulder, quickly turning and stepping into the shower, rushing through my routine so I can make it to the bakery on time.

On my way out, I'm not sure if I should—but I can't stop myself. I grab another neon-pink sticky note and scribble a thank you on it, sticking it to my landlord's door as I pass by.

KNOX

While going over my schedule for the next couple of weeks, I catch myself smiling over getting Indiana's note on my front door this morning. *Had she gone three days without hot water just to avoid me?* I had planned on seeing her, but when Hazel and I stopped by, she didn't answer. Her car was still parked out front. We checked the dock but found it empty. Maybe she was out for a walk. I saw no one come to pick her up. I hope she had pepper spray with her. We don't have a large bear population, but there have been some mountain lion sightings in the area.

I had let myself and Hazel into the house with my key, walking to the closet that houses the hot water heater. It looked like I had forgotten to turn the thermostat back up after having it at a lower temperature for the winter when it sat unused. A quick turn of the dial was all that was needed, and we were able to be on our way. Hazel was disappointed she wasn't able to see Indiana. After talking with her a few nights ago, she has been the main topic of conversation in our home. All while I've been doing my best to avoid the beauty living next door.

From her hair to her camera to the little gold hoop in her nose, Indie has been discussed at length.

I can't blame all the curiosity on my daughter though. I was also left wanting to know more about the woman next door. Wondering about the shirt she might have on today and what it might say. If she's at work or not. *Maybe my last few hours here at the office require coffee.*

Locking the front door on my way out and taking the sidewalk to Thistle and Sage, I'm at war with myself, not wanting to admit that I'm hopeful I may catch a glimpse of her. I shouldn't care if she's there, but I find myself searching through the glass windows as I get closer, looking for her. It felt weird leaving this morning without having seen her come back to the guesthouse. I don't see her in the bakery—which is probably best. I don't need to concern myself with what she's doing with her days.

The bell chimes with the door when I walk in. There's a small line, but it's late enough that the morning rush has cleared out. Winnie pops out from the back carrying a small tray of cookies. She narrowly misses the edge of the counter, avoiding taking a spill. I swear, sometimes she trips over nothing but air.

She glances up at me while placing the baked goods into the glass case. "Hey, Knox. A little late in the day for you," she greets me, smiling at me from her place in front of the door to the kitchen.

"Hey, Win. How's it going?"

"Good. How are things with you? Everything going okay with Indiana?"

"Fine" is all I say, hearing the door chime behind me.

"Yeah? Well, I'm glad to hear it. I'm happy things are working out."

"I wouldn't go that far. I'll be glad when she's off my property and out of my hair," I tell her, instantly regretting my words. It's not really the truth, but at this moment, I'm not sure how I feel about the situation, or if I want anyone to know I'm feeling anything. A throat clearing has me turning to see none other than Indie, head bent down toward her feet, a look I'm starting to recognize as embarrassment on her face. *Shit.*

"Excuse me," she says quietly, gesturing to the door behind Winnie. I move to the side to let her move past, she smells like clean clothes drying in the breeze. Warm and sunny. *I want to bury my nose in her neck.*

"Hey, Indie!" Winnie greets her before sending me a glare.

"Hey. Let me just put my things in the back, and I'll be right back out." I can hear the strain in her voice. I hadn't meant for her to hear that. I hadn't even meant the words at all. She disappears through the door, and I feel like a grade-A jackass.

"Jeezes, Knox. You could attempt to be nice. She's done nothing to warrant that kind of behavior from you," Winnie scolds me. She's right.

"You could have warned me that she had just walked in," I accuse, knowing full well it's not Winnie's fault that I acted like an asshole.

"How was I supposed to know you would say something so rude? I know you can be crabby, and when someone gets on your bad side, you don't mind setting them straight, but this isn't that. I'm not sure what's gotten into you, but you need to apologize. She already felt bad having to stay at your guesthouse when it's *my* fault she has to be there. Are you going to be mean to me too?" Winnie is a good friend. Loyal. I hadn't realized she and Indie had become friends already, but it's apparent from the berating I'm getting that she already counts her as one.

"I'll apologize," I say before leaning in to kiss the top of her head.

She lifts her chin. "You better. I just hope she accepts it."

I nod, reaching up to scratch the back of my neck. "I do too. What I said didn't have anything to do with her, and I'll tell her as much. I have a feeling she's waiting to come back out after I leave, though, so I'm gonna go."

Winnie blows out a breath. "Hold on." She walks behind the counter, grabbing a to-go cup before filling it with coffee. She puts a lid on it and offers it to me.

I grin at her. "You're too good to me," I say, hoping to lessen some of the tension between us. Winnie has been like a sister to me long before she was engaged to my brother. I may be ten years older than her, but between her, my mother, and Florence, I'm effectively kept in line by the women in my life.

She sighs but smiles back at me. "Maybe, but I'm pretty lucky to have you in my corner—most of the time. I don't want you running her off."

I put my hand over my heart as I walk backward to the door. "That doesn't sound like me."

She gives me an exaggerated eye roll. "Doesn't it though? Bye, Knox."

"Bye, Win." I step out into the bright light. The day is warming up with the sun sitting high in the sky, blazing down. I look to the mountains in the distance. Since Winnie and Rhett are keeping Hazel overnight and tomorrow, I think I'll try to get a hike in tomorrow. It's been a while since I've been able to do anything too challenging. I bring Hazel with me on the milder ones, carrying her on my back most of the time.

She used to fall asleep in her carrier while I kept hiking. Now, she gets a little restless if we're out there too long. I love exploring nature with her though. Seeing views I've seen before—through her eyes—is one of my favorite things I've experienced as a father. Thinking about her turning three soon has me remembering those first days of just us.

THREE YEARS AGO

Soft humming fills the room. It's calm now—quiet, a stark contrast to the last half hour. To anyone looking in on the scene before them, they would think it's peaceful. But inside my head? It's loud. The quiet surrounding us leaves me with no choice but to let thoughts in that I've tried so hard to keep out for the last five days. *I don't know how to do this. How does anyone do this?*

A few months ago, I was just getting used to the idea of doing this at all. Now, I'm coming to grips with the fact I'll be doing it alone. I'm angry, maybe even a little scared. Neither feeling is one I'm familiar with. I've always been able to face any situation head-on, with a calm mind. It's how I was raised. It's ingrained in me to find a way forward, to push myself.

I've made sure that everything I have done thus far in my life has been given my all. I'm responsible according to anyone's standards. Which makes finding out you're having a child, with a woman you had no contact with for six months, that much more shocking.

The situation I currently find myself in may be glaringly

different from any other I've been in before, but *I'm the same, aren't I?* I guess I'll add that to the list of things I need to figure out. I'm learning so many new things these days. The last few months have reduced any time I spent studying for the bar, any court case I've spent hours dissecting, to a mere blip. I won't fail at this. I won't let myself—neither will my family. *Thank God for them.*

I realize, after having this thought, that I'm not really alone. I'm a little overwhelmed at the idea of not having a partner in this, and it kills me that this tiny angel won't ever know her mother.

There's been a flurry of activity at my parents' ranch today. Food and diapers were dropped off. A community that's ready to stand in the gaps that I will inevitably leave. As much as I try to be, and as much as I try to pretend, I'm not perfect. No, Hazel won't have a perfect father, but she will never wonder if she's loved. That's something I *can* promise.

She stirs, the motion is small, but I catch it, looking down at her perfect sleeping face. Dark curls are already starting to form around her tiny ears. She was born with so much hair. I didn't know babies could be born with so much hair. My baby sister, Florence, was practically bald when Mom and Dad brought her home from the hospital. I guess there are advantages to being almost fifteen years older than your youngest sibling. For one, I already knew how to change a diaper.

I can swaddle, I can soothe, I can hum, and I can cook. Tom and Mary Holloway didn't raise incapable men. Because of my upbringing, there are a lot of things I'm prepared for. A lot of things I can adapt to. But as I look down again at this perfect little angel, so peaceful and safe in my arms, I'm struck by how unprepared I was to love someone so much.

INDIANA

"He's gone now," Winnie says, poking her head into the back kitchen.

Doing my best to appear unaffected, I ask, "Who?" while tying my apron strings.

She huffs a little laugh. "The grump who was just in here and unfortunately lives next door to you."

"Oh. *Him*." I smirk.

"I'm sorry he said that. I don't think he really meant it, but it's not my place to apologize for him."

"I agree and also see his point. He didn't agree to this because he thought it was a good idea for himself or his family. He only did it because he cares about you." I pause, sighing. "Which unfortunately means he's not all bad," I surmise.

"Oh...you're one of those glass-half-full people, aren't you?" she accuses.

"Guilty." I chuckle.

She grins back at me, grabbing a bright-yellow water bottle

from the counter. "I'm working on being more like that. I can be a little doom-and-gloom at times."

"Really?" That surprises me. I haven't gotten that vibe from her at all. She takes a drink, nodding as she sets the bottle back down.

"Yep. I struggle a lot with anxiety. It's taken some time, but I've been able to get a handle on it. Living in this town helps—a lot. I hope you feel welcome here. It's a really great community to be a part of," she tells me.

I grin. "I must have missed the parade in my honor," I quip.

"Stick around. I'm sure you'll get one. Hell, I'll throw you one just for working here. I don't think I could have kept going on like I was. I was here just about every day of the week from morning to night. And as much as I love this little bakery of mine—I was starting to get burned out," she admits.

"Honestly, I'm more than happy to be of service. I'm still a little in shock that you wanted me here. You *did* read my application all the way through, right? And you heard me when I said I have zero bakery experience?" I question.

"I wouldn't say zero. You baked a loaf of bread just a couple of days ago, and it looked amazing."

"Thank you. For this opportunity." For some reason, Winnie's hands-on approach to me makes me feel emotional. I've always been an emotional person. Mad, sad, angry, even hungry. I feel it all and feel it deeply. Han's always been the stoic one. She's always kept herself in check, never giving too much away. My chest aches. I miss her. I'll call her tonight, maybe after a glass of wine—or two.

"You don't have to thank me again. I'm happy you're here, but I do need to get into the zone back here to get all the breads ready for tomorrow morning so Anna actually has food to sell."

"Say no more. I'm heading out front to learn the ropes." Giving her a salute, I back out of the kitchen to shadow Anna the rest of the afternoon.

A few hours later, I'm parked in front of the guesthouse. I'm covered in flour, and there's a big coffee stain on my white tennis shoes. I probably shouldn't expect my shoes to stay white, but I'm still going to try to scrub them. It's still light out. Hours still until the sun starts to set. I get out of my car, and before I even hit the steps, a bright-orange square catches my attention. I groan. *Great, I'm probably being evicted.*

Marching up the stairs, I snatch it from the door; a soft metal clink sounds against the porch at my feet. There's anger gathering inside me at the nerve of this man. Does he think living here was my first choice? I've done nothing wrong here. I'm quiet, I don't bother anyone. *Well, there was kicking him into the lake—and seeing him naked, but not since then!* The swirling feelings completely dissipate as I bend to pick up the metal object, reading his note.

> I'm sorry I was rude. I'm not used to having neighbors. Here's a key to the shed between our houses. The paddles for all the boats are in there. And LIFE-JACKETS. Help yourself.
>
> Knox

I grin like a full-fledged idiot. He's not kicking me out. He's letting me in.

Well, he's letting me into his shed. That counts for something. Running into the house and grabbing a bag that I need to unpack into the dresser soon, I find my swimsuit and a linen button-down to put on over it. Smiling, I pull out my leather, wide-brimmed hat next, another gift from Han. A replica of Indiana Jones's. My parents' names may have been on the tag that Christmas, but I knew it was from her.

I rub some sunscreen on, tying a white bandanna around my neck, and grab my sunglasses before sliding into my strappy water sandals—a new purchase but one the salesperson at the outdoor store said would be a good investment for the terrain here. *Whatever that means.* I bought them because they're a pretty terracotta color, and I am a slut for fun-colored footwear.

Making my way around the side of the house, I see a trail that connects each of the houses' respective yards. I follow it to the small shed and use my newly gifted key to unlock the door. Before I step into the dark shed out in the middle of nowhere, I quickly look around. I've watched enough documentaries, Lifetime Movie Network, and listened to enough true crime podcasts to know that maybe accepting the key and going to this man's shed is *just* on this side of *not safe.*

Well here we go, it's either some type of weird-ass trap and I'm about to be murdered, or and I'm really hoping it's this one, it is a true olive branch, and I'll find the paddleboard paddle in here so I can teach myself out on the lake. I take that first step and see a light switch just inside. I flick it, and the whole room is illuminated by soft amber lights. I don't see any chains or a chair with restraints, but the way it's so organized *is* giving me serial-killer vibes. Heavy.

I walk down the row of paddles, there are wooden ones, aluminum, rubber, thick plastic, short, tall, two-sided, and finally I see the one with a teal handle that matches the paddleboard out at the dock. After removing it from the hook, I'm set but don't leave just yet. Framed photos on the shed wall draw my eyes to them. There are three boys in one; I can see it's Knox and Rhett, the other boy must be the third brother. Winnie wasn't even kidding about good genes. Then there are a few of her in a group of people. I see a recent one of Hazel with an older couple, most likely her grandparents.

There are lots of fishing poles and those rubber waders I've seen in magazines and on TV. Hats and rain jackets are all neatly stored and hung up. There's a small bench and a wooden desk on the other side. I see a tabletop magnifying glass and colorful threads and hooks. He must make his own fishing bait. My lips curve thinking about that big man sitting out here making tiny little lures with his big hands.

When I take in all the items, it makes me think about home. The Holmeses are a family of collectors, and if this shed tells me anything, it's that Knox may be too. A more *organized* one, but a collector nonetheless.

Curiosity satisfied, I take my paddle, grab a bright orange vest, and locking the door back behind me, hustle down to the water. Sally is already out on the dock, and even though I'm sure it's just a coincidence, it almost feels like she's waiting on me, which I know can't be true, but I still like the feeling.

"Hey, girl. Are you going to come out on the boat with me?" She cocks her furry head to the side in response. "Yeah, I don't blame you. I have no clue what I'm doing and will most likely end up in the water," I tell her. She whines in answer. "Oh, don't be so nervous. I'll be fine," I mutter, mostly to myself.

I've seen people sit on them, so surely I can handle that. I untie the knot where the board is tethered to the dock and lay the paddle out onto it. Slowly, like I'm trying not to spook it, I lower myself onto the board. It's wobbly, but I can balance. Actually, I feel pretty secure on it. With that newfound confidence, I rise to my knees—still balancing. Okay, I work one of my feet forward until I'm in some sort of low lunge. Less comfortable, but I'm okay.

As gracefully as I can, I take the paddle and push myself backward away from the dock. I inch myself up on my last leg, coming to a full stand. *Now what? Should I paddle?* I'm not sure how to paddle. *No, stop it, Indie.* I know how to paddle. Sweeping the paddle through the water on one side then the other annnd...I'm just going straight back to the dock. New plan. I paddle backward on my right, and I turn a little fast, almost falling off, but I'm able to recover. Instead, I keep going and pretty soon, I am out on the lake.

I paddle around until the bottoms of my feet start to feel sore, then sit down again. The sun is starting to set, and my view is—stunning. I wish I had Han's camera. This would be a perfect postcard if I didn't drop the camera into the water, that is. Grinning, imagining what she would say if she were here. *"Oh, so she's outdoorsy now? Okay, Granola Gal!"* I close my eyes, soaking in the last of the sun as a tear makes its way to my chin. I wipe at it. *I'm fine. I can be alone.*

"You think it's about time to call it an evening, Indiana?" a deep voice calls from behind, startling me and causing me to almost knock my paddle into the lake.

"Well, hello to you too, Knox," I quip.

"You've been out there a while, and the sun is going down. You shouldn't be out on the lake after dark," he reprimands. *Has he been watching me?*

"I'm not on the lake after dark. I was enjoying the sunset before paddling myself back in," I retort.

He grunts in reply.

"Come on now, Knox. Don't ruin that nice apology with those grouchy noises," I tease.

He huffs, and I chuckle. *Well, I tried.* I paddle myself back to the dock, he catches the board before it hits the edge, looping the rope through the hook at the end and expertly tying it off. That's kinda hot. *Shit, can I think that?* He may be with someone.

"Are you single?" Holy mother of god. I did not just ask that out loud—except I did. And now Knox is looking at me with an expression that equally says *where the hell did that come from?* And *that was forward.* "I'm sorry—that came out a little weird. I just hadn't seen anyone else out here, and I was going to bring her flowers, or a plant,—your girlfriend—if you have one, to say sorry." The ramble is rambling.

"Huh. And what would you need to apologize to her for?" he asks. Surely, he knows, and he's just giving me a hard time.

I clear the frog from my throat. "For uh-walking in on you the other day—or well, seeing you naked." I must be a shade of red that can be seen from space.

He laughs. Not a snicker. Not a chuckle. A real laugh. My chest warms from the blush, but also with something else. Pride? At getting the man to laugh? Maybe. I don't analyze it too long.

He locks our eyes, his crinkled at the corners, a deep shade of blue like a sapphire in the sun before speaking to me. "There's no one to apologize to, Indie."

"Oh. Good." *Oh. Good?* Oh my god. Oh my god. Lake, please swallow me. What if I rolled off this paddleboard and swam to shore? Would that be more or less awkward? And what does it say about me that, since he said he didn't have a girlfriend, all I can think about is his mouth? Is that bad? *If it is, I don't wanna be good.* Who am I? He makes me so...horny? Yeah, but also scattered. Incoherent.

He holds out his hand to me, and I take it, standing on wobbly legs before stepping onto the dock.

"Thanks. And thank you for the key. I've wanted to try this since I saw it the other day."

"You haven't done this before?" he asks, a little surprised. I shake my head. His surprise turns to admiration. "Well seeing as you're still dry, I guess you figured it out fairly quickly, although I still would have preferred you have the life vest *on*."

I notice then that I left the vest on the dock beside the key. "Oops. I wouldn't say I'm a professional or anything, but I held my own out there." Knox just hums in response. "So where's Hazel tonight?" I ask, hoping to shift the subject off me.

"She's at Winnie and Rhett's for the night and tomorrow for a sleepover," he tells me. I'm not sure why, but him saying the word *sleepover* is really adorable.

"I bet she loves that. Winnie's great."

"She is. My brother lucked out when he got her to say yes to marrying him."

That makes me smile. "I'll put the paddle back where I found it and let you get to your child-free evening," I say, awkwardly sliding by him.

He grabs the paddle, stopping me. "I can get it." We're face-to-face now—well, face-to-chest. Looking up at him, the top of his head is cut off from my view by my hat, but his mouth is on full display. *Has he thought about me?*

"I don't mind. I got it out; I can put it back," I insist. He lets his hand drop to his side, giving me a nod. "Thanks again."

"You're welcome to anything in there," he tells me. That sounds like a subtle gesture of goodwill.

"I'll keep that in mind if I start making my own fishing baits," I tease, and he flashes a smile at me. "Do you do that often?" I ask.

He shakes his shaggy hair. "Not so much anymore."

"I've never been fishing. All my knowledge of it comes from TV. If I'm being honest, most of my outdoor knowledge is from a book or TV."

"You've never been fishing? Not once?"

"I'm a city girl, Knox. Remember where we met?" I ask, wanting him to say I'm memorable to him. If he doesn't, he'll have to admit it to me now and put me out of my misery.

"I remember," he confirms. I'm dizzy with relief, which is so stupid. *He stood me up.* "You didn't say much the other day, so I wasn't sure you remembered me all that well," he tells me.

"I didn't want you to think I was a fangirl or something. 'Hi, remember me? From three years ago when we briefly met? Yeah, now I'm going to live in your guesthouse.' It sounded just a little stalkery to me," I tease.

"Wait. Are you saying you're *not* my stalker?" he asks, sounding offended. I'm loving this little peek at a different side of him. I like playing with him.

"No, I am. I just didn't want it to *sound* that way," I deadpan.

One side of his mouth kicks up into the most devastating

lopsided grin I've ever laid eyes on. Uh-oh. This could be bad. *For me.* I mentally gulp. On the outside, I give him a flirty grin. At least I hope that's what it looks like. He walks toward me and takes the trail that leads to the shed. I follow him, paddle in hand.

"So how *did* you end up in Silverthorne, Indie?" His question is not one I can easily or quickly answer, and his use of my nickname has butterflies swarming in my stomach. I need to get a handle on my emotions.

"Is seeing me again so bad?" I ask.

"That's not what I said."

I sigh. "Honestly—it's a bit of a long story."

"I've got time." His response surprises me. *Does he really want to know?*

I clear my throat. "Okay. Well, I had a pretty big fight—"

"With your boyfriend?" he cuts me off.

"No, I had a fight with my s-sister," I explain.

"Ah, fights with your siblings can be brutal," he sympathizes.

I nod slowly, even though he isn't facing me. The fact that he isn't makes it easier to talk about. I try to be as honest as possible. "Yeah, well, this was—more than brutal. I said some things...some *really* awful things." I close my eyes against the onslaught of words. *Just because I've always let you get your way doesn't mean the whole world revolves around you, Hana. I'm so done with your shit. Just fucking grow up.*

I open my eyes and hurry to catch up to Knox. "Anyway, we had this fight, although she also didn't ever really like that I was with my boyfriend."

"That's rough. I love all my siblings' partners—at least for now. I'm not sure I'll ever like the guy my baby sister decides to settle down with." I snicker at that.

"Ohh, so you're the overprotective big brother, huh?"

He grunts. "We all are. She had no chance with three of us."

"Are you all these huge, hulking men?" I ask, and it gets me a huffed laugh.

"I don't know if I've ever heard us described quite so eloquently, but we're all around the same size, yes."

"Damn. That's some intimidation there. Poor baby sister." We reach the shed, and he opens the door, holding his hand out for the paddle. This time I give it to him.

"Did I mention we call her Baby Lo?" he offers.

"Oh nooo. I mean my sister and I had nicknames for each other growing up, but none that were spoken outside the house. That was agreed on once she hit middle school," I tell him, laughing.

"What were they?" I notice he hasn't flipped the light on in the shed, so I lean my back against the doorframe, and he walks to the peg where the paddle belongs.

"Weren't you listening? We swore an oath," I tell him seriously.

"Oh, of course." I like this side of him. I like all sides of him. He's a walking fantasy. But I like him being more open with me; I decide to take advantage. My curiosity won't let up.

"So, the last we spoke, you were going to meet me for pizza. Did you get lost on your way there?" I ask, laughing a little. It's not like we're old friends, but I would be lying if I hadn't thought about this man on occasion over the years. I slide my hat from my head, letting it fall to my back, and I fidget, running a hand through my messy hair.

"Okay, let's just get right into it," he says, blowing out a breath, reaching for the back of his neck again. "First of all, I want you to know that I had every intention of meeting you. I had a lot of intentions where you were concerned," he tells me, eyes boring into mine, and I think I see a glimmer of the man I met in that bar. "I got a phone call on my way home that night. One that sort of rearranged my schedule."

I'm on the edge of my seat, dying to know more about these intentions, but what I need is his reason for not showing up right now. Wondering what you did to make someone stand you up is hard to get over, and being stood up by Knox was one of the biggest pills I've had to swallow.

"Rearranged your schedule? So what, a work thing popped up?" I ask, a little miffed. *A work call? Really?*

"No, *my daughter* popped up. Or her mother did, letting me know about her," he tells me pointedly.

Oh. "Holy crap on a cracker. That's a big schedule rearranging."

He hums. "It was. One I'm grateful for every day. I do regret not being able to get a hold of you though. If you recall, *you* had *my* number. I had no way of contacting you."

"That's valid. Wow, playing the adorable daughter card so soon. I guess I have no other option but to lay all the resentment I've held for you over the years down."

"Have you held that much resentment? Have you thought about me that often?" he quips. I'd like to play hard to get, but if Knox is *trying* to get—he's going to get.

"I'll admit to the occasional thought of you. I'm not ashamed." *But I might be embarrassed now that I've told him. Hard to get is looking more appealing.*

"I may have been harboring some curiosity of my own." His admission has me taking in a deep breath. "So this is a big change from Atlanta, are you settling into small-town life okay?" *Whoa. Subject change.*

"It's been an interesting introduction. But now that I feel a little stability in my living situation, thank you for that, yes. Being here, in the mountains, is starting to feel like an adventure to me, and nature makes me feel small. Manageable," I confess.

"You *are* small," he points out.

I roll my eyes. "I don't mean physically. Although looks can be deceiving. I may be small, but I'm pretty tough."

"I have no doubt. I know a tiny-but-mighty when I see one, and I felt that kick." He grins that crooked grin again, and my heart stutters at the sight. Does he know how gorgeous he is?

"So the boyfriend in the city?"

"What about him?"

"He was fine with the long distance?" *Is he asking if I'm single?*

I let out an exaggerated sigh. "You can ask if I'm with someone, Knox. It's only fair since I asked you the same thing," I say, poking fun at myself and poking him in his chest with a finger.

He doesn't laugh, but there's humor in his eyes before he leans in, causing me to press my back against the doorframe, and asks, "Are you with someone, Indie?" His breath on my bare skin sends goose bumps down my arms. I'm becoming very aware that I'm still in my blue bikini. I shake my head in response, unable to locate my voice. The air between us is too thick. Too tension filled. I fight my hands, hugging them to my sides as tightly as I can. Then he keeps talking, causing me to doubt the function of my ears—or maybe I'm just having trouble hearing him over my own heartbeat.

"Do you wanna be?"

KNOX

It's as if my brain is completely separate from my mouth. Indie weaves some strong magic. The only thought I have is that I don't want to stop being around her. Before I know what I'm doing, I'm asking her to my place for a drink.

"I'm sorry. What?" Indie asks. Like maybe she's misheard me, or maybe my invitation is a complete surprise. I had thought there was some flirting happening, but now I'm feeling like I read this all wrong.

"Do you want to have a drink? With me?" I repeat, scratching at the back of my neck.

"Like at your house? Now?" The shock on her face is... confusing. How had I misread this so completely? I lean back, putting a little space between us.

"Unless you don't want to," I say, trying to sound more casual than I'm feeling. Having never been good at anything resembling dating, I'm doing my best here but flying blind.

"I want to," she blurts, reaching out to grab my arm. My lips curl into a smile at her acceptance and her hand on me.

"Okay. Good." I turn and walk to the house, somewhat awkwardly, just hoping she's following.

"Your place is beautiful," she says after we walk a few steps.

"Thank you. The renovations were a lot more extensive than I had originally planned, but I'm happy with them," I tell her honestly.

"Did you do all the renovations yourself?"

"Not all of them, I hired out most of the heavy lifting, and my family helped with the more cosmetic issues."

"That's nice. No one in my family is very handy, so it probably would have ended up in worse shape than when we started if we took on that kind of project," she muses, and I laugh.

"Not everyone in mine is, I found that out the hard way."

"Now, if we're talking design or interior decorating, the Holmes family are your people."

"Oh yeah?"

"My parents are both artists. Dad works on movie sets, and my mom does oil paintings."

"What about you?"

"What about me?"

"Are you an artist?" I clarify.

She laughs. "If you had ever seen a drawing of mine as a kid, you wouldn't be asking me that."

"No one can draw when they're a kid," I tell her, thinking of the last thing Hazel has proudly presented. Did I put it on the fridge? Yes. Do I know what it is? No.

"Maybe. But if I showed you one I did today, you wouldn't be able to tell the difference." That makes me laugh.

"You laugh, but it's actually kind of sad." She chuckles.

"Sad how?" I ask, reaching the side door of the house and sliding it open.

"You try growing up in a family that paints murals and makes everything they touch beautiful." I consider her words. We may not have had similar childhoods, but being in a family that feels different from you is something I can sympathize with.

"Well, I guess it wouldn't be fair if you looked like you do *and* you could make everything beautiful," I tease, taking off my shoes by the door.

She smiles at me, tucking some hair behind her ear. It's shy, and so fucking sweet, and I want to reach out to feel the strands between my fingers.

"How do I look?"

"Don't act like you don't know you're beautiful, Indie."

Her smile widens, and I'm rewarded with a blush. She dips her head to the shoe rack, eyebrows raising.

"What size shoe do you wear?" she asks, then snaps her head up. "Sorry, you don't have to answer that. What kind of drinks are we having?"

I laugh; it would seem both of us are having trouble with our filters tonight. "Twelve," I answer, even though she said I didn't have to. "And do you have a preference? I was going to have a beer, but I have some wine or whiskey," I offer.

"A beer sounds great," she tells me, taking a seat on a stool at the island, then asks, "So...what do you do for work, Knox?"

"I'm a lawyer," I answer, grabbing two cans from the fridge and handing one to her.

"That sounds exciting." She pulls back the tab on her beer and takes a drink.

"It can be. Silvethorne is a little slower paced than New

York, but I find it a bit more rewarding." I crack open my own can and take a long sip.

"How so?"

"Well, for one, I would say I know 98 percent of my clients personally, so it's nice to have that personal connection. Knowing the people I'm helping are good ones."

"That makes sense."

"It's really nice to be back home. With my family and friends. This community really cares about its people." Indie hums in response. "What?" I ask.

"Nothing, it's just that Winnie said the same thing to me. I'm looking forward to being a part of that." She looks at her hands.

"Yeah? Planning on sticking around for a while then?" There's probably a little too much hope in my voice. I may not want to admit it, but I do want her around.

"Well, not *here*. I'm hoping to be *out of your hair* as soon as I'm able to." She throws my earlier words back at me. "But in town? Yes, that's the plan."

I nod. "Did I mention that I'm sorry for saying that?"

"I think I got a note or something," she teases, taking another long drink.

"It wasn't about you," I start. "You've been nothing but nice and—" I clear my throat. "Well, that was more about me."

"I see."

I laugh. "I don't think you do because I'm not sure I really understand myself."

"You caught me." She sighs, making me laugh again.

"I haven't had a neighbor in a long time, Indie. I haven't made a friend in even longer," I admit. *Friend. The word feels wrong.*

"You're doing fine, Knox, I should probably get back home though.

"Sure." I step toward her, reaching behind her head for her hat. Her eyes flick back and forth between my eyes and my mouth, a light blush on her cheeks from the beer or maybe something else. Her big, brown eyes meet mine with curiosity, like she might be okay with me doing something other than getting her hat. I grab it off the hook and set it on her head, adjusting it to fit. "You're really leaning into the whole name-sake thing, aren't you?" I'm close enough now to feel the breath from her answering chuckle.

"This was a gift from my sister. My parents are big film buffs. They love Harrison Ford, hence the names Indiana and Han," she explains.

"It suits you," I tell her. And it does. She looks sexier than she has a right to in that hat, and I can't imagine another woman with her name. "Come on, Indie. I'll walk you to your place."

She shakes her head at me. "Not necessary, Cowboy."

I smile down at her. "Cowboy?"

"Isn't this the Wild West?" she asks with a flutter of her eyelashes.

"I wouldn't describe Silverthorne like that exactly."

Smiling, she slides open the glass door, and I follow her through it. "You really don't need to walk me. It's what? Half a mile?"

"More or less, but it's dark."

"Do you think something is going to get me? I'm a pretty fast runner, you know," she jokes.

"Oh yeah? I might believe you, but if you can't see it coming, then how will you know to run?" I flinch in her direction, causing her to scream. *Loudly*. We may not have neighbors, but I would be shocked if someone in the next county over didn't hear it. I laugh. Hard. *Why is it so fun to tease this woman?*

"Asshole." She shoves at me, but I don't move. Her hand lingers for a few seconds on my stomach. I may or may not be flexing for her.

"A lot of the time I can be," I agree quietly.

"That must be freeing."

"How so?"

"Not worrying about everything that comes out of your mouth and how someone else might take it? What that must be like?" she says dreamily.

"Is that really how you go through life?" I ask.

She nods. "For the most part."

"I'm not an expert, but I don't know if that's healthy," I tease.

"Oh, it's not. Rest assured, the experts all agree with you."

I hum, but don't comment.

"Got any big plans for tomorrow?" she asks.

"I'm going for a hike."

"I've been wanting to go on a hike. I even made a list of trails in the area I want to try." I think she might be fishing for an invite, but I've been wrong before.

"Have you ever been hiking before?"

"Not exactly, but I went for a run on the trail that cuts off the main drive here and made it back in one piece," she tells me quickly. Eagerly. There is no pretense now.

"Would you want to go, Indiana?" The question hangs between us. It's not like I've asked her on a date, but close enough.

"Oh. Um, sure. What time?" I can tell she's excited, but she doesn't want me to know. Her mouth is tilted up, and I want to kiss the corner of it.

I grin. "Seven?"

"Perfect. I'll be on your porch ready to go," she says, moving to take the steps up to the front door. I don't try to stop my eyes from watching her ass as she goes. She turns back to me when she reaches the top. "Goodnight, Knox."

"I'll see you in the morning, Indie. Goodnight," I say, before walking back to my house in the cool evening air. I can feel her eyes on me until I make it to the edge of my yard.

When I lie down in bed, it takes me much longer than usual to fall asleep. Thinking of Indie being right down the road, within walking distance, has me wired. When I do succumb to sleep, she's there too. In that blue swimsuit, smiling at me.

KNOX

The smell of coffee wakes me in the morning. I've only just realized the full potential of the fancy coffee machine that Florence got me for Christmas. Being able to time my coffee with my alarm is a luxury I didn't know I needed. Flinging my blankets off, I plant my feet on the floor before stretching out my back. I may not feel forty-one by this afternoon, but I sure as hell do every morning. Moving my body through my daily morning routine, I think about the night before and the woman who it revolved around.

Having met her years ago, I already knew that there was attraction between us, but the easy conversation wasn't something I had expected. I haven't been on a date with a woman in three years. There has been some interest, but there hasn't been anyone I've cared to spend any more time with than necessary. But Indie? I want to spend time with her.

Hence, the inviting her on my solo hike this morning. I run a hand down my face. Yes, she had basically invited herself, but I didn't have to ask her to come. I want to know more about her. I realized last night, after getting into bed, that she had somehow steered the topic back to me when I asked about her. I said more to her last night than I've said to anyone outside my family or my business associates in—I'm not sure how long—but it's been a while.

I pour myself a cup of coffee in the kitchen and take it back with me to the bedroom to get dressed. It's supposed to be warmer today, and there's a waterfall on the hike we're going on, so I pull on a pair of shorts and a T-shirt, throwing a flannel over the top to combat the morning chill. Grabbing my backpack, I stock it with plenty of water, some granola bars, and some sunscreen. I only have baby sunscreen, but it smells good and it's the organic shit that I pay twice as much for.

Zipping the pack, I check the time on my phone to see it's 6:45. Glancing at my messages from Winnie, there are two pictures that I've already saved to my phone. One is of Rhett, his hair pulled tight into a ponytail on top of his head with a pink bow. The other is of Hazel sitting on their kitchen counter, helping Winnie bake. I smile at the tiny chef's hat sitting on top of her little head.

Out back, I water the plants that Hazel helped me pick out and plant, along with the small herb garden I'm trying out. Cooking is something I really enjoy doing, and a lot of times, I end up helping my family out with recipes. Hazel isn't always thrilled with my offering unless it's covered in cheese. I guess I can't be too offended by her three-year-old's palate.

I check my phone again and see it's now 6:59. Hmm, still no Indie. Only when I make it to the side of the house with the hose, she's there. She's standing on my porch in one of my old ball caps and a sweatshirt that says: Adventure Is Out There, But So Are Serial Killers. I've never wanted to kiss someone more in my life. I'm not sure how she managed to get her hands on my hat, but it's hers now.

"Hey," I call, and she looks up at me from her perch against the porch railing.

"Hi." Her voice is still sleepy sounding. Knowing I'm the first person she's spoken to today does something to me.

"Morning. You ready to head out?"

"Mm-hmm."

"Just let me grab my pack; I'll be out in a minute."

"Sounds good," she says, smiling at me.

Gathering my things quickly so I don't keep her waiting, I meet her back at the porch.

"Is the trail around here or...?" Her question hangs in the air.

"It's only a fifteen-minute drive to the trailhead," I tell her, locking my front door.

"Should I follow you?" She hitches a thumb over her shoulder at her car.

"Not unless you have an objection to being in my truck." *I want her to be in my truck.*

"No objection...but since I did *kind of* invite myself on your hike today...I thought I would give you the chance to not be stuck with me on the drive as well." She gives me a sheepish grin.

"I wouldn't have invited you if I didn't want to, Indie."

She nods her head at that, biting her full bottom lip. "I guess I'll have to believe you."

I hum. "After you." I hold out a hand toward my truck, watching her skip down the steps to the passenger door. When she opens it, Sally jumps inside.

"Oh, hey, Sally girl!" Indie says giving her full attention to the dog now sitting in the middle of the bench seat.

"Do you mind if she tags along?"

"Are you kidding?" she asks sliding in beside Sally, shutting the door but rolling the window down so if she wants, Sally can lean her head out of it. I shake my head. The girls in my life will be spoiled with or without my help.

"How long have you had her?" Indie asks me as I shut my own door and turn the key in the ignition causing the truck roar to life.

"A couple years. She made her way onto my parents' ranch, and Hazel fell in love with her." Indie smiles widely at that.

"I'm guessing Hazel gets what she wants most of the time." It's not a question, but it's also not said in a way that suggests that would be a bad thing.

"Well, when you have three younger siblings and yours is the first grandbaby in the family, I suppose it comes with the territory," I muse.

"As it should," Indie agrees. "I know if I had a kid, my sister would have spoiled them rotten, and my parents, while being incredibly theatrical, are extremely loving." I notice that while petting Sally, Indie gives me a lot more information.

"How was growing up in Atlanta?"

She bites the side of her bottom lip into her mouth before answering. "It was good. Busy. A lot more public transportation." She laughs. "I didn't learn to drive until I was twenty-one."

"You didn't drive until you were twenty-one? Why wait so long?" I can't fathom not driving the day you turn sixteen. I was so excited to drive to school the very next day.

"Well, like I said, there were options, we took the train most places—everywhere really. My family still doesn't own a car, and the one I'm driving now is a rental. Actually, I need to find a car so I can stop paying for that, but I just haven't wanted to. It feels a little overwhelming. I don't know what kind of car I need, or should I get a truck? I kind of like the idea of a truck. Can't you just picture it?" Her question is directed at Sally, but that doesn't stop the image from popping into my mind. Her tiny frame sitting behind the steering wheel of a massive truck makes me laugh before I can stop myself.

"Could you even see over the steering wheel of a truck?" I ask, turning to see her face. She narrows her eyes at me, nose scrunching, and fuck me that's cute.

"Go ahead, cowboy. Underestimate me. I'm no stranger to proving someone wrong." I'm not sure why, but the idea of this woman having to overcome anything has me ready to fight someone.

"I was only referring to your size, not what you're capable of," I amend.

She smiles at that, and a swell of emotion fills my chest. Unsure what's causing it, but not wanting to question it because I like the way it feels. *I like how being around Indie makes me feel.*

"When you're five foot one, I guess it comes with the territory," she tells me, using my phrasing from earlier.

"What little territory there is," I mutter.

"Okay! That's enough about my size! We can't all be six five and built like Paul Bunyan." A hoarse laugh sputters out of me, and she giggles in response.

"Been a while since I've heard a good Paul Bunyan reference, and never have I been compared to him."

"What about his Ox?" That makes me laugh again, even

harder. God, this woman. She makes me feel young, which reminds me of another question I've been meaning to ask her. Winnie mentioned her age, but I can't remember it. *Twenty-something?* I know there comes a time when you aren't supposed to ask a woman her age, but I can't imagine Indie's old enough to worry about that yet.

"How old are you, Indie?"

"I just turned twenty-seven. How old are you, Knox?" Knowing my answer puts me in another generation than her is a tough pill to swallow, but I do.

"I'm forty-one, forty-two in a month."

She whistles low. "Oh wow, so you're like...really old," she says in exaggerated surprise. I look over at her, and she winks, causing my chest to heat in the crisp mountain air.

"It's fourteen years older than you," I state.

"I may be a bit younger than you, but I *am* out of grade school." She laughs at herself. "High school and college, too, just so we're clear. I'm caught up on basic math, old man," she adds.

"Oh, not you too." I groan. "You sound like my siblings."

"Aww, do they pick on the elderly in your family?"

"Excuse me?"

"Did you need me to speak up? Can you not hear me?" she asks, speaking loudly and slowly. Without thinking, I lift my hand off the gear shift and grab her exposed knee. She pulls away from me, giggling while Sally lets out a couple of barks at us.

Smiling, I turn us onto the side road that takes us to the trailhead.

"Sorry, I couldn't resist with how you went on about my size," Indie says, still smiling, Sally all but on her lap now.

"You can tell her to get down; she'll listen."

"I wouldn't dream of it. Growing up, my parents wouldn't let us have pets. We tried to convince them, but to their point, we lived in an apartment with nowhere for a dog to run, and my dad isn't a fan of cats."

I put the truck in park when we reach our destination and feel behind me into the backseat to grab my backpack and Sally's dog pack that has her water bowl and some food.

"Tough break. We've had so many animals at our home over the years, I don't think I could name all of them," I tell her, opening the truck door and stepping out. Sally jumps out after me, and I fasten the pack around her.

"That many animals? Like what? Did you have pigs?" she asks curiously.

I think about it for a minute. "For a little bit. My mom wasn't a big fan of the smell."

"I hadn't thought about that part of it. I'm imagining mini pigs that fit in your purse," she muses.

"Think more like a baby elephant that would eat you if you gave it the chance."

She laughs. "You can't be serious."

"I am. Those pigs were mean as fuck." Her laughter grows, her eyes going squinty.

"What else? What other animals?" she demands.

"Goats, cattle, horses, cats, llamas, chickens...Florence had a duck for a bit." I list all the animals I can think of. When she doesn't respond, I look over to find her mouth open.

"You had all those pets, and I couldn't even convince my parents to let me have one teeny tiny goldfish? Although that didn't stop us from trying—" She proceeds to tell me about stealing a neighbor's cat and keeping it hidden until her parents found it. The way she speaks is so animated, arms slicing through the air, hand gestures to emphasize everything she's saying. For someone so small, she makes sure to take up space when she's talking. "So from then on, we started collecting things," she finishes.

I start walking toward the trailhead, Sally trotting in front of me and Indie falling in step right behind me. "So, what did you collect?" I ask.

"What didn't we collect? We started with rocks, but Han liked every single rock she laid eyes on, and our apartment was overflowing with them. After the rocks, we started pressing flowers. I still do that every spring, and I cannot wait to catalog the wildflowers in Colorado. We had so much fun collecting things that my parents started doing it. Mom has a small army of ceramic frogs, and my dad started finding and repairing German cuckoo clocks."

"Cuckoo clocks?"

"Yes." She chuckles.

"Like with the bird that comes out of the door and loudly squawks?"

She giggles. "That isn't how I would describe them exactly —but more or less, yes. My dad would repair them, and sometimes he would let Han and me paint some of the pieces."

"Sounds like you're really close with your family."

She doesn't answer right away. I look over my shoulder and see her looking down at her feet as we hike. I barely hear her response.

"Not as much lately, but there's a lot of love there." I just hum in acknowledgment. I'm not usually one to pry, but asking her why is on the tip of my tongue when she speaks again. "I guess I should have asked, but how long is this hike we're on today?" she asks, effectively changing the subject. She's good at this evasiveness.

"It's only a three-and-a-half-mile loop. The trail you ran yesterday would have been more challenging, but this one has some bouldering routes on it that I like to climb."

"Rock climbing?" she asks.

"Yeah, have you ever been?"

"Not really. I've never been climbing outside, but I did have a pass to my indoor climbing gym in Atlanta." That surprises me. It doesn't exactly fit in with the picture I've drawn of her life in my mind.

"Do you boulder?" I ask her.

I hear a huffed-out laugh. "Not well. I'm more of a sport climber. I am belay and lead climb certified though. At least that's what the little tag on my harness says."

"Impressive; if you like climbing, then you've come to the right state," I tell her as we continue through the forest. The sun is out, and the day is warming up. It's quiet out here, only the sound of our boots and Sally's happy panting.

"I do enjoy climbing. I'd really like to start doing it outside. Do you have any recommendations on where I should start?" I wonder if she's fishing again, wanting me to ask her to come with me sometime.

"Yeah, there are a few places to boulder. If you're looking to sport climb, then you'll need a partner," I tell her. *Now who's fishing?*

"If you want to come with me, you can just ask, Knox." I'm glad she's behind me so she can't see the grin on my face. Now that she's put the thought in my head though? I really wouldn't mind having her on the other end of a rope.

"Oh wow," I hear her breathe out behind me. Turning

around, I find her staring behind us into the valley we've just hiked out of. I like that she's taken the time to take in the view. Sometimes I'm too focused on the destination.

"It's so beautiful out here. Just—everywhere. Even the gas station on my way into town was pretty," she muses.

"It is. Just wait until you see where we're going." She spins back to me at that.

"Well, what are we waiting for then?" she asks me, laughing. The excitement coming off her in waves when she moves past me and now leading the way with Sally. My old ball cap looking better on her than it ever did on me.

"After you," I mumble, not used to following anyone. Indiana is sure in her footsteps though. I would venture to say that she's no stranger to taking the lead.

"So, you grew up here?" she asks after we've been walking for a few minutes.

"I did."

She laughs. "And? I met you in a dive bar in New York. How long were you living there?"

I nod. "I was in New York working at a law firm out of college and was there for the better part of a decade before moving back home," I answer.

"Were you a fancy lawyer in a big office?"

"My office wasn't that big."

"That means it was." She sighs. "So, how was it readjusting to life here again? It's only been a couple of weeks for me, but I'm already missing a few things from living in a city."

"Like what?" If it's anything I can remedy, I will.

"Maybe it's not so much that I miss it, it's just going to take some getting used to, but the convenience of delivery. I tried looking online and on a few of my apps, but there are zero grocery or food delivery options. I've never been a great cook. Honestly, I've never tried too hard, but Silverthorne is forcing me to put all the recipe videos I've saved to good use," she says wistfully. In my head, all I can think is: *I wouldn't mind cooking for her.*

But out loud, I just hum in agreement. "Yeah, that will take some getting used to. You forgot something at the store? It's another trip to town, or you have to go without."

"It doesn't help that I didn't make a list when I went shopping. I'm pretty good at staying organized, but put me in the grocery store when I'm hungry, and there's no telling what I'll come out with or how many things..." she trails off, making me look over at her. Indie has stopped moving, and if I didn't already know this trail, the look on her face would tell me we've made it to the waterfall.

INDIANA

From the moment I hopped into Knox's old truck up until now, I had thought I'd seen some really beautiful views around the world. I haven't traveled a lot, but my last job took me to some pretty places. Looking before me now though, I'm not sure seeing something is the same as what I'm doing now.

We're up on top of a huge waterfall, with another one above us just to the right that flows into this one. I can see the stream down below. The rocks are covered in moss, and all along the sides of the water are colorful wildflowers. It's beautiful and *right in front of me.* I can smell the water, reach out and touch it if I want. I'm *in* the postcard right now. "I've never been inside the postcard before," I whisper.

"Do what?" I hear Knox's deep voice ask from behind me.

I laugh. "It's just that I've seen a lot of pretty things. A lot of nice views. I pick up postcards from every place I visit. But I've only ever seen them from hotel rooms or from the air. I've never been *in* the view before," I try to explain. When I look over at him, he looks thoughtful. I miss Han in moments like these. I never have to explain anything to her; she just gets it.

"You're experiencing it in real time," he says, surprising me.

"Yes, exactly." I smile, fighting the tears that being seen by someone brings.

"Want to explore a little before we head back?" he asks.

"Absolutely. Please."

He starts walking down a small trail to our left, Sally following him, and me following her. I pull Han's camera from my backpack, looping it around my neck. I take a couple of pictures from up here before making my way down the pathway to get a few from a different angle. Still in awe of my surroundings, I barely notice Knox leaning against a boulder by the water's edge.

I wonder then for a moment if this is a typical hike for him. If maybe this is a place he brings other people—*other women.* The thought leaves behind a bitter taste. One that, instead of examining further, I push to the wayside, along with all my other unpleasant thoughts, feelings, and concerns. Knox takes a drink of his water and draws my attention back to him. His hip propped against the large rock beside him, he's looking out over the river that the waterfall flows into. I lift my camera and, without thinking, take the photo. He turns, and I snap another.

"I believe it's common courtesy to ask someone before you take their picture," he scolds me. If I thought he was serious, I might blush or drop my gaze, but the lazy drawl in which he delivers the remark puts me at ease. He's only teasing me. *He's only teasing me, and it makes me think of other ways this man could tease.*

"I'm not sure what you mean. I'm only capturing the beautiful landscape. If you happen to be in some of the photos, then that's completely by accident." I give him a shrug and keep moving down the riverbank toward some wildflowers. I picked up a book before moving that has all the Colorado state flowers categorized. There are these little slots after each description to place a real flower.

Once a collector, always a collector.

I guess you can move thousands of miles from your family, but the habits you pick up from them stay with you. Thinking about all the collections I've seen through the years tugs at my heart. I miss the eclectic apartment I grew up in sometimes. The tight quarters and colorful whimsy are one half of the mold that worked to shape me into who I am today. Various items on shelves or in cases. I can still see the walls lined with art and hear the clocks.

"Do you ever get desensitized?" I ask when I feel Knox walking behind me.

"In what way?" I've noticed he does this a lot. He's good at answering a question with a clarifying one. Must be the lawyer in him. I'll play along.

"Now that you mention it, I think I'd like to know all the things you *think* I could be referring to, but in this instance, I mean to the scenery. I'm not sure I could ever get tired of it."

When I turn to look at him, his gaze is fixed out on the water again. I put the lens cap back on the camera and stow it in my pack. I remove the old ball cap I found this morning and run my hand through my hair while I wait for Knox to respond. The sun coming out has brought the temperature up, and it's time for my sweatshirt to come off.

I'm beginning to wonder if he's going to answer me. I swallow, readying another prompt, wanting to get to know him better, but when I look back at him, I see his eyes are locked on my waist, where I'm fastening the sleeves of my discarded sweatshirt into a knot. I'm delighted that he looks interested in the skin I'm now showing. I watch his throat work before his sapphire blues flick up to my eyes. *Busted, Mr. Holloway.* It's nice to know maybe I'm not the only one feeling the attraction between us grow. I grin and tilt my head to the side, raising my eyebrows in a silent question.

He clears his throat. "I think if you live anywhere too long, you might get complacent. But if the question is do I get tired of the views? Then no. I could go on the same hike, the same climb, the same turn around the lake, and each time I would find something different to appreciate." He continues to walk down the river while I trail behind.

I nod. "I don't know how anyone could get tired of this," I say, gesturing to the picturesque scene before us.

"You'd be surprised. Small-town living isn't for everyone." he tells me then grabs the back of his shirt, slipping it over his head and off his body in one swift motion. The defined lines of his back and the tattoo he has in the center of his shoulder blades has my hands twitching in his direction, aching to trace it.

At my silence, he turns to face me, and oh god, forget the waterfall, *this* is the view.

"You okay?" He's smirking at me.

I gulp. Honesty is the best policy, right? "I'm trying really hard not to completely objectify you, Knox." He raises his eyebrows for a second, then his face relaxes into a knowing grin. Of course he knows he's hot because how could he not? Was taking his shirt off premeditated?

"Don't try too hard," he teases and then *winks* at me. I'll be riding this high for days. That crinkled eye smile is already embedded behind my eyelids.

I clear my throat. "No, I guess small-town living isn't for everyone. I've lived in a big city my whole life, and although it has its perks and opportunities, I'm more than happy being here. I've never in my life been able to look one way or the other and not see a building. It's...freeing? Exhilarating? Is that at all how you feel?" I ask, turning to face him.

"I'm not sure if those are the words I would use, but freeing comes close. When I was living in the city, I did feel homesick from time to time. My plan was always to be back here. Things just fast-tracked as soon as I found out Hazel's mother was pregnant."

I have a lot of questions on the tip of my tongue that may be too personal to ask. So I ask one that feels safer.

"Last night you mentioned you didn't have a girlfriend—"

"You *asked* if I had one, but go on," he prompts, and I have to fight my smile.

"Was that how it happened? It's not really important." I brush him off. "Anyway, I guess I was wondering if you have Hazel full time or if she spends time with her mother too." I can see his shoulders tense in front of me. Was that too personal? It was the least personal question I could think of. "I'm sorry. You don't have to answer that," I rush out. We continue to walk, his footfalls never faltering.

I stare at my feet, at my bright-blue tennis shoes. I need to watch each step carefully so I don't trip over any rocks or roots. I take Knox's silence as he doesn't want to answer me, maybe he doesn't even want to be out here with me after my rude question. I hate that sometimes I find it impossible to read the room. Try as I might, that seems to be a skill I still lack. I open my mouth, ready to tell him that he can take me home if he wants, but he surprises me by speaking first.

"I have Hazel full time. Her mother passed away not long after she was born, so it's just me—and my family." An overwhelming sense of sadness takes hold of me at hearing that.

"I'm so sorry, Knox." I wish I had something better to say, but sorry is what I feel. Sorry that Knox went through losing someone and was left to raise Hazel alone. Sorry that Hazel won't meet her mother, and sorry that a mother had to leave her child.

"Thank you" is all he says. I decide that dropping the subject and *not* asking what happened is the best course of action. It's none of my business, and asking would most likely be insensitive. He would share with me if he wanted to.

We spend the rest of our hike quietly exploring. I snap a few more pictures, and there's some small talk. We keep it light; I do my best to steer clear of topics that could be seen as probing. I ask about foods he likes to cook, the things Hazel's into—sharks and princesses—a combo that I am thoroughly intrigued by. And after hearing him talk about his daughter, I come out of this hike with a new fear.

Knox Holloway is even better than I had originally thought, and I'm in very serious trouble of falling for him.

KNOX

Candy-pink bows and plastic dinosaurs are sprinkled over a three-tier birthday cake. Winnie has gone all out for Hazel's third birthday party—she's gone all out for all her birthdays really. There is a station in the yard specifically designated for princess gowns that Hazel and the other guests can dress up in. My baby brother, Rhett, and his best friend, Colt, have graciously offered to take up post there—complete with their own princess crowns. The dinosaur bounce house was not approved by me, but I couldn't be upset when I saw my daughter's face light up at the sight of it.

Three years old. I'm having a hard time figuring out where time has gone. Months of my tiny baby needing help adjusting to a life without her mother, weeks of no sleep, and the endless diapers and bottles that felt like they would never end have somehow gone by in the blink of an eye. Now she's this perfect little person. Walking—running—around in the yard with other little kids. It makes me wonder how fast the next few years will go by.

Looking out across the yard, I see my whole family scattered and enjoying the party. Ivy and Florence made sure the whole property was decorated, and Winnie and my mom handled all the food. To no one's surprise, Alder is responsible for the bounce house. He and Ivy are making sure no one is injured, which is the only reason I let it stay up. I grin seeing my father twirl my mother in a circle while they dance to the music playing over the outdoor speakers.

Scanning the party again, I see Indie walking down the road that connects our houses. She's carrying a big, green box with a frilly pink bow tied around it, perfect for the theme. Hazel invited her the night after our hike, followed by a pretty please. She had looked up at me to confirm it was okay to say yes before telling Hazel she could come. I had appreciated it and at the same time wished I had thought to ask her first, so she would know she was welcome. That thought had caught me off guard. I'm not exactly the first person someone would think of when thinking *welcoming*.

"Indie!"

"Hi, Hazel!" I watch Hazel's green princess dress swish behind her as she runs to meet Indie at the edge of the yard. Setting the present on the ground beside her, she bends down to greet my daughter.

"Happy Birthday, Hazel Emilia Holloway."

"Thank you. Is that mine?" she asks Indie. Practically vibrating with anticipation.

"It is! I couldn't come empty-handed." Hazel grabs her hand and tugs her toward the party. Indie picks up the present, letting herself be pulled.

"Hey, Indie!" Rhett calls from his position at the dress-up station.

"Hi, Rhett. I love your crown."

"Thank you," he says, then curtsies, causing her to giggle. In all the years since middle school, I don't remember ever wanting to be the reason a girl giggled. Until now.

"Hey, Knox. Thanks for the invite," she tells me while Hazel drags her past me over to the present table. I nod at her and take a sip of my beer.

"It goes here," Hazel tells Indie, pointing at the table.

"Oh my goodness. This is the coolest party I've ever been to."

"It's my birthday!" Hazel shouts.

Indie laughs with her. "It's your birthday!" she shouts back.

"Will you jump with me?" The face she gives Indie is one I've been met with many times. It's nearly impossible to say no to, I'd say even harder when you aren't used to it.

"Hey, Hazey. Why don't you give Indie a minute to say hi to everyone? I'll send her in to play with you soon."

"Okay!" she agrees easily, smiling as she runs into Alder's arms so he can jump into the bounce house with her.

Indiana places her present with the others and turns to face me. "Hi."

"Hi. I'm glad you came," I tell her honestly, moving closer to her.

"I wanted to. There's no way I could say no to an invitation from the birthday girl." She looks to Hazel then back at me. We just stare at one another for a few seconds.

"Hey, Indie!" We turn to see Winnie and my mom coming out of my house, holding platters of toppings for the burgers and hot dogs my dad is grilling. He waves at us, wearing his new apron proudly. This one reads "It's All Fun And Games Until Someone Burns Their Weiner." It's pretty tame for him, probably because this is a children's birthday party. What started as a prank apron has turned into a full-on collection at this point.

"Hi! I feel like I haven't seen you in days," Indie tells Winnie.

"I know! I was getting used to seeing you every day." Winnie sighs. "I'll see you tomorrow, though, right?"

"Absolutely! Reporting for duty." Indie gives her a little salute. It's awkward and adorable.

"What's going on?" I ask.

"The Spring Festival. I'm helping Winnie prep all the items for Thistle and Sage's booth. I'm making all the new signage."

"Wait! *You* made all the new branding?!" Florence has appeared seemingly out of nowhere with three presents in her arms. Indie moves to help her with them, guiding her to the table to set them down.

"I did. Winnie hired me on as a part-time manager but also for some branding and web design," she tells my sister.

"Yeah? How would you feel about helping me with some branding for the hotel?"

"Really? I would be more than happy to. I already have so many ideas."

"Are you trying to poach my employee?" Winnie asks.

"Not poach—share?" Lo suggests.

They grin at each other. "Deal," Winnie agrees.

"Do I have a say in this?" Indie chimes in.

Both girls look at her. "No," they say in unison. Indie just laughs.

"Did I show you the pictures she took for the website?" Winnie asks, practically buzzing with excitement.

"No, do you have them with you?" Lo asks.

"I would like to see them, too, if you don't mind. I was thinking of updating The Edgemont's site as well," Ivy chimes in. Since moving to town last winter, she joined Alder in running the ski resort up on the mountain during the winter and turned it into a mountain bike destination in the summers.

"I have them all on my laptop back at the house. Do you... would you guys want to come by after the party and see?" she asks hesitantly. They all give her a resounding yes.

"Count me in too!" another voice yells from the other side of the yard. Marigold walks over to the group, still in her hospital scrubs.

"Hi, big brother. Sorry I'm late. I had to deal with a small mishap at work," Lo says, giving me a hug and kiss on the cheek.

"Everything okay?" I ask, it's not like her to complain about anything.

"Fine. Just a guy on the phone today. He made a big stink about talking to me on the phone and then called me a—" she cuts herself off, looking around to the kids then whispers, "bitch, when I couldn't get him a room. We're booked, it's a busy season," she finishes, reaching for a glass of pink lemonade from the table behind me.

"He what?"

"I know! Such a jerk."

"I hate that you have to deal with rude assholes."

"Them's the breaks," she says breezily. "I'm fine. Shaking it off to celebrate now!" she tells me, walking back over to the women gathering.

I leave them to their conversation and walk over to the bounce house to spend some time playing with Hazel.

"Are you having a good birthday, dragonfly?"

"The best!" she yells, jumping and falling over.

She's having a hard time staying up, so I bend to help her stand.

"Thank you, Daddy," she says.

"You're welcome."

It's not long before we're joined by Indie. She pops her head into the opening in the net.

"Can I join?" she asks us.

"Yes!" Hazel screams, then giggles like she's never had sugar before in her life. Indie jumps in with us, twirling around as she does, her hair fanning out with each motion.

"Can you do this?" Hazel asks her, then proceeds to do her version of a somersault.

"I don't know, that was pretty good. I'll try if your dad does," she answers, then looks my way.

"Okay! Do it, Daddy! Do it, Daddy!" Hazel chants.

I narrow my eyes on Indiana. Her front two teeth are sinking into her plump bottom lip to hide her smile, eyes glittering when she opens her mouth and pushes me further to the edge. "Yeah, let's see it, *Daddy*."

I almost choke on my tongue. *Daddy?* Thinking of her calling me *that* in a more private setting has my heart rate picking up.

Reining in my racing thoughts, I hold up my hands. "Alright, alright," I tell them, holding my arms over my head. "Are you ready for this?" I ask them.

"We were born ready," Indie says, and Hazel says, "Yeah!" I somersault as gracefully as I can, making a show to stand up again to take a bow. Both girls jump around clapping.

"That was so good, Daddy!" Hazel cheers for me.

"Truly. I can only think of two somersaults in all my life that rival that one," Indie mutters.

"Two? Better than that? Whose?" I ask. My tone playful but demanding. She's jumping toward me and laughing with me. Grabbing my arm for support to steady herself, my skin heating at the feel of her hands on me.

"Well, Hazel's obviously," she says, waving a hand toward her.

"And the other?" I question, feeling light and carefree.

"You're about to witness it," she tells me before lunging forward to a handstand, tucking and rolling out of it. She stands with a flourish, giving Hazel a wink. We're both a little starstruck by her. Hazel claps loudly, jumping over to her, hugging her legs. Indie bends to lift her up, bouncing in a circle with her. At the sight of her holding Hazel, their laughter contagious, I don't even try to fight the smile spreading across my face.

Someone rings the dinner bell, followed by my dad telling us that the food is ready. I help the girls out of the bounce house before making mine and Hazel's plates. We all settle into the picnic tables I set out earlier. As we eat, my eyes wander back to Indie. She looks beautiful in her jean shorts. Her white shirt is loose, and it looks soft like her tanned skin.

She starts laughing at something Florence says; the sound is melodic. It scratches an itch I didn't know I needed scratching, and I'm jealous—I want it to be me who makes her laugh. I seem to be *wanting* a lot the past few weeks. I haven't wanted anything for myself in years. But Indie has me wanting.

After our lunch, we sing Happy Birthday while Hazel blows out her candles, getting all three of them in one go. Everyone erupts into cheers for her; Alder, Colt, and Rhett let out whistles. She smiles bashfully—so delicately sweet. I'm always grateful for my family, but times like these make me just a little more so. Each one of them takes their turn kissing my daughter's adorable cheeks before we dig into the giant cake Winnie made.

"Hey, Knox. We need more ice. Will you grab some from your freezer?" my mom asks.

"I can get it!" Indie says, already walking to the door.

I scan the party, seeing Hazel being entertained by Colt and Rhett before making my way in after her. *She may need help.* I tell myself. Walking in the side door, I see her bent over looking for a bowl in my kitchen. I clear my throat, and she straightens, gasping and holding a hand over her chest.

"You scared me." She laughs.

"I can see that," I say, gripping her upper arms, moving to her side to open the next drawer over, and removing a large metal bowl.

"I would have found it eventually," she says, looking up at me.

"I have no doubt."

We're standing close now. Just a breath between us. I briefly wonder if I lean down right now, if she'll let me kiss her. She's looking at me like she might. My hand reaches out, letting the back of my fingers skim down her bare arm.

"Indie—" I start.

"Hey! Can we get a rush order on the ice, brother?" Alder yells from the side door. We jump apart, even though there's no reason to.

I sigh. *Perfect timing.* "Yeah, I'll be out in a second," I call back to him before filling the bowl with ice from the freezer. I shut the door, finding Indie staring at me intently and smiling softly.

"Um, can I use your restroom?" she asks.

"Just down the hall on the right," I say, grinning back at her.

"Thanks, I'll be right out." Again, the urge to tease her, to flirt with her, is too strong to deny.

"If you're not, I may have to come back in to find you." Her eyes widen, glowing as she backs herself toward the hall.

"That doesn't sound so bad," she says quietly before turning and disappearing through the bathroom door. I'm left feeling lightheaded; all the blood in my body rushing other places.

An hour later, the party is winding down. I had planned on Hazel opening her presents, but she's slumping against me, and I just heard her yawn.

"Are you tired, Hazey?"

"Mm-hmm..." she hums, nuzzling deeper into my chest.

"We'll get things picked up out here, Knox. Go ahead and lay her down if you want," my mom tells me, picking up some trash and closing the lids on the food containers.

"Thank you. For everything, Mom." I kiss her cheek before turning Hazel to face the rest of the crew. "Birthday Girl is headed to lie down for a while. Thank you all for coming."

"Thank you for coming," Hazel tries to yell, but it's sleepy. The yard is full of smiles as the sun sets. We hear a chorus of happy birthdays while we walk into the house.

Inside, I wipe Hazel's face and help her change into her birthday pajamas. Green with tiny dinosaurs on them. She looks at me with sleepy eyes so full of love it makes my heart feel too big for my chest.

"I love you, babygirl. More than sunshine, air, and the moon."

"I love you, Daddy. More than dinosaurs," she tells me softly.

"That's so much? How lucky am I?"

"Really lucky," she says quietly, settling into her bed. I'm not sure how, but I did manage to get extremely lucky to call this little girl mine.

"Happy Birthday, dragonfly. Sweet dreams."

INDIANA

The air is starting to cool as I walk back to the guesthouse. After spending an unexpectedly great day at Knox's house for Hazel's birthday party. When I left this afternoon, I'd expected to be coming home alone. Instead, there are four other women walking back with me. I wasn't even sure I would go today. My hike with Knox a couple of weeks ago left me feeling on edge, thinking it may be intruding, but ultimately, I couldn't stomach the thought of disappointing Hazel in any way after she asked me to come.

"I've never seen Colt look so in his element before," Winnie says, her arm linked with Ivy's.

"You know, the tutu really is one of his better looks," Marigold muses. "Definitely better than the iced tips in high school."

My mouth pops open and laughter bubbles out. "He didn't."

"He did," they both say together.

"So did you grow up around here too, Ivy?"

"I did not. I just moved here from California after Thanksgiving last year."

"California? That's a big move. Can I ask what brought you here?"

"That's kind of a long story, but the highlight reel is that my dad manipulated me, and I fell for it. Hook, line, and sinker," she says, then adds, "Joke's on him though. I now have a smokin' hot, action hero boyfriend and am going to have a baby with him in three months." When I look back at her, I catch the look on her face. It's a perfect mix of love and devotion.

I smile in response. "Alder is a lucky man."

"He really is," she agrees, causing a few chuckles from us. I take the steps up to the house, opening my front door. I hadn't bothered locking it since I was only down the road.

"I know you've all probably been here before, but welcome to my place. Make yourselves comfortable, and I'll grab my laptop. I'm thinking I can cast it to the TV so we won't have to crowd around it."

"Thanks for having us over, Indiana," Florence says.

"Of course. If you ladies hire me, I may be able to support my novelty shirt collection," I call over my shoulder, walking into my bedroom to grab my computer.

"You have to see these pictures. I cannot wait to have a couple of them blown up and on the walls at home," Winnie says, talking me up a little bit. I only took a couple of photography classes. My skills lie more in the website-design realm. But I'll take it. Taking photos is something I'm finding I really enjoy.

"I'm not sure if they're *wall-worthy*, but I am really happy with how they turned out."

"She is absolutely being modest," she tells the group.

"We're gonna have to work on that," Ivy says.

I grin. "Actually, that would be great. I've never been that good at taking a compliment. That's more my sister's area of expertise." I regret the words as soon as they're out of my mouth. Bringing up Han means that I'll get questions. Questions I'm not ready to answer. I need to derail the line of questioning before it begins. "Are y'all looking for more interior shots or landscapes? I did a mix for Thistle and Sage." Opening my laptop, I tap a few buttons to connect the screens, and they all glance to the TV.

"Here are some of the town I chose, and I can even walk you through adding them to the site if you want."

"Wait, wait. Go back," Marigold shouts. I click the arrow, and the screen fills with a shirtless Knox. Oops. I forgot those were still in here.

"Holy fucking shit."

"Sister present!" Florence yells, and I laugh at her horrified expression.

"It's a torso. Nothing that scandalous," I remind the room.

"*That* is more than a torso. When did you take this, and can I have a copy?" Marigold asks.

"Mare!" Florence gasps while the rest of us laugh.

"We went on a hike a couple of weeks ago. It wasn't a big deal." Can they all tell that I'm lying to myself? Playing it cool is not something I'm very good at. "Moving on...this is a few of the interior shots I got of the kitchen and Winnie baking."

"Oh my gosh, stop. Winnie. You are so freaking adorable. If that's on the website, Rhett is going to demand your ring be front and center. You look hot," Ivy tells her. I smile, happy that I have successfully steered the conversation back to familiar and comfortable territory. Well, for me. Winnie is blushing at the compliments.

"I think Indie just got some good angles is all," she deflects.

"That's bullshit. I mean, I may have gotten some good angles, but you don't have a bad one," I tell her.

"Okay! Move on to the ones of the food and the bakery, please." She laughs.

I finish showing them the rest of the photos and demonstrate how I'm planning to showcase them online. I'm met with admiration. It feels nice to be validated by women who all run their own businesses and are their own bosses.

For much of my life, I didn't think I was capable of handling everything on my own. Other people's problems? I've always been able to solve, but my own always feel bigger. I start feeling out of control. Scared to let anyone down if they were counting on me. Lately, though, I've been thinking that there's a lot more I can do on my own than I've given myself credit for.

Florence gives me a hug, and I let myself sink into it for a moment. I miss Han. I miss my mom and dad. I didn't realize until this moment that I needed a hug this badly. "Thank you again for having us over, Indie. Can I call you next week and work out some dates for the hotel?"

"Yes, that sounds great! Do you need my number?"

"Nope, I already have it." I don't ask *how* she has it; I just accept it.

"I'll be calling you too! I'm thinking we could do something with the mountain biking and then maybe update with the snow once we open for the ski season," Ivy tells me.

"Absolutely, I'd love to be involved."

"I'll see you tomorrow at work, Indie!"

"And I'm hoping to see you out at AJ's. Have we set that up yet?"

"What's AJ's?"

"That would be my uncle's brewery in town," Winnie says. "And it's kind of the last step in a welcome to Silverthorne."

"Oh yeah?"

"I'm thinking a night out is in order. I'll talk to you more tomorrow about it." Everyone gives me one more wave before walking back over to the big house.

I watch them laugh as they go. They're all so close. It's nice to be welcomed into their group. Smiling, I make my way back inside. My photos are still up on the TV, and I tap my laptop screen to pull up the picture of Knox I took on our hike. I sigh. Yeah, this is frame-worthy. I allow myself a few more moments to appreciate the hard planes of his body before disconnecting the screen. I pour myself a glass of wine and sit out back at the small, metal bistro set.

I'm enjoying the cool evening. It's been a good day, and I'm really starting to feel like I have my footing here when my phone rings. I flinch. Now that I've given more people my number, I'll have to check who's calling. I blow out a breath and walk back into the house and into my bedroom to pick it up. One look at the flashing name tells me it's not a call I'm ready for.

I ignore it, dump the rest of my wine into the sink, and crawl under the blankets on the bed, like sinking into them could keep the thoughts and dreams away from me.

Knox

"I think that's enough water for the fairy pond, Hazey."

"Almost," she says while dumping the rest of the watering can out.

"You sure are doing a good job with that."

"Thank you." She smiles sweetly.

She's been three for less than a week and already feels bigger—talking bigger, acting bigger. Every day, she finds something new to tell me or a new word I'm surprised she knows and knows how to use it correctly. I watch her carefully place pebbles as a walkway for her fairies, singing softly.

Sally's bark has us both turning our heads down the road. She's running toward us beside my not-so-temporary tenant. Winnie called yesterday to say that when the pipes in her house were getting replaced, they found mold. It's going to be a while before anyone is able to live there. I may have put on a little show of being annoyed, but when Florence called saying she could probably swing a room for her to stay in, I told her it wasn't necessary if Indie wanted to stay here longer.

"Indie!" Hazel shouts as she approaches us. Sally comes up to nudge my hand with her wet nose, so I'll scratch her head.

"Hi, Hazel. What are you up to?" she asks, only a little out of breath.

"Making a fairy garden! Come see!" Hazel walks over, grabbing her hand and pulls her along. Indie catches my eye as she passes. She's not wearing one of her T-shirts tonight, in its place is a tight, pink jacket that isn't zipped up completely. The color matches the stitching on her black shorts.

"Hey, Knox," she greets me softly, that sweet-as-honey smile on her face.

"Indie." Her name is all I manage as a greeting.

"Look here," Hazel tells her, and Indie crouches beside her to examine the little moss houses and acorn people we've made.

"Oh my gosh, did you do all of this yourself?"

"No. Daddy helped."

"Not much," I add.

"Well, it's lovely. So magical," Indie says, standing and shifting her weight from leg to leg. "Thank you for showing me. I should probably get home and let you guys get back to your evening."

"Do you want to stay?" My invitation takes me by just as much surprise as it does her.

Eyebrows raised, she cocks her head at me, fighting a smile. "Are you asking me to dinner?"

"I've already made chili, so it's not that big of a deal." I shrug.

"Right, well, I'm sure it's better than whatever boxed dinner awaits me. I'd love to eat with you guys."

"Yay, come see my new books!" Hazel cheers, already running to the house.

"Right behind you!" Indie calls after her. "Is that okay?" she asks me.

"Yeah, it's okay." *Having her here is more than okay.*

After putting away all the garden tools we used to make the fairy garden in the shed, I make my way into the kitchen to get everyone some dinner. Taking out bowls from the cabinet and I ladle some chili into them, and set them at the table.

"Dinner's ready," I call to the girls.

"Coming!" I hear Indie's yell, followed by Hazel's little feet hitting the floor as she runs.

"It smells good in here," Indie praises.

"I hope it tastes that way."

I'm surprised at how easy it is for us all to fall into sync together. Without being asked, Indie helps Hazel into her chair, making sure she can reach her drink and spoon. I pour Indie a glass of tea while she tucks a lock of hair behind her ear, smiling at me.

"Thank you."

"You're welcome."

"So, what have you been up to with work recently?" she asks. I'm not used to anyone asking about my day besides my mom.

"Well, I was able to close a case for one of my clients before it went to a trial. The other party wasn't happy with that, but there was no evidence to support his claim. Now I'm working with a new client. A horse he was caring for passed while at his stable, and he swears it had nothing to do with him, but the owner is spewing some vicious rumors now about how animals may get treated there."

"That sounds awful. Do you have any reports from a vet or

a police report to go on?" Her questions surprise me—like she knows exactly what I would need to make a case.

"I have the police report, I'm still waiting on the official cause of death."

Indie hums. "Yeah, that will help the case move along," she says casually, taking another bite of chili. She looks like she has more to add, so I probe.

"It could, is there something else?" She turns to face me then, setting her spoon down and folding her hands on the table.

"Well, I'm definitely not an expert, but if I were you, I would make sure I was documenting all his online comments. A few bad reviews, and some accusations could ruin a business, and if what he's saying *isn't* true, then maybe you'll have a case for defamation." I'm stunned. Not that she's smart. Her wit alone tells me that. It's that she's thinking about this in a way that a good lawyer would.

"Were you previously a lawyer?" I ask.

She laughs. "No, no. I'm sorry. That was probably dumb."

"Not at all. It's a great suggestion. One that I'll be taking—if I can figure out where to look," I tell her. I'm not online—like at all. Besides sending and receiving emails, I don't spend time on the internet.

"Probably his socials would be a good start...see if he's in any groups or discussion boards." Her words are a little tentative, like she doesn't want to step on my toes. "I can help if you want," her offer is tempting for more reasons than those having to do with my case. I could probably figure it out on my own, but wouldn't it be nice to have a partner?

"That would help me out a lot," I tell her, and she beams at me.

"Then I would be happy to help."

"Is this beans?" Hazel asks, causing Indie to laugh.

"Yeah, dragonfly, it's—" I'm cut off by Indie's spoon clattering against her bowl.

"Sorry. Um I'm just going to go to the bathroom real quick. I'll be right back."

"Sure, second door on the right, across from Hazel's room," I tell her.

"I like beans," Hazel tells me, happily eating another spoonful of chili.

I'm not sure what would have caused it, but Indie looked upset. Sad somehow, seemingly out of nowhere.

When she gets back, the look is gone. Her sweet smile and happy-go-lucky attitude are back in place. I've noticed she has these moments every now and then. When she directs the conversation to a new topic or gets quiet before answering a question. Curiosity isn't something I like to get entangled in, but I think I'd like to get tangled up in Indiana Holmes.

INDIANA

After my morning run, I step out of the shower, wrap my fluffy towel around me, and swipe the steam from the mirror, catching a glimpse of myself. Five weeks in Silverthorne, and I'm turning into a version of myself I didn't realize existed anymore. My skin has deepened into a golden brown, and afternoons spent on the lake are causing more of my freckles to stand out.

Which is how I'll be spending my day off. With my e-reader loaded with books and my tote bag filled with snacks and sunscreen, I slip into my blue bikini. It would be a lie to say that I didn't have *him* in mind when I laid it out. It's almost the same color as his eyes. I grab my wide-brimmed hat and put on my sandals, pick up my tote bag and head down to the dock. Only when I get there—it seems I won't be the only one.

Three heads turn to see me coming down the trail. Sally comes to meet me at the end of the dock.

"Hey, Sally girl," I coo, stepping onto the wooden slats and bending to pat her head.

"Indie!" Hazel shouts.

"Hi, beautiful. How are you today?"

"Good! We're swimming!" she tells me as Knox continues to rub sunscreen on her face before putting a little sun hat that matches her pink swimsuit on her head.

"Do you mind if I hang out here with you guys today?" I'm asking Knox because, as much as he's warmed up to me the last few weeks, I still don't want to intrude.

"Yay!" Hazel shouts. I smile but keep my eyes fixed on Knox, waiting for his response. Wanting him to want me here, not just tolerate my presence. His answer warms me from the inside out.

"We'd like that." *We.* Not just Hazel but him too.

I'm not sure in what capacity he wants me around. Maybe he's starting to see me as a friend, or maybe he's just being neighborly. I don't care if it's that he likes looking at me in a bathing suit, as long as he wants me close by.

Spreading out my towel, I sit down on it criss-cross applesauce. Hazel joins me, the smell of her sunscreen floating in the air. Her water wings squeak with each movement.

"What's that?" she asks, looking at my green beaded anklet. I stretch my leg out so she can get a better look.

"It's an anklet. Do you like it?"

"Yes," she says longingly. I grin, digging through my tote bag to see if I can find—yes, there it is. I pull out one of my many bracelets. It's too big, but maybe if I tie it a little tighter, it'll work.

"What do you think of this one?"

"It's so pretty," she tells me, eyes wide like she's never seen such treasure.

"I think so too, but I think it would look even better on someone else I know."

"Who?" I smile at her. I've sort of fallen for this little girl since the moment she told me chocolate was the superior ice cream choice.

"Would you like to match with me?" Her eyes grow as big as saucers before they turn squinty with her beaming smile.

"Yes, yes!" She claps her hands as I carefully untie the bracelet and take off some of the beads.

"Okay, which foot do you want it on?" She sticks her left one out and scoots closer to me, so it's resting on my thigh. I tie it on her, making sure not to get it too tight. "How does that feel?" I ask.

"Good!" she says, stroking it with her little fingers. Once she's done inspecting it, she jumps up and runs over to where Knox is sitting in his chair sans shirt. Will I ever get tired of this view? Now *this* would make one hell of a postcard.

"Look, Daddy!" Hazel holds her foot up, almost losing her balance until Knox reaches out to steady her.

"Look at that. So pretty. Did Indie make that for you?"

"Yes!"

"That was nice of her. Did you say thank you?"

"No," she tells him, then yells in my direction. "Thank you, Indie!"

"You're welcome, Hazey," I call back to her, laughing.

I slip my hat off and lay back onto the towel, pushing my sunglasses up on top of my still-damp hair. I use my hand to shade my eyes for a moment before closing them. There's not a cloud in the sky today; the sun is out in full force. I let it heat my bare skin for just a few moments before sitting up and reaching into my bag for my sunscreen.

Rubbing it in, I catch Knox's gaze and hold it, smiling at him. He doesn't look away. Opting to scan my body instead. It's thorough, his examination of me. He starts at my face, and I can pinpoint the moment he gets to my pink toenails. The right side of his mouth ticks upward into a smirk. It's not the sun now that warms me.

"You missed a spot." His deep voice draws me in.

"Yeah? Where?" I ask, hoping to sound flirty.

"Here!" Hazel tells me, running to stand by my side and tapping the center of my back.

"Do you think you could help me?" I ask, grinning at her over my shoulder.

"Yes!"

"Okay, hold your hand out for me." She does, and I squirt a little lotion in her hand. "Can you rub that on my back?"

She does for a few seconds. "Done," she announces.

"Thank you, Hazey."

"You're welcome," she says sweetly. I smile at her, and she grins back before reaching out to touch my nose, specifically my nose *ring*. "What's this?"

"That's my nose ring," I tell her.

"I like it."

"Thank you. I like it too."

"Dragonfly!" she exclaims, and for a second, I forget that I have the tattoo. A delicate little thing, between my collarbone and shoulder. It's a reminder. "Like Daddy's." *Daddy's?*

I look over at Knox and find his eyes locked onto the strap of my bikini, or more the tattoo that sits beneath it.

"Alright, Hazel. Let's let Indie get back to her day," Knox tells the curious little girl in front of me.

"Okay, Daddy." She leans forward, catching me off guard in a hug. Wrapping my arms around her, I lift her slightly and tickle her sides as she runs off toward her dad. I eye him openly.

Turnabout is fair play after all, right? His torso really is a work of art. All rippling muscles, and I don't know what it is about his chest hair, but something about it has me wanting to tangle my fingers in it. Yes, he's a beautiful man. One who's unforgettable and possibly a little forgetful when it comes to me. *Had I been forgettable to him?* I drop my gaze when doubt starts to creep in, understanding that he had much bigger things to focus on than me. It mixes in, causing my emotions to muddle.

Hours later, when I've shared all my snacks with Hazel and paddled around the lake with Sally, I excuse myself and start walking home. I don't make it all the way when I hear him yell at me.

"Indie!"

I turn to face him, exhausted from being in the sun all day, even though I mostly just laid in it.

"Yes?" I ask, looking at him standing on the road holding a dozing Hazel.

"Do you want to come to our place for dinner?" His question is unexpected, but Han has always said the best things are. I think I'm starting to believe her. My hopes could be getting a little too high for comfort. I shouldn't want to penetrate this man's walls so badly, but I do. I want to know him. Better than anyone. And maybe more than anything. I want him to really know me.

"Yes."

KNOX

I work hard to control my gaze. Indiana makes it difficult for me to focus on anything but her. She's telling Hazel about the big zoo in Atlanta she loves—complete with sound effects for each corresponding animal. My lips twitch when her elephant impression has Hazel belly laughing in earnest. I'm trying to cover my laugh with a cough when she imitates an orangutan.

It's nice. Having her here. I wasn't prepared to enjoy her company on a regular basis. We started having Indie over for dinner a few weeks ago. After Hazel's birthday party, I was left with more questions for her than I liked. She makes me curious. When Hazel begged her to come see her fairy garden and then to stay for dinner, I didn't fight her on it; in fact, I was happy to have an excuse to get closer to her. Her presence is like a beacon that draws me in at an alarming rate.

Alarming because never in my wildest dreams would I have thought that watching a woman sit on my front porch pretending to be the whole zoo would absolutely captivate me. Also, it's been years since I've thought about spending time with a woman who wasn't a member of my immediate family or marrying into it.

Indiana's voice carries through the open door and into the kitchen to me while I stir the butter sauce for our gnocchi. "What is your favorite animal?" she asks Hazel, coloring on the roll of paper between them.

"A shark!"

"A shark? Oh my goodness. I don't know a lot about them other than what I read in a fact book that there are over 450 different kinds," she says absent-mindedly, still coloring with her black crayon.

"They swim in the ocean," Hazel informs her.

"Have you ever been to the ocean?"

"No."

"Me either. Do you think we could draw it?"

"Yes!

"Perfect. What colors should we use?"

They carry on like that, Hazel asking Indie if she likes what she's drawing over and over, and Indie patiently answering and reassuring her that her colorful fish are a work of art until I call them in for dinner. When they make it to the kitchen, I notice that Indie's handkerchief of the day is now tied in Hazel's hair. It's light blue, the same color as her socks. I've never made the connection before and wonder if she always matches them.

"Oh, shit," I mutter, having spilled the glass of water Indie left sitting on the counter beside me. She's always leaving her cups around, which leads to a lot more spills than usual, and I'm not used to having to navigate having another adult in my space like this. I walk to the linen closet to grab a towel, and when I get back, I don't see the girls on the porch anymore.

I lay the towel on the counter and look out the window to

see them walking down the path to the dock. Indie holds her camera up, snapping pictures of Hazel as she goes. I watch for a minute before wiping up the rest of the water. Turning back, I catch sight of the sunset over the lake, then I see a small figure out on the dock—alone.

My blood runs cold as I take off out of the house.

"I want to show my dance moves!" I hear Hazel yell, twirling in place. With each spin, my panic rises.

"Oh my, that was a big one," Indie calls from the edge of the dock—several feet from Hazel.

"Hazel!" I yell, my voice so loud, both of them flinch at the sound, heads snapping toward me. "Off the dock. Now."

"Knox?" Indie questions. I'm only a few steps from her now.

"What the hell were you thinking?" I accuse.

"W-what?" she asks timidly as Hazel hops off the end of the dock onto solid ground.

"You let her out on the dock alone?" I ask, picking Hazel up.

"It was only a few feet from me. I wasn't going to—"

"And without a life vest?" I accuse, adrenaline still pumping through me. Her face crumples at that.

"Oh god. I'm so sorry. I wasn't even thinking about—"

"You weren't thinking about her falling off and not being able to see her? I don't have that luxury, Indiana. Hazel is at the forefront of my mind every second of every day."

"I understand that. I do. I'm sorry. I would never put her in any kind of danger. Not on purpose. Never," she apologizes in a rush. The look on her face shows me she's terrified at the thought of something bad happening to my daughter.

"I'm okay, Daddy," Hazel says, leaning her head onto my

shoulder. The weight of her in my arms helps to calm me down. I look at her sweet face, smiling at me. "I was a balletina!" she says excitedly. The way she says ballerina softens my stony disposition.

"I really am sorry. Maybe I should just go home. I'll catch you guys later." She takes a step back, away from me, the distance and the look on her face extinguishing the fire. I can't hold onto my anger anymore.

"Indie, stay!" Hazel pouts.

Her eyes are a little glassy, but she smiles at my girl, trying to put on a front. "It's okay, Hazey, I'll—"

"Stay," I blurt. Shock registers on her face, then confusion.

"You don't have to do that, it's okay. I'll come another time." Her words don't convince me. If I don't convince her to stay now, I may not be able to ever.

"I want you to," I say.

Still looking mildly confused, she nods, accepting my re-invitation, and walks back toward the big house with us, Hazel a few feet ahead of us.

"I—" we both start at the same time.

"You go," Indie offers.

"I'm sorry about my reaction. Hazel's safety is my number one focus, and seeing her out there." I pause. "It scared me."

"I can't tell you how sorry I am to have been the cause of that. I would never do something to hurt her. Please tell me you believe that," she pleads. If it were anyone else, I wouldn't. But I hear the honesty in her voice. The conviction behind her words. She really does care about Hazel.

"I *do* know that, which is why I shouldn't have come down on you so hard."

"No, you were right. Completely justified. I'm on high alert now."

"Welcome to the club," I tease.

"It must be exhausting doing this all on your own," she muses. *She doesn't know the half of it.*

"It can be, but Hazel is worth every gray hair."

"You only have a few of those," she smirks.

"You're not going to tease me about my gray hair?"

"Why would I do that? It's a good look for you." I grin.

We make it back inside, and I set Hazel down. The awkwardness from before not completely forgotten, but on its way to being.

"It smells good in here. What's for dinner?" Indie asks.

"Gnocchi in brown butter sauce with parmesan cheese."

"I like cheese!" Hazel chimes in.

"So do I," Indie tells her, then looks to me before adding, "I should attempt dinner for you guys soon. I appreciate you feeding me."

"The word *attempt* puts me a little on edge," I say, pouring the sauce over all our plates. She laughs and without me having to ask, starts to get Hazel's highchair set up.

"Har-har," she says with an eye roll. I smirk.

"Up you go, Hazey," she says, spinning her in a circle before setting her in the seat. "Do you want the purple bib or the red one tonight?"

"Red!"

"You got it, sweets." She turns to retrieve it from the drawer and ends up chest-to-chest with me while I carry Hazel's food to her. "Sorry," she whispers, but her hands stay on my chest and seem to linger there for a moment before she slides out from under my arm and passes by. I grin. Glad I have an effect on her, seeing as she has an astronomical one on me.

I am painfully aware of her every movement. From her hand brushing her hair back from her face to the way she absently rubs at her shoulder when she's nervous. Yesterday I had to force myself to focus on my research for the upcoming case I'm presenting instead of staring at her in her bright-blue bikini out on the dock.

After dinner, I start cleaning up in the kitchen, and Hazel requests that Indie read her a bedtime story. She's wearing her birthday present from her, a pink nightgown with a dinosaur on it, holding a cup of tea that says: Tea-Rex. She's worn it almost every night since opening it. I place the plates in the dishwasher just as Indie appears in the hallway smiling.

"I'm not sure how, but that little girl gets more charming every time I see her," she whispers to me.

"I think she's been spending too much time with Alder," I tell her, and she snickers.

"I don't think he's her only influence in that department." I think that's a compliment, and I think I really like getting them from her.

"Thank you for inviting me for dinner. You don't have to feed me all the time though. You've already let me extend my stay at your guesthouse—which I am incredibly grateful for by the way," she adds.

"I like feeding you," I answer honestly. I feel like we've been doing this dance for weeks now, and I'm not the best at making my intentions known with words, but I had hoped my actions might have conveyed a measure of how I'm feeling.

With each week that's gone by, each dinner where she's fumbled around my kitchen until she finds what she's looking for, or each day in the sun we've shared, I find myself missing her when she's not with me. Indie is quickly becoming a part of my life—a part of Hazel's. Happiness and doubt war inside me at the thought. She may choose to spend time with us now, but she's so young. Her whole life is really just beginning. I shake my head, ridding it of my uncertainty, and let myself enjoy her company. "Do you want to stay for a glass of wine tonight?" The look on her face is slightly confused and possibly amused.

"I could use a glass of wine," she says after giving it some thought.

"I'll pour us a couple of glasses and meet you out back," I tell her. She nods and walks out the back glass door. I watch as she picks her chair, opening one of the bottles Winnie gave me. She and Rhett gave everyone a bottle from the vineyard they visited last month in California to choose wine for their wedding. I may as well try some with Indie.

After pouring the red liquid into two stemless glasses, I take a quick peek into Hazel's room and find her already fast asleep. Smiling, I make my way out back. I haven't been on a date since I was in college, and this may not be an actual date, but it is time spent with a woman I'm interested in. I hand Indie her drink, then I grab some wood to start a fire in the pit between us.

"It's nice out tonight," Indie says, drawing my attention from the fire to her legs thrown over the side of her chair.

"It is. The weather will only get better from here on out. You'll like summer."

"Why do you say that?"

"You like being outside, and you seem to like the lake. Summer's the best season for it. You'll have more daylight." I light the fire, then I sit in my chair to the side of hers, stretching my legs out in front of me. Only a small end table separates us.

"In that case, I'm really looking forward to it. I've been wanting to get out on the paddleboard more." She sighs, tipping her head back against the wooden slats. "There are so many things I want to do here, and I feel like there's never enough time."

"There'll be time. If you're planning on sticking around, that is." I'm trying not to make it sound like my happiness may depend on her answer.

She smiles, that sweet fucking smile that makes my chest feel funny again. "I plan on sticking around," she confirms.

"Good." She laughs at my response.

"Is it good? You're not dying to get me out of your hair anymore?" she teases, throwing those words from over a month ago back at me. Had I ever thought that I wanted to be rid of her?

"You're growing on me," I tell her.

"Enough with the flattery, Knox. I can't take much more of it." She's grinning at me. Her nose slightly scrunched as she settles further into her chair. Her sweatshirt tonight has a velociraptor on it and the words "clever girl" underneath. Her shirts have become something I look forward to, and I'm not sure if she realizes it, but I don't compliment women often—not because they aren't deserving, but because I don't know how to without sounding cheesy or like I've never said words before.

Growing up, it became obvious that I wasn't as outgoing as either of my brothers. Rhett is the definition of lovable. Kind-hearted to a fault, he's always well-intentioned and never quick to anger. Then there's Alder, from the day he was born, he's demanded attention without even trying. He's funny and charming and being around him is as easy as breathing. I'm lucky to have them in my life—I've also compared myself to them more often than I should.

"I'll dial it back a bit," I tell her. She tosses her head back in laughter. More of this. More of her. That's what I want, but I don't know how to tell her that. I'm forty-one years old, forty-two in a matter of weeks, and I don't know how to tell a woman I want to spend time with her. Asking my brothers for advice is an option, but I would never hear the end of it. I could maybe ask Florence, but asking my baby sister feels embarrassing.

Also, calling her my baby sister when she's the same age as Indiana reminds me that Indie is so young. She has so much of her life ahead of her, and I'm not interested in going out every night or traveling the world. Being saddled to me wouldn't be doing her any favors.

"That would be appreciated. So how long have you lived here at the lake?"

"A couple of years now." I clear my throat, unsure if bringing up some of my past is necessary, if it's something she cares to know. I decide I want her to know me and know my daughter. "Hazel and I lived with her mother for a few months after she was born while I had this house renovated. After she passed away, we moved here." I watch her face change, the blush from her wine draining from her face. Her eyes shine with sadness.

"I'm so sorry, Knox."

"It was a long time ago. Emily and I may not have been together, but she was Hazel's mother and a wonderful woman."

"She would have to be to help create Hazel." Her care for Hazel is obvious.

"It's funny, sometimes Hazel will do or say something that reminds me so much of Emily."

"She must have been beautiful."

"She was. Hazel has her eyes and her smile."

"How did she die? Oh, my god. I-I'm so sorry. You do not have to tell me that." I look back at her. Her expression is a mix of embarrassment and apology. I don't talk about Hazel's mother with anyone. Some of that stems from having to explain how Hazel came to be, but also it brings up painful memories of watching a woman I cared deeply for wither away. I'd like Indie to understand though. If I want her to know me, that starts with opening up.

I clear my throat. "She had cancer. They found it when she was in her second trimester of pregnancy, and Emily refused treatment until after Haze was born."

"Oh god," Indie gasps.

Nodding, I take a sip of my wine before speaking again. "By the time they found it, she was already stage four, and because she waited on treatment, they told us it was a miracle she lived as long as she did. Emily was resilient, though, so I wasn't surprised." I smile thinking about her. How strong she was, even after being told treatment wasn't an option. Indie swipes at her cheeks. Is she crying?

"Sorry, I don't mean to get this emotional. That's just one of the most equally beautiful and heartbreaking things I've ever heard. She sounds like a great mom." It's this part of her that intrigues me the most. Indie is stunning and funny, but her heart, the way she openly shows it to people. It's admirable.

"She was an amazing mother." From the first conversation I had with Emily about Hazel, it was obvious she was already in love with her. Her phone call to me wasn't only to tell me that she was pregnant with my child, but when I look back on it now, with a lot less bitterness, I realize it was making sure Hazel would be cared for if she wasn't around to do it herself. It hurts me to know that Hazey won't know Emily's love for her firsthand. I've kept photos in a book for her as she gets older and starts having questions.

I want her to know that she has been loved from the moment her mother found out about her existence.

"Knox?" Indie's amused tone tells me she's either asked me a question or I've been staring into the fire while she's been trying to have a conversation with me.

"Sorry, did you ask me something?"

"No, I just said I should probably get going. I have to be up early in the morning to help Winnie at the bakery. Thanks for the wine and dinner—again. It was really nice."

"Of course, let me walk you. I just need to check on Hazel," I tell her, standing.

"You don't have to do that. It's only half a mile."

Two thousand five hundred feet, but who's counting? "It's dark, I'll be right back." I take her glass from her and walk back into the house to set them in the sink. Tiptoeing down the hall, I peek into Hazel's room and see that she's sleeping peacefully, gripping her stuffy close. Her little body is spread-eagled with her tiny foot hanging off the edge. I tuck it back into the blankets and kiss her cheek before heading back out to see Indie home.

"All good?" she asks as I step out the back door.

"Out like a light." I smile at her.

"She was pretty tired when I was reading to her, lots of yawning."

"She's always gone to bed easily—barring a few of her

newborn months," I amend. "I've never seen a kid wake up as happy as she does. Not that I have much experience, none of my siblings have kids yet, although Alder and Ivy will have one soon."

"You know, your brothers have fantastic taste in women," she tells me.

"They do," I agree, laughing. "Winnie's been like a sister to me since I met her, and Ivy may be rough around the edges, but I think that's something Alder needs."

"Mmm, it's nice that you're all so close." I hear the sadness that creeps into her tone when family is brought up. I want to ask her about hers, but I don't want to push too far too quickly.

"It is. It's also a little annoying to have your family so wrapped up in your personal business. I wouldn't trade it though." We're nearing the small, white house now. Our evening is coming to an end, and I'm more surprised than anyone to realize that I don't want it to. It'll be past my bedtime soon, but I want to stay up late, talking all night with Indie.

"Thanks again for tonight and letting me hang out with you and Hazel. It's nice to have friends when you're still new to town." I'm not sure how to respond. *Friends* isn't what I want to be, but if I tell her that now, will I scare her off? I decide to make a move, as subtly as I'm able. I run my fingers through the ends of her short hair before tucking it back behind her ear.

"You're welcome anytime, Indie. Goodnight."

She leans into my hand slightly before I drop it. "Goodnight, Knox," she says softly, backing away and jogging up her stairs. I start back toward the big house but stop after a few steps to look back at her. She's looking at me, so I flash her a smile. I could be wrong, but I think Indie wants more than friendship too.

Indiana

I'm practically skipping when I make it to Thistle and Sage this morning. Not only am I riding the high of a morning run, but last night's dinner with Hazel and Knox was the most fun I've had in I don't know how long. Playing with Hazel reminds me of taking care of Han when we were young. Being six years older than your sibling could have been an issue, but it wasn't for me. From the first day she was brought home from the hospital, she was my baby.

"Good morning, Indie!"

"Good morning, Winnie! How are you? I feel like I haven't seen you in weeks."

"I know. We've been working opposite shifts, and I took a few extra days for a wine tasting for the wedding."

"Did you decide on one?"

"We did! It's from this beautiful family-owned vineyard in California. I'm sorry I abandoned you! Are you settling in okay?"

"Don't be sorry! That's so exciting! And I'm fine. Good, um, great actually. Silverthorne is already feeling like home."

"That makes me so happy to hear. So, you've been in town almost two months now...I think it's time you come out to AJ's with everyone."

"I'm in! I think a night out would be good for me, and who is everyone?" I ask excitedly.

She giggles. "Yes! I need a night out, too, and everyone is a lot of Holloways, my brother, Marigold and her boyfriend, and anyone you've possibly seen in town will also probably be there," she tells me.

"Oh, is that all? So a small, intimate gathering?"

She laughs, a small snort slipping out. "Yes, exactly. Oh, and maybe have a karaoke song lined up," she says, walking back into the kitchen. I follow after her to set my purse down in the back and get my apron on.

"Karaoke? Okay, now I'm even more in than I was a few minutes ago."

Winnie claps her hands. "I can't wait! I'm so excited for you to hang out with us!"

"I'm excited too. I'm a little short on friends at the moment, and it means a lot that you've included me so much."

Her lips curl into a smile, but it doesn't reach her eyes. "Did I tell you I moved here when I was thirteen?" she asks.

"You didn't."

She hums, nodding. "My parents passed away in an accident right before Colt and I came to Silverthorne to live with our Uncle Buck." My heart sinks into my stomach, feeling connected to Winnie in more ways than one.

"I'm sorry, Winnie." My words are so cliché, but she accepts them with grace.

"Thank you. They were really wonderful parents— wonderful people. Moving across the country so young can be really hard, but this community made it bearable for us. We were welcomed with open arms. Now my heart is so invested here that I can't imagine living anywhere else." Her smile touches her eyes now. "I guess all that is to say, I hope you'll feel that way here too—eventually."

"I'm starting to," I say, not wanting to admit that a huge part of that is due to my dinners with Knox and Hazel the past few weeks.

"Excellent. I'll ask you again after karaoke and the festival this weekend. Town events are one of my favorite things about Silverthorne."

I laugh, tying my apron on. "I've been looking forward to it since you told me."

"Perfect," she says, looking up from her phone. "Tomorrow night!"

"Wow, you work fast," I tell her.

"I texted the Holloway family group chat. Ninety percent of the people coming are in it."

"Is Knox in that?" In an attempt to keep my tone casual, it comes out very *not* casual.

"He is..." Winnie says, her voice going up at the end.

I roll my eyes, mostly at myself. "Did he say if he would be there...?"

"Knox doesn't usually come out with us; he would rather stay home and hang with Hazel. I think the last time we got him to come out was months ago, and his brothers practically had to drag him there."

"Yeah, I'm getting the vibe he's more of a homebody."

"You're getting vibes from Knox?" she asks curiously.

"I mean...not a lot or anything. I've had dinner at his house a few times, and last night, it just seemed like he was more relaxed there," I comment.

Her head whips to me. "You had dinner together?" I'm not sure if Knox wants that information out or that I have dinner at his house more often than my own.

"It's really not that big a deal. I was walking by and Hazel waved me over. I was talking with her and picking flowers; I think Knox felt like it would be rude if he didn't ask me in. Then he found out that I can't cook—it's probably more of a pity thing," I try to explain, but not liking the sound of the words I'm saying. *Is it a pity thing? It doesn't feel that way.*

"I know you're just getting to know Knox, but I feel the need to tell you that man doesn't mind being rude. In fact, the Holloways don't do anything they don't want to," she muses.

I laugh at that. "I also got that vibe from him. It was a bit of a mixed-vibe bag."

She grins at me. "That sounds about right. Don't get me wrong. I love Knox. He's always been like a brother to me. He's protective and kind, and he's the best dad to Hazel. He just likes his privacy and isn't a big fan of socializing." Winnie starts putting things into the oven, then walks to the fridge to gather items for the cookies she's making for the Spring Fling Picnic event happening this weekend.

Nothing she told me about Knox surprises me, but I would be lying to myself if I didn't kind of hope he would be there. I would love to see him in a different setting, out at a bar with friends. I can't stop the giggle that escapes me at the image of Knox singing karaoke. Winnie looks at me.

"Sorry, just had a funny thought. Thanks for inviting me out tomorrow and for welcoming me into the friend group. First rounds on me."

"Oh, you're gonna be the favorite if you keep that up." She snickers.

"Excellent, that's all part of my plan," I say mysteriously. Winnie laughs so loudly that I almost drop the bowl I'm carrying to the sink. I love it. Her laugh is so infectious that I start laughing along with her. We carry on for so long that my stomach starts hurting. Winnie puts her hand on my shoulder, and the action knocks a memory loose. One I can usually keep contained.

Han and I on the front steps of our apartment building. Her shoving me in the shoulder, causing me to slip down a step. We had been out day-drinking at a baseball game in the city, and I lost my keys. I *miss* her.

Heat behind my eyes pulls me from the memory, and I swipe at them, keeping my smile in place. I put the bowl in the sink, running some water in it before splashing a little on my face to get myself together.

"So, do you need my help back here today, or should I head out front?" I ask.

"Out front for a while, please. I'm going to try and get these cookies and croissant dough made up for the weekend. Then do you want to come back here when Anna gets here? I'm going to show you how to make some blueberry muffins today if you're up for it."

"I am so up for it! My family's never going to believe that I can bake something."

"Not just *something*. Something delicious," she says seriously. I grin at her before walking back out front to open the door for the day and get the coffee ready.

A few hours later, I've done all the weekly cleaning up front, made a list for the grocery store, and learned how to make blueberry muffins. Winnie said the recipe is interchangeable with most fruits, but I have to be careful with any that could be considered "wet." Tomorrow I'm going to learn how to bake a chocolate croissant, and I'm scared to have that information because I'm not sure there will be a day when I don't eat one if I know how to make them myself.

I walk into the grocery store, list in hand this time, and grab a cart from the front. I don't know how to cook many things, so my list is basic, but I'm proud of it. Growing up in the city, we ate a lot of takeout, and even when my mother did cook, Han and I never asked her how to make anything. That being said, I follow a lot of online chefs who make meals that are at a level I think I can manage, so my menu for the next week is a lot of pasta. I'm making spaghetti, ziti, chicken alfredo, and an attempt at mushroom ravioli. Just in case, though, I have frozen pizza, Uncrustables, and popcorn as a backup.

I'm having trouble steering my cart with all the people packed in here. The whole town is a flurry of activity, and I'm assuming it has something to do with the spring event this weekend. There was always something going on in Atlanta, but for the most part, it was a sports event that brought people in or the odd movie was being filmed. My dad was usually involved if it was the latter.

I sigh, wistfully thinking about my parents. I do miss them. None of this is their fault. *It's mine.*

I pick up the varying pastas needed for the internet meals and then walk to the produce section—avoiding the zucchini entirely—and grab the rest of my groceries. All I need now is some cheese. I'm almost to the dairy when I see Knox. He's standing right in front of all the cheese and yogurt, which wouldn't be a big deal except he's talking to someone. Not just someone though. A woman. A gorgeous woman.

She looks to be around my age. Long, blonde hair and bright, blue eyes. She's much taller than me, maybe six or seven inches at least. Her legs go all the way up to my chest, and now she's laughing, and it's delicate like bells tinkling in the wind. I don't like the feeling snaking inside me right now, causing my face to heat and my mind to race. *And I'm staring.* I'm staring at her so hard that it looks like I'm trying to use my pyrokinesis to set her aflame.

I avert my eyes and realize that Knox and I have nothing going on. A few dinners at his house, some mild flirting, and I'm what? Ready to call him my boyfriend? Fuck, I *am* ready to call him my boyfriend. I'm contemplating whether I actually need the cheese or if I should just try my hand at making my own when the woman speaks—to me.

"Hi, are we in your way?" she asks, and it's not passive-aggressive—it's sweet and genuine. *How annoying.*

"Uh-I'm...I just need some cheese," I blurt.

She smiles at me. "I'm so sorry. I would never stand between a woman and her cheese," she jokes. Cool, so she's beautiful *and* funny.

"No, you aren't—" I cut myself off, trying to string together a full sentence in my head before letting anything else come out of my mouth. "Excuse me. I'll just grab this and be out of your way." I reach for a block of cheddar, two wedges of smoked gouda, bleu cheese crumbles, and a bag of shredded mozzarella. *Okay, so I needed a lot of cheese.* I'm a little embarrassed. I need to get out of here.

"That's a lot of groceries for someone who doesn't cook," a deep voice drawls from my side.

"Yeah, I'm attempting to cook a few meals for myself this week," I say, tossing the packs into my cart. "It could end very badly, but I want to try."

Blonde goddess chimes in, "I don't cook. It's safer for me and the fire department. This one though? He is an amazing cook." She elbows Knox in the chest, and I fight my eye twitch. "I haven't introduced myself yet. I'm sorry, I'm Cora. I work with Knox. You must be Indiana," she introduces herself. The snaking feeling I mentioned earlier coils tighter. I'm not sure I like how wound up I am.

"Oh, hi. It's nice to meet you. Will you be at AJ's tomorrow night?"

Knox looks back at me. "Will *you* be at AJ's?" he asks.

"Um, yeah. Winnie invited me and called in the cavalry to show me a night out." I laugh.

"I'll be there.I wouldn't miss a night out with everyone. You'll come, right Knox?" Cora asks the man towering over us.

"Great, I'm glad to be joining. I've heard a lot about the place," I tell her, but I can't help the way my eyes flit toward Knox. I find him looking at me. Eyes a little narrowed. Does it bother him that I'm hanging out with his family—his coworkers? "I guess I'll see you tomorrow, Cora. Knox, see you around." I give them both an incredibly awkward wave, halfway between a homecoming queen and a soldier, before making my escape. Oh god. *Am I cursed to become an idiot around him?*

I carry my bags out to my car and try to stop the nervous laughter that's threatening to be set loose on the good people of Silverthorne, but I'm stopped in my tracks by the mountains. I'm still not used to these views. I need to get out there again. Maybe this weekend. I'm helping Winnie at the festival, but I have Sunday off, and I'm thinking I need to start exploring my new home state.

I'll consult my list when I'm home and try to pick one close by. I may have already run this morning, but I'm thinking I'll try paddleboarding around the lake for some exercise this afternoon. It will do me some good. I have to get some of this energy out of me before I go full green-eyed monster on anyone who looks in my landlord's direction.

I didn't plan on showing up at AJ's tonight, but after watching Indie paddle around the lake last night in that tiny, red bikini, the draw to be near her was too strong to ignore. From the way she looked at Cora in the grocery store, I could tell she was jealous. Maybe I shouldn't have, but watching her react that way, *over me,* gave me the impression that she might see me as a little more than a friend.

So now I'm here, in a familiar setting but for a very unfamiliar reason. Stepping outside my comfort zone for someone isn't something I expected this soon after meeting them, but I wasn't expecting Indie. I certainly wasn't expecting to walk in here tonight and see her dancing with another man. The man in question may be Colt and Winnie's sixty-two-year-old Uncle Buck, but still another man.

Indie's laugh is loud and obnoxious, and I want to swallow the sound with my mouth. We've been toeing the *friendly* line for weeks now, and the tension that's built between us is enough to make me snap—or go to a bar on a Thursday night where I'll probably have to answer some prying questions from my siblings.

"As I live and breathe. Knox, is that really you?" Alder calls from their table in the corner. "How long has it been? It feels like years since I've seen you out of your house." Colt chuckles beside him.

"Oh, shut up. It's maybe been a month, and that's not long enough," I tell him, walking over. My eyes go back to the tiny brunette in the tight jeans that look like they were made for her. The white shirt she has on fits her like a glove, showing a small sliver of smooth, golden skin above the waistband of her jeans.

Her short hair is whipping around her face with every turn on the small dance floor. Uncle Buck's eyes are lit up as he tosses his head back at something she says, the two of them laughing loudly. I look back at the table to find everyone's eyes trained on me.

"What?" I snap, and they all avert their eyes.

"So what brings you out tonight, Knox?" Winnie asks sweetly.

"Yes, what made you decide to grace us with your presence?" Mare follows up.

"I wonder if it could have anything to do with the interesting conversation I had yesterday about dinner guests," Florence adds.

These women. I'm always either getting interrogated or manipulated by them. "Dad came by and picked up Hazel, so I thought I would come out and get a drink. I *was* invited. Is that okay with everyone?" I ask.

"Absolutely. Let's get you that drink. I could use another one," Colt says, standing and making his way to the busy bar. I follow just to get away from all the prying eyes. He may not be related by blood, but Colt Parker's been like another little brother to me since I've known him. "What a fucking joke." I hear him mutter under his breath, but I'm still able to make it out.

"What is?"

"Just the guy Mare's decided to slum it with." I follow his line of sight and find Mare cuddled up with her boyfriend.

"Yeah, she's really slumming it with that doctor of hers," I joke.

"Oh, shut up."

"So when are you gonna stop talking about it and do something?"

"I don't know what you mean. There's nothing to be done. She can see whoever she wants," he says casually, turning back to the bar and cutting off his view of them. He's fooling no one. But not being one to press for information or to talk about feelings, I let that sleeping dog lie.

"What can I get you boys?" Cecily, our bartender, asks us.

"Two beers. Whatever IPA you have on draft is fine," Colt tells her with a wink.

"Coming up," she says, drumming her hands on the counter.

"Not to pile it on, but—what *are* you doing out tonight?"

I sigh. "Is it that insane that I would be at AJ's?" Cecily sets our glasses in front of us, and I take a sip.

He chuckles. "No, but I have to admit the timing is a little suspicious." He shrugs.

"Suspicious?"

"Listen, I don't know the whole story, but from what I could gather from the women—your new tenant mentioned she would be here—tonight—and you haven't been out with us or responded to the group chat invites until tonight."

"How would you know? You left the group chat months ago."

"Yeah, because as happy as I am for Rhett and Winnie, I didn't need to see one more innuendo about my best friend and my sister," he explains. "I only know this information because it was a topic of conversation before you got here." Of course it was. No one can stay out of anyone's business around here.

"My siblings are annoying."

"Are they wrong though?" he asks before walking away and back to the table. I stay on my stool a couple of moments longer. I'm not usually someone people talk about, and I can't say I care for it much. People may have had a few things to say when I moved back to town and a few months later had a child, but my family really rallied around me then, keeping me away from too much of the idle gossip.

"Hey, Knox," Cora greets me, coming to sit beside me. Then to Cecily she asks, "Can I get a glass of white and a rum and Coke?"

"Cora. How are you?" I ask, trying to be polite. I forgot she said she would be here tonight.

"Good. You know, it's good to see you out and about. I hear we have Indiana to thank for that," she says pointedly.

"Just decided to get out of the house." *She doesn't need to know that Indie played a role in that decision.*

"Right. Well, whatever the reason. I'm glad you're here. It feels like we haven't hung out in forever." She places her hand on my shoulder as she speaks. I'm assuming she means *forever* literally because we have never hung out.

"Excuse me." Indie's voice is soft as she reaches in to grab a drink sitting on a napkin beside Cora.

"I'll just take the rum and Coke. Thanks for ordering it for me, Cora," she says, backing away.

"No problem," she tells Indie, lightly rubbing my arm. *What the hell is that about?*

"Hey," I blurt, trying to catch Indie's eye. For what I'm not sure, I just know I want her attention.

"Hi," she says back, eyes directed at the hand on my shoulder. She pinches her lips together, gives me a nod and turns to walk back to the table. I shrug out from under Cora's hand, moving to stand.

"Good talking to you, Cora."

"Yeah, sure." Her smile is forced, but she takes the hint, slipping off her bar stool to leave. I'm thinking of something to say to Indie when Alder plops into a stool beside me, tossing an arm over my shoulder.

"We're taking shots, and one has your name on it."

"No, it doesn't."

"Oh, come on. When was the last time you took a shot, old man?"

"I don't take shots anymore, and you'll stop taking them soon enough," I tell him.

"I'm going to become a dad—not lame, big brother." He laughs at his own joke.

"Ha-ha. You'll see. One day, maybe not so far in the future, you're going to take a shot, and it's going to wreck you."

"Don't curse me, old one." He hisses, crossing his fingers in front of his face.

"Enough, idiot."

"Do you not want Indiana to know your age?" he stage whispers. At that, I let the eye roll I've been fighting go.

"She already knows." I don't know why I said that. He doesn't need to know.

"Oh really? So you've had *the talk?* How much time are you spending with her exactly?" Alder questions.

"Not a lot." Three nights a week is a lot for some and not a lot to others, so it's not really a lie.

"Hmm, I'm not sure I believe you. You're not really a very good liar."

"I'm not lying. She lives next door. I see her. Hazel wanted her to stay for dinner a couple of times."

"Ah, and Hazey gets what she wants," he says. "Kinda works out that her dad reaps those benefits too."

"There are no benefits," I tell him sternly. *Not yet. Not that I don't want there to be.* I don't need people talking. More laughter makes its way to me, and I look to find her bent over with Colt, hand on his shoulder. He looks past her, giving me a wink before whispering something to her. *Ass.*

"Not yet," Alder says, mirroring my thoughts. "You better head over to the table before Colt decides Indiana should hang out with someone her own age." I just grunt in response but find myself walking to the table and sitting directly across from her, unable to look anywhere else.

She glances in my direction, her eyes widening marginally when she notices me. "I didn't think you'd be here," she says, smiling at me, like me being here makes her happy.

"Wasn't planning on it, but Hazel went to her grandparents," I explain.

"Well, I'm glad you could make it," she says, and I don't miss the blush on her cheeks.

A smile tugs at my lips at her admission. I like that she wants me here. I only nod at her. Mare stops back by our table, and she and Winnie invite her to their next wine night. Indie grins, accepting all open invitations, glancing back and forth between the two. I can only look at her.

She's so beautiful. Her short hair just brushes her shoulders with every move she makes, reminding me of another night in another bar in what feels like another life. I wonder if it tickles, what it would feel like brushing my skin. Her brown eyes are shiny and full of excitement, but there's something else there. I would almost miss it if I weren't fully staring at her. *Studying* her. Her pink, plump lips curved into a smile, and the gold hoop in her perfect upturned nose has no business being as sexy as it is.

Her eyes shift to me, catching me staring. I become aware of more than just her and realize someone has asked me something.

"Knox?" Winnie prods.

"Sorry, what?" I clear my throat.

"Can we come have a lake day? The weather is getting warmer, and I think it would be fun for us all to get together out at your place," she explains.

"We could camp!" Mare cheers.

"Where are we camping?" Colt asks.

"At Knox's," Winnie answers.

"I'm in," he says.

"I'll have to check and see if Ivy's down. Being six months pregnant changes the camping experience. If I bring a bed, she might be more willing," Alder muses.

"I haven't agreed to anything yet," I object.

"She could have mine," Indie chimes in. Everyone at the

table looks to her. "I mean...unless she wouldn't want to? It's just I-well I don't mind sleeping in a tent. I never have before, and it sounds fun. And my b-bed or house is just right there." Her rambling subsides, and I find myself smiling.

"That's really sweet, Indie," Winnie tells her.

"If you really don't mind, I'll tell Ivy that when I pitch her the idea," Alder tells her.

"Not at all," Indie confirms.

"You've never been camping?" I ask. She shakes her head.

"I'm not big on outdoor activities, so I don't really do camping," Winnie tells her.

"It's not that exactly. I mean, no one would call me outdoorsy or anything, but I actually think I would like it; there just isn't anywhere to be in nature in Atlanta. Not like here," she says, swinging her arm in the air.

"Well then, let's go camping," Colt says, smiling at Indie like she's one of his weekly conquests. *Not gonna happen.*

"Alright, fine," I relent. Indie bounces up and down in her seat; Winnie and Mare squeal and clap their hands along with her.

"I need a tent," Indie announces excitedly. "And probably some other things."

The words are out of my mouth before I can think about them. "I have a tent you can use."

"I'll bet you do," Alder jokes and elbows Colt. *Children.* I sigh.

"Between all of us, we'll have everything you need. Don't worry," Mare assures her.

"Aww, thanks, guys. I'm gonna get another drink. I saw moonshine is available, and I've never had it before. Anyone else want something?" she asks, looking around the table.

"I'll have another beer, and I'll come with you," Colt tells her. I clench my jaw. He's doing this on purpose, and I'm getting tired of it.

Alder checks his phone. "I better get going actually. I need to get some oranges and get home. It was nice meeting you, Indiana. Ivy will be grateful for your offer, I'm sure, and probably call you to say so. If not before, we'll see you at the Spring Festival," he tells her.

"Call me Indie—and absolutely. I'm looking forward to it."

He grins at her. "Goodbye, family. Make good decisions. Don't do anything I wouldn't." We all have a laugh at that. Something that, up until the last eight months or so, would have been something we said to him.

"We have shots!" Indie yells, approaching our table. *Shots?* What is this, her second one of the night? "Round three!" *Third* shot of the night?

"What the hell, I'm off tomorrow," Mare says.

"I'm in!" Winnie squeals.

"What are you in? Trouble?" I hear Rhett say from behind us.

"Hi, handsome! I didn't know if you would make it!" Winnie cheers.

"I thought the staff meeting would never end, but I snuck out when they started debating if we would be allowing metal water bottles inside the school anymore," he says, sitting next to her, keeping an arm around her.

"You're so bad, Coach Holloway," she teases, and he whips his head to her. A knowing grin on full display.

"Alright that's enough of that." Colt groans.

I laugh. I can't imagine seeing Florence like this with a guy. I feel for him.

"Oh, come on, Colt. We all know you're not a prude," Mare says in an accusing tone.

He cuts her a dirty look that ends up looking more predatory than threatening. "Why don't you come home with me tonight, and we'll test that theory, Goldie." Marigold holds up her middle finger in response. Colt takes it in stride, smiling widely. "I'll take that as a maybe and definitely don't tell Dr. Grant," he says, shooting her a wink. I fight my smile, as does everyone at the table except for Indie, who looks mildly confused. I can't blame her. The tension between these two is hard to figure out.

We all take our shot, and it goes down like I imagined it would. Tasting like I won't be having another drink the rest of the night, and my beer will be abandoned. I have a beer here and there occasionally. Hard liquor has never been my friend, and even though I've been called a stick-in-the-mud, I have never had any interest in drinking to excess. I do like to watch all my family have a good time though.

A few more rounds for the table, and a soda for me later, and everyone who's still here is well and drunk.

"I'm going to dance!" Indie announces, waltzing out in the open with a few other couples. She dances alone. Not caring who's looking. Her body sways to the rhythm, enchanting me. I can't take my eyes off her.

"You should dance with her, Knox," Colt tells me before taking a long sip of his drink.

I scoff. "I don't dance."

"No, but I do, and if you don't get out there soon, I may have to make sure Indie doesn't have to dance alone."

"Oh, fuck off."

"I'm serious. She's a great girl. Smart, funny, beautiful, and don't get me started on her a—"

"Finish that sentence, and you won't be able to breathe without pain for the next month," I threaten.

He holds his hands up. "I'm just saying, if it's not me, it'll be someone else." I mull over his words and am contemplating the alternative when I see Darrin Ward head toward her on the dance floor. Darrin without a doubt will be a handsy motherfucker. I'm up and out of my chair in an instant, whistles and cheers from the peanut gallery following me.

I grab one of Indie's hands, spinning her into me. She gasps and giggles at the motion. I twirl her around again, pulling her close to sway for a couple steps before twirling her out again. Her laughter is like a drug to me. Her body pressed in tight to mine; hands sliding up my forearms, leaving behind a trail of goose bumps.

"Where did you learn to dance like this?" she asks, breathless.

I lean in close to her ear before answering. "Would you believe me if I said TV?"

She laughs, it's husky and tempting. "No, I wouldn't. You're good."

"Well, a man has to have a few secrets. I can't go giving it away all at once," I tease.

"Mm. Secrets aren't any fun though. I should know," she mutters.

I pull back to look at her face, hoping to get a read on her mood, but all I find is a tipsy smile and eyes full of warmth.

"You're so handsome," she whispers, then those soulful, brown eyes go wide, like she's just realized what she's said.

I chuckle and spin us around a little more until Indie tells me she needs a glass of water through her giggling.

An hour later and Winnie and Rhett are dancing while he serenades her out on the floor, Colt is on his third table of women, and Marigold and Indie are talking about a podcast that *dropped a new episode* this morning. Whatever the hell that means.

"We need to call Ivy. She'll have the best theory," Mare slurs.

"She's a muderino!?" Indiana asks, her hands flying up in excitement.

"The biggest! She's who got me into them!"

"Okay, let's call her!" She pulls out her phone. I'm about to call it a night when Indiana reaches across the table, grabbing my arm.

"Knox, do you know Ivy's number?" she asks me, her big, brown eyes glazed with alcohol and a dopey smile on her lips.

"I do, but I don't think she would appreciate your call as much after midnight as she would tomorrow," I tell her.

She giggles, causing her grip on my forearm to tighten. "You sound s-so serious." She hiccups. Mare starts laughing with her, and Winnie joins as she and Rhett make it back to our table.

"What's so funny?" Rhett asks.

"Me, apparently. I think it's time for us to clear out. Last call was twenty minutes ago. Can everyone get home safe?"

"Grant's picking me up," Mare says.

"We're walking," Rhett answers, kissing Win's temple.

I look over at the table Colt was at and find him missing.

"Colt slipped out a few minutes ago," Winnie tells me, then

turns to my neighbor. "Indie, do you want to stay at our place tonight?"

"Um, I don't want to impose," she murmurs. A sleepy look covers her face. Between that and the flush on her cheekbones that runs down her neck to her chest, it's obvious she's incapable of getting herself home on her own.

"Come on, Indie. I'll give you a ride home," I tell her.

"Um, I don't want to bother—"

"It's not a bother," I say. So much about this woman *bothers* me, giving her a ride home isn't one of them. "Do you have your jacket, your purse?" I ask her.

"Uh...yeah, I...I didn't bring a jacket. It was warm earlier," she explains. I catch what she says, but with every word, they start running a little more together. She grabs the thin strap of a small, black leather bag and slings it over her shoulder. "Thank you for inviting me out," she tells Winnie and Mare. They both get up and smother her tiny frame with their bodies. I reach forward to steady them before they knock one another over.

"Okay, ladies," Rhett says, grabbing Winnie, pulling her to him. She turns into his embrace and snuggles.

"I'll see you this weekend! And I'm s-so excited to g-go camping! In a tent! I have to tell Han!" Indie's shouting, swaying on her feet. She steadies herself with her hand on the table, but it's obvious she won't be making it to my truck without help. I lean down without thinking and wrap my arms around her knees, swinging her up over my shoulder. I hear a gasp followed by giggling. "Are you manhandling me, Knox Holloway? I've never been tossed over someone's shoulder before—I've never been tossed around at all actually. I don't hate it," she announces. She's drunk. Really drunk, and she's so fucking cute.

"Night, guys," I call, heading for the exit. Uncle Buck meets me there, holding the door open for me.

"Goodnight, Indiana. Come back soon. I haven't had a dance partner in forever," he tells the woman dangling from my shoulder.

"Please call me Indie! You're a wonderful dancer, Buck. I would be honored," she tells him earnestly.

"The pleasure is all mine," he replies, then to me adds, "Will you be okay getting her home, Knox?"

"I think I can manage," I tell him before walking out into the now-cool night.

"Speaking of managing things, I think I can walk to your truck," she says. "Although the view from back here is..." she trails off, when I let her slide down the front of my body. "Your eyes...are so blue, Knox." Her voice is low, the compliment coming out slowly. Lazily.

"Thank you," I tell her. Eyes roaming over her flushed, heart-shaped face.

She smiles at me. "And your teeth. Oh god, they're so nice. When you smile at me, it makes me want to..." she trails off again, and I wish she would keep talking. Her feet fully planted on the ground now, she's not swaying anymore when I unwillingly pull away from her. I'm stuck between wanting to know what she was going to say and making sure she isn't going to be sick.

She leans back into me, her lips curved into a devilish grin, looking up at me, biting down on that full bottom lip. I feel the leash I have on my control loosen.

"Fort Knox..." she muses.

"What was that?"

She giggles. "I called you F-Fort Knox." She hiccups.

"You're just so hard to get to know. Your walls are so high, like a fortress. I'm trying though. I'll keep trying," she says wistfully, trailing her fingernails down my chest and nuzzling into me. I'm in trouble.

"Indie, I think you overestimate my willpower."

"Really? I think I estimate it just fine," she quips.

"If you did, you wouldn't be rubbing yourself against me right now, Honey." Her eyes spark at the nickname.

"Are you flirting with me, Knox?" she teases.

"If I was?"

"I might flirt back."

She's still leaning into me, looking up at me with kiss-me eyes. I only want one thing more than to kiss her pretty lips swollen, and it's for her to be stone-cold fucking sober when I do.

INDIANA

My head throbs. Like there are little people with hammers inside it, trying to get out. I'm afraid to open my eyes because I'm worried it will make me nauseous. I had three too many shots last night. The last time I had more than two glasses of wine was months ago, and for a very different reason. I snuggle deeper under the soft blankets and inhale. It smells like trees and mountain air. Crisp and clean—like Knox.

At that, I do open my eyes, taking in my surroundings. The first thing I see is a glass of water and two pills on a sticky note placed on a nightstand beside the bed I'm in. I smile before reading the note.

Take these for your head and then come meet me out on the dock.
I laid some clothes on the chair for you.

Grinning, I take the pills and guzzle the whole glass of water. I swing my legs over the edge of the bed, my eyes searching for the chair in the corner—noticing my jeans folded over the back of it—then down at my bare legs. I'm in my shirt from last night and my blue panties. That's it. My skin heats at the thought of Knox's calloused hands working my jeans down my thighs, touching my bare legs—*focus, Indie.*

I stand slowly and wait for a moment to move, making sure I'm not going to feel sick. Surprisingly, I feel okay. I go to put my jeans on but see that there is a clean pair of shorts and a sweatshirt on the chair beside them. Did Knox go get me clothes from my house? If it were anyone other than him, I might think it was odd, but since it *is* him, I find it endearing.

I pull the shorts up and slip the sweatshirt over my head. It's the one with women holding hands around a fire. Above them it says: It's Nice Here, and then under them: In The Cult. I laugh at his choice, but I love that he picked it for me. I know for a fact this one wasn't just lying on top. He had to dig for it. I make a quick stop in the bathroom, splashing some water on my face.

Last night comes back to me in pieces. Dancing with Buck, laughing with Colt. Shots. Cora's hand on Knox. *Now,* I feel a little bit nauseous. Knox offering me a ride. Standing on the sidewalk by his truck. Had I nuzzled into his chest? Oh, yes. There was definitely nuzzling. One more handful of cold water to my face, and then I head outside and down to the water.

The sun is already out, making the lake sparkle. Sally is basking in it on the porch, but she gets up to walk with me.

"Hey, Sally girl." I pet her head as we walk.

When I get to the edge of the dock, I stop to admire the view—and I don't mean the mountains. Knox Holloway is standing on a paddleboard, coming this way—shirtless. His abs flex with the effort, and my mind conjures lots of images that involve the motion. Lots of dirty images.

"Well, good morning, Tiny Dancer," he calls as he steps off the board, tying it off on one of the boat cleats. I'm assuming the new nickname has something to do with last night, but it all gets a little fuzzy after Knox offered me a ride home.

"I'm not sure what I did to gain the title, but there are worse things than being called 'Tiny Dancer' I suppose." His teeth flash with his smile. The sight makes my knees wobble. I want to be bitten by those teeth. *Okay, rein it in, Indiana. Horny much?*

"Well, there was the dancing," he says thoughtfully. That could go either way. I'm not completely uncoordinated, I'm only worried the alcohol may have thrown me off balance. "Then there was the singing in my truck."

Oh, no. Oh, no, no, no.

"The singing?" I hedge.

"The singing," Knox confirms with a smug grin.

"Was it that bad? Er—was *I* that bad?"

"Bad? No. Entertaining. Yes."

"Oh god. So pretty bad," I surmise.

"I found you entirely captivating."

I snort. "I'm sure. Captivating as in a car crash you can't look away from?"

"Captivating as in a sight I didn't *want* to look away from."

I grin. "You're being nice to me," I accuse, and he surprises me by laughing. He has a great laugh; he has a great everything.

"Is it so hard to believe that I would be nice?" *It's not actually. It's not surprising at all.*

"Thank you for taking care of me last night, by the way. I'm never drinking again."

"You weren't hard to take care of. And if you do decide to drink again, I recommend skipping the moonshine; it has a history of sneaking up on you."

"Now he tells me," I say. "Well, I think I'll go home and shower; let you get on with your day."

"Do you think you can postpone that for a while?" he asks.

"I could be persuaded. What do you have in mind?"

"Come out on the water with me."

"On the paddleboard?"

"You don't think we can manage?"

"Honestly, I'm not sure. I'm still pretty shaky when I stand up on it."

His smile is...sweet. Teasing. Almost boyish. "As certain as I am that we could, I was thinking we should take the canoe out."

"Oh, that sounds like fun. Yes, I would love to. I need to help Winnie later this afternoon, but I've got nothing this morning since my run got canceled." *By three shots, a rum and Coke, and some moonshine.*

"I'm picking up Hazey later, so I thought we could take a tour around the lake before."

"I'm in."

We paddle around the edge of the lake for a while. I spot some adorable little otter-like creatures that Knox tells me are marmots, bighorn sheep, and some elk. I'm kind of wishing I had my camera but also really enjoying myself.

"I've never done anything like this."

"Been in a canoe?"

I laugh. "That or been out on a lake like this. I've been swimming, but only in a pool. I mean, I've been in nature, but only at one of the nature centers in the city. Nothing like this.

This? It's like experiencing something for the first time, and you hadn't even realized you were missing it or that you knew to want it. Does that make sense?"

"I think I'm following," he says from behind me. I smile. "So tell me more about you, Indie. What was it like growing up in a big city?" My instinct is to redirect back to him. To not talk about me, but Knox is letting me into his life, I think it's time I crack a window.

So I tell him. I tell him about the tiny apartment. The collections. The cuckoo clocks, the ceramic frogs, the shirts, the rocks. He laughs at my puns and sympathizes with me when I tell him that we had to return the cat Han and I stole. He doesn't make me feel like I'm rambling. Just lets me tell him stories that make up who I am.

"I need to ask you a question," I say after finishing the story of how my pants ripped in half in sixth grade when I tried to scale the fence at recess.

"Shoot."

"I woke up without pants on this morning."

"I assumed you would." I turn to look at him. He's staring at me, amusement spilling out of him.

"Well...I was wondering how I ended up like that, Mr. Holloway."

"You don't remember?"

"I wouldn't ask you if I did."

"You took them off before we made it inside the house last night. Then you did two really impressive ballerina turns. Where did you learn that, by the way? All while singing "Tiny Dancer." I followed you into the bedroom to find you already in the bed. I just laid them over the chair and figured you might want something else to wear this morning, so I ran over to your place early to get a few things. I didn't snoop," he promises.

I'm a little mortified at my behavior.

"I hope you know that I don't go out and get drunk. That's not really my thing. Last night was an exception. Well, not the ballerina turns, I do those every now and then to make sure I still can."

He chuckles. "You're young, Indie. You should be enjoying your nights."

"I would rather be having a glass of wine by the fire after reading a book to Hazel," I admit. It's blatant now. That I like him. That I want to spend time with him.

"I would rather you be doing that too," he says. I whip around to face him, wanting to make sure I heard him correctly. *Does he feel what I do?* Only when I do, he stands, getting ready to step onto the dock, and we tip. I try to overcorrect us, but end up making it worse.

My head is under the water before I have a chance to look up at him.

KNOX

My head breaks the surface, and I look around for Indie. She's barely treading water, laughing so hard she's having trouble keeping her head above the water. I swim over to help her, bringing us closer to shore. She's laughing still, her strong legs folding around me. I can just stand in this spot, my shoulders out of the water. I hold her to me, and she wraps her legs around me tighter.

"Can you touch the bottom here?" she asks me, amused at the possibility.

"I can," I tell her, slightly distracted by having her in my arms.

"You're like the Jolly Green Giant." She laughs at her own joke.

"Is that what you're into, Indie?" Her eyes warm at the question.

"It would appear that I'm into all sorts of things if they involve you, Knox."

Her laughter slows as she stares at me, slowly placing her arms around my neck, the wet sleeves of her shirt cold on my skin. I move a hand up her back to the base of her neck, supporting her with one arm now. Gripping her hair in my hand, her eyes blink slowly, her mouth falling open in a small gasp. Heat bursts in my veins at the feel of her against me.

"I-I'll be honest with you, Knox. I'm not exactly sure what's going on here. I spend a lot of time with you, with Hazel, and I'm starting to get used to it—starting to look forward to it." She swallows, looking up at the sky. "If we're friends...I can do that, right? If that's what you want. I can be your friend." Her fingers deftly comb through my hair as she speaks. There are so many things I want when it comes to Indie, but being her friend might kill me.

"I don't want to be your friend, Honey."

"Then what do you want?" she whispers, staring at my mouth. Leaning forward, I ghost my lips over the side of her neck, murmuring against the tender skin.

"I'm not a subtle man, Indie. If you don't want me to kiss you, you need to tell me now." She grinds herself against me in answer. I groan, feeling her heat through our clothes. She does it again, and I snap. I take one last look into her clever, soulful, deep-brown eyes, ones that pulled me in the first night I met her, searching them for any hesitation before pulling her mouth to mine in a kiss that sends shockwaves through my body and across the damn lake.

At first, our kisses are drugging, lazily exploring one another's mouths. I haven't kissed someone in a so long, but I know for certain I've never been so fucking starved for someone's mouth like I am right now. Kissing has always been a prelude to the main event—but kissing Indie is the headliner. Tongues teasing parted lips. Breathy moans mixed with the sound of the water lapping around us.

She continues to grind herself into my near-painful erection. I take what she'll give me, letting her set the pace for now. Our mouths find their rhythm, in sync with Indie's movements as she sucks my bottom lip into her mouth. She bites down on it, rolling her hips faster, making these sweet, erratic whimpers that have me loosening the reins on my control.

"You're a greedy little thing, aren't you?" I ask, pulling her hair so her throat is on display for me. She gasps when my teeth graze her neck before licking and sucking my way back to her mouth.

"Knox, I—"

I groan. Saying my name in a breathy voice is almost enough to send me over the edge.

"That's it, Indie Baby. Fuck me through these clothes and use me to make yourself feel good."

"Oh god," she whines, grinding a bit harder, picking up the pace. I'm seconds away from losing all semblance of willpower.

"Please, Indie. Let me see what you look like when you come for me." I move my hands to her hips, gripping tightly and working her body against mine.

"Fuuck..." She cries out, her voice echoing on the lake, going slack against me. The noise I make as white hot pleasure shoots down my spine is somewhere between a moan and a whimper. She lays her head against my shoulder, her breaths puffing out on my neck.

I slide my hand through her wet hair and kiss her temple. "Fuck, Honey. I've just come in my pants for the first time since I was fifteen years old." She giggles, kissing my mouth, my cheeks, my neck.

"I haven't done anything like that since I was a teen in my room humping a pillow," she admits. A laugh barks out of me.

"Please tell me this was a slightly more stimulating experience."

Her body shakes with quiet laughter. "Considerably," she says, tilting her head up to look at me. She grabs my face and pulls it closer to hers, kissing my lips softly. Once. Twice. Three times. It's so sweet and unexpected. This whole day has been so surprising. I walk us out of the water, and when we make it to shore, I don't bother setting her down. As I carry her to the house, she kisses on my neck, running her hands through my wet hair.

"Do you have time to come in? I was going to take a quick shower," she offers.

"I'm not sure if I get in there with you, it will be very quick."

"I'll take my chances," she tells me, smiling.

We remove our shoes, and I set them on the porch railing. Indie unlocks the door, and we walk inside back to the bathroom. She grabs a couple of towels for us, and I get the shower going before removing my wet clothes.

"I'm freezing, it's lucky for us that someone fixed my hot water or—" her words cut off when she enters the bathroom, seeing me naked. This time she doesn't hide her face or turn away from me—her eyes roam over my body lazily. Taking her time, getting her fill of the sight of me.

"God, Knox. You're perfect," she whispers, stepping toward me. Her cold hands press into my stomach, and I flinch slightly at the temperature. "Sorry."

"Please don't ever be sorry for touching me." She hums in response. "Let's get you out of these wet clothes. Arms up, Honey." Her smile is shy, but she lifts her arms for me. I peel the clingy fabric of her sweatshirt from her skin, so she's left in her white T-shirt, no bra. "Fuck, just the sight of you is going to have me coming again." I run my thumb over her nipple and watch it harden under my touch.

Exploring her body like this; unfettered access to her makes me dizzy.

She sucks in a breath. "Please," she moans out. I've been imagining the feel of her for weeks. How she would feel under my hands, what noises she'd make. She could ask me anything right now, and I would do it.

"Please what, Honey?"

"Please touch me." My dick is hard again—harder than it's ever been in my life. Her breathy plea is so fucking sexy, so fucking tempting. I'm a man starved for her. I give in to what my body wants, letting myself be selfish with Indie.

"You're so sweet for me. So polite. Is that what you want to be for me, Indie Baby? Polite?" She shakes her head slowly. "What do you want to be then?"

"Everything," she says, bending to pull her shorts and panties off, then she slips the last remaining thing that's separating us over her head. Bare before me, she's a vision. Her body is better than I could have dreamed up, and I'm stunned by the sight. Strong toned legs and tits I want to suck. "I want to be everything for you; do whatever you want me to do."

"Are you asking me to wreck you?" I ask, running my thumb over the dragonfly tattoo on her shoulder, so similar to mine.

She shivers, her eyes almost glowing when she answers, "I want you to fucking destroy me." *Fuck, she's so fucking captivating.*

"You're stunning, Indie," I tell her before pulling her into the shower with me and under the spray of the warm water.

She kisses my chest, then lower down on my stomach. She lowers herself to her knees and looks up at me. I palm the side of her face, taking in the sight before me. Indie on her knees, water sluicing down her face, her body, her thighs spread wide, and her hands resting on mine.

"I want you to use me too, Knox." I rub my thumb over her lips, and her mouth pops open in offering. *Fuckkk; she's going to be the one who wrecks* me. I spread it wider, guiding my dick to her waiting, sweet mouth and have to close my eyes and take a deep breath so I don't come on contact. Indie takes me in her hot mouth, moaning around me, the vibrations nearly taking me out. Then she sucks, and I lose all thought, I'm only running on feeling now. I grip the back of her head and guide her up and down on my length slowly.

"You okay, Honey?" She hums again, nodding, letting me know she wants this. "Think you can take all of me?" She takes me deeper in answer, gagging on me, eyes watering in the corners as she stares back at me. "Fuck, that's good. So fucking good. Do you like sucking my dick?" Her knees squeeze together in response to my question as she bobs her head up and down on my dick.

"Touch yourself, Indie. When I come, I want you there with me."

She does as I say, and her moaning increases along with the pace she sucks. When I can't hold back anymore, I pull myself out of her mouth, coating the delicate column of her neck in ribbons of my cum as she stares up at me, mouth hanging open in a lust-filled haze. "Fuck, Indie." I grab her underneath her arms and haul her against me. Kissing her within an inch of her life. "That was the single hottest thing I've ever seen or done in my life."

"Thank you," she says, a nervous giggle bubbling out of her.

"So fucking beautiful." I kiss her again before running my fingers through the mess I've made of her. She smiles at me. It's shy and so fucking alluring.

"Something funny?" I ask, grinning back at her.

"No, it's just that—I've never done that before," she tells me quietly. *She's never done that before?* Why does that make my chest fill with pride like some kind of neanderthal?

"Fuck, Honey, I'm gonna get hard again if you keep saying things like that." She nods, then reaches up on her tiptoes to kiss me long and deep.

"I would say I don't see the problem, but I need to actually get clean now," she says.

"Then let me help you," I say, pulling her closer to me and gently rubbing my release from her neck, watching it slide down her body. I grab the shampoo bottle and squeeze some into my hand. "Turn around," I order her.

"Are you going to wash my hair?" she asks, smiling widely.

"I am."

"You like me, Knox Holloway," she accuses.

"Yeah, Honey. I like you," I confirm, dipping my face to hers, pressing a hard kiss to her lips. "Now turn around." She does, and I lather the shampoo in my hands before massaging her head with it.

"That feels really good," she moans.

"Good. Lean back and let me rinse." She does, and I repeat the steps with her conditioner. I take a little longer when I scrub the rest of her, finally getting my hands on these torturously sculpted legs, but hearing her enjoy it is too fun for me. "All clean," I announce.

"Thank you," she breathes, turning in my arms to face me.

"Knox, I-," she cuts herself off, shaking her head and smiling before trying again. "Last night, this morning, and now this. I might start getting used to this." She plants a kiss to my chest, giving me a grin as she slips from the shower to go get dressed.

"I might want you to," I whisper to the empty shower.

KNOX

I'm mesmerized by the smiling beauties illuminated by the soft, amber glow the lantern casts in our makeshift tent. Indie has completely transformed the living room into a magical looking safari camp. Lamps from every room are lit around the room. We're lying on the soft cushions she pulled off the couch along with most of the blankets and pillows she could find in the rest of the house. Me lying one way with the view of Hazel tucked in tight to Indie's side, attention locked on gentle hands, reaching up and sweeping through the air to set the backdrop.

She's weaving together a story for Hazel that has all her favorite animals in it. I could watch this woman tell me what it looks like to watch paint dry and be completely captivated. Watching Hazel's face, eyes so full of wonder, grinning ear to ear, has my mind racing. After my morning with Indie, I haven't been able to focus on much else.

"Is the baby tiger okay?" my daughter asks.

"Of course he is. He was only hiding in the basket because

he didn't know if he was allowed to be in the human's camp, but once they find him they'll make sure he knows it's safe," Indie assures, looking down at her and smiling.

Hazel smiles back at her, then settles back in for the end of the story, reaching for one of Indie's hands, holding it in her tiny one. I grip Indie's ankle and her soft gaze meets mine. We stare at one another for only a few seconds. Some kind of silent conversation passing between us. My adoration for this woman, my want for her, only grows at the sight of her with Hazel. Fear fights with desire, and when Indie finishes her story and we get Hazel tucked into bed; desire wins.

I catch her in the kitchen getting a drink of water. Walking up behind her and placing my hands on either side of her body, I drop my head to her shoulder, placing a small kiss there.

"Thanks for inviting me over tonight, I had a lot of fun with Hazel. I think she likes my stories," she muses, setting her glass down and turning into me.

"I don't think it's possible not to enjoy one of your stories, Honey." Her arms reach up to thread her hands together behind my neck, softly playing with the ends of my hair.

She grins, her nose scrunching and a flush staining her cheeks. "Is that so, Mr. Holloway?"

"Yeah, I tried to fight it, but I might be in need of a bedtime story from now on," I tell her, gripping her hips and lifting her onto the countertop.

"I make no promises, but we may be able to come to some kind of arrangement."

"What's the trade off?" I ask, running my nose up the side of her neck.

"I would say a dinner for a story, but you already feed me

most nights as it is." Her voice is barely a whisper. I place a kiss to her jaw and her fingers tighten in my hair.

"I'm sure we can come up with something, can't we?" I bring my nose to hers now, waiting for any sign that she doesn't want me to kiss her. All I've been able to think about since this morning is kissing her again. Her eyes bore into mine, a heat simmering behind them. She tugs at my hair once more but her hands stay fixed where they are. I brush my lips gently over hers and her legs flex around my own. I reach down her thigh, gripping behind her knee to hitch her leg higher over my hip, pressing into her so she can feel how badly I want her.

Letting out a sound between a whimper and a sigh, she moves her other leg up my side, squeezing, before our mouths collide in a kiss that's full of need and longing. She sucks my bottom lip into her mouth and I groan, my hands sliding under her ass to pull her as tightly to me as possible. I lift her from the counter, walking us down the hall toward my bedroom, kissing as we go.

"Shit!" I whisper curse when I stub my toe on the corner of the trim in the hall. Indie tucks her head into my neck, trying to smother her fit of laughter.

"You think that's funny?" I ask, swatting her on the ass once before we make it through the threshold of my room and shutting the door behind us.

"A little, yeah." Laughter still in her voice.

"I'll give you something to laugh about, Indie Baby." I lay her onto the bed and tickle her side a little and her giggle burts free."Knox! Knox, d-don't! Stop, I can't be quiet if you do that!" She flails in an attempt to get me to stop. I do, but it's more about how utterly stupefied I am at the sight of her. Face flushed, bright smile, shirt riding up revealing the smooth tanned skin of her toned stomach.

She rises up onto her elbows. "What?"

"I like you in my bed," I tell her.

"Aw, shucks I bet you say that to all the girls," she teases.

"Honey, I've never had another woman in this bed." Her eyes flare, smile turning more serious.

"Kiss me in your bed, Knox. I want to be the only woman you've ever kissed in your bed."

I crawl over her body until I'm hovering over her then slip a hand behind her head and kiss her. Slowly at first, tenderly. But it's not long before it turns into something more. We kiss for what feels like hours, at some point both of us losing our shirts. She's straddling me now, strands on her hair falling around my face like a curtain. I run my hands over every exposed inch of her warm skin. I feel like a teenager again, making out with a girl in my bedroom and trying to be quiet.

"Daaaddyyy!"

We both turn our heads toward the sound of Hazel's voice drifting down the hall, Indie climbs off my lap and starts for the door before remembering she doesn't have a shirt on.

"I got it," I say, jumping up as she bends to grab a shirt off the floor and slips it on over her mussed hair that I've been running my hands through. I open the bedroom door and look back at her. She giggles, drawing my attention to her swollen lips, looking like every fantasy I've ever had come to life in my old T-shirt.

I quickly walk to Hazel's door and open it to see her sitting up in the moonlight coming in from her window. Crouching beside her bed, I place my hand on her head.

"Hazel? Are you okay, babygirl?"

"I'm thirsty," she says with a yawn. "I have some water, please?"

"Yeah, sweetheart. I'll get you some and be right back," I tell her, kissing the top of her head before walking back out into the hallway.

"Is she okay?" Indie whispers, leaning against the opposite wall.

"Fine. Just needed a drink," I tell her.

She nods, grinning at me. Her eyes full of the past hour's memories. I hold out my hand to her and when she reaches out for it, I grab her wrist and pull her to me, placing a quick kiss to her mouth before pulling her to the kitchen to get some water for Hazel.

"I should get home," she says as I secure the lid onto the sippy cup.

"Should you?" I question. I can't think of anything more important for her to be doing than what we were just in the middle of.

She laughs under her breath. "I should," she confirms, then stretches up onto her tiptoes to kiss my neck, then my cheek, then grabs my head to kiss my mouth. "I'll see you tomorrow though. Big spring festival, right?"

"Yeah, we'll be there."

"Good. Goodnight, Knox." I don't want her to go, but I'm not sure if she wants me to ask her to stay. This is all still so new.

"Goodnight, Indie." I kiss her forehead and she walks over to the front door, sliding into her shoes. She opens the front door but pauses, turning around to blow me a kiss. My heart beats out of rhythm at the sight. Then without my permission I reach up to catch her kiss. Not willing to waste even one of them.

Her answering grin tells me it was the right choice. I'm afraid of the things I might do to put that smile on her face. Then she's bounding off my front steps and jogging down the path connecting our houses and I'm wishing she would have stayed, that there will be a time that she doesn't ever leave.

Indiana

The string lights over my head make me think of the farmers' markets my family would go to when I was a kid. It's noisy and loud, and there are booths lined up as far as I can see. I'm walking down one of the lanes, thinking about how much Han would love it here. The colorful people and the live entertainment. It's just the sort of thing we would have dreamed up while telling stories to one another.

I've been here since seven this morning, helping Winnie set up all the baked goods, and I even helped Ivy and Florence get some packages together for the auction they're having. Free nights at either The Edgemont or The Holloway Hotel sound amazing, but the packages now both include a spa treatment and an outing.

"Indie!" I turn to see Hazel up on top of Knox's shoulders. She's waving at me frantically. The sight gives me that fuzzy feeling I've become well acquainted with. They both feel like mine.

"Hi, Hazey!" I yell back to her. Beside Knox are his parents. I smile at them.

"Hello, Indiana. It's good to see you again," Mr. Holloway greets me.

"Very good to see you again," Mrs. Holloway chimes in.

"It's great to see you both. Please, call me Indie. Are you enjoying your night?"

"Oh, yes. We always like to come and see the sights. This town is always celebrating something," she comments.

"That's something I'm looking forward to. I love this kind of thing," I say, looking out over the festival.

"Me too!" Hazel yells. "I have cotton candy!"

"I see that. And it's blue. That's my favorite, you know?"

"Want some?" She holds it out to me in offering. It's not as fluffy as I assume it used to be, and there's some melted sugar in spots, but I will not reject this very gracious offer.

"Indie, you don't—" Knox starts, but I lean forward and bite a small piece off.

"Mmm. Hazel. That is the best cotton candy I've ever had. I have to get some for myself before I eat all yours," I tell her seriously. She grins at me.

"I can share!"

"That's okay, baby. Why don't we go get Indie her own?" Knox encourages shooting me a wink. With that wink, that boyish gesture, I melt like the cotton candy on his daughter's sticky fingers.

"Okay!" Hazel agrees, and I grin at her easy-going nature. So unlike her father in that way.

"We're going to stop by the bakery booth; we'll catch up with you in a bit to get Hazel and head home," Mrs. Holloway tells us.

"Yay! Sleepover with Grammy and Grandpa!" Hazel cheers.

Knox smiles but shakes his head. "It's not like you don't have a sleepover every week or anything."

"Time with grandparents is very important for her development, son. It also keeps us young," Mr. Holloway says.

"Studies have also shown that grandparents who spend time with their grandchildren retain their memories longer. You wouldn't want me to lose my mind, would you?" Mrs. Holloway asks Knox pointedly.

"More than you already have?" Knox mutters. His dad laughs, and I bite my lip to stop mine.

Mrs. Holloway gives me a look. "It's like he doesn't remember that I know all the embarrassing moments of his life, and I really enjoy talking." At that, I can't stop the bubbling laughter.

"See you in a bit," she calls over her shoulder as she walks away, Mr. Holloway beside her, reaching for her hand.

"Your parents are really great. They remind me a little of mine," I tell Knox.

"They're the best. I just like giving my mom a hard time every now and then. She would keep Hazel at her house permanently if it were an option."

"She does give that impression," I muse.

"But you want to stay with Daddy, right?" He looks up at Hazel, and she leans her head down to look at him.

"Forever and ever," she says sweetly.

"That's my girl." She giggles at him, kissing his face.

We walk around the grounds for a while. I get my cotton candy, and we watch Hazel play some games. I try to get a hold of my heart when Knox throws a tennis ball at some milk bottles, winning her a giant dinosaur with a tutu that's bigger than she is.

"Can you keep an eye on her while I throw this away real quick? I think I saw a trash bin just around the corner." On the outside, this seems like such a small thing, but I know differently. Hazel is Knox's entire universe, and he's trusting me to keep her safe. Even if it's only for two minutes.

"Of course! We'll be just fine."

"Indie, look at her!" She holds the green dinosaur up for me to get a good look.

"Oh my goodness. That's the biggest dinosaur I've ever seen, and she's beautiful. What are you going to name her?" I ask her, squatting down to see her better.

She looks at the dinosaur, smiling so big her eyes are squinting, then back to me. "Greenie!"

"Greenie? That's the perfect name for her because of her green scales!"

"I like her skirt."

"Did you know that's called a tutu when you're a ballerina?" I ask her.

"I want to be a balletina!"

"You do? I bet there are some classes you could take. Would you like that?"

"Yes!" she shouts, hugging me and knocking me off balance, so I fall backward. I laugh as my back hits the ground with Hazel on top of me.

"What's going on here?" I hear Knox's deep drawl from above us. I rise into a sitting position and then stand with Hazel and Greenie in my arms.

"We named our beloved dinosaur."

"It's Greenie, and I want to do dance!"

"You want to do dance? What does that mean?" Knox asks her, slightly amused.

"She said she wanted to be a ballerina, so I said maybe there was a class or something," I say, shrugging.

"I'm not sure if that fits into our schedule." Oh. *Do I fit into their schedule?*

"I could help out, maybe take her or something?" I offer, hoping to understand his mood change.

"Maybe. We'll see what happens." *Okay? Maybe I've gotten a little too comfortable.*

"Hello! Oh my word, Hazey! What do we have here?" I file that response away, turning to see Florence walking over to us.

"It's Greenie, Andy Lo!"

"That's perfect! Greenie is bigger than you!"

"I know!" Hazel shouts back excitedly.

"Hi, Indie. How are you? My brother being nice to you?" I can't stop my blush in response. *If by making out like we're horny teenagers, letting me hump him in the lake, and then washing my hair after sharing one of my most intimate moments is nice? Then yes, Knox has been very nice.*

"Am I being nice to you, Indie?" Knox gives me a knowing grin, echoing my thoughts.

"I was wondering if you could stop by the hotel in a couple of weeks to work on the website with me."

"Absolutely. Just say when."

"Perfect, I'll text you. I'm heading over to a friend's. Someone left a note on my car after work, and I'm not sure what it meant, but I don't want to be out, and I don't want to be at home tonight."

"Someone left a note on your car? What did it say? Did you see anyone? I told you to get outside cameras." Knox is the picture of concern, and I can't say I blame him. Safety isn't something you mess around with.

"Easy, big brother. I'm fine. It was probably one of the guests. I turned a guy down when he asked for my number earlier. He's harmless." Her words come out easily enough, but I'm not sure she's convinced either of us. "I just wanted to stop by and drop off my auction items. I'm visiting Winnie's booth for some baked goods, and then I'm off. Love you, Hazey!" She drops a kiss onto Hazel's cheek and heads off.

"I guess I need to order some cameras," Knox says.

"I guess you do," I agree.

We get a corndog at the fried food station, and Hazel and I try a fried Oreo. It was delicious, and I could probably go the rest of my life without ever having another one. Knox has twined our fingers together more than once, run his fingers down my arms, and wrapped his around me while playing carnival games. The tension from earlier seems to be forgotten, and I shake it off. It wouldn't be the first time I read something wrong.

Mr. and Mrs. Holloway, or Tom and Mary as I have been instructed to call them, came by and got Hazel. So now it's just Knox and me—and Alder and Ivy, Colt, Mare and her boyfriend, and Rhett and Winnie. We're crowded around a small arena, and in the middle sits a mechanical bull. I've already signed both of us up to ride it.

"You know I'm more grateful to be pregnant now than I was a few minutes ago, knowing I don't have to get up there," Ivy comments.

"Oh, come on. I bet you'd absolutely crush it," I say.

"Crush it and look so hot doing it," Ivy agrees.

Winnie sighs. "I think we all know it's better that I stay out of the ring." A chorus of agreement follows.

"Agreed."

"Yes."

"Affirmative, baby sis."

"Okay! Rude! Let's see you get up there!" Winnie says to Colt.

"More than happy to demonstrate a successful ride." His look at Marigold is anything but subtle, and I fight a blush.

"I wanna go!" I say, and I'm met with cheers from the crowd.

"You gonna be okay on that thing?" I spin to face Knox, grinning.

"Are you worried about me?"

"Should I be?"

"It would be the *friendly* thing to do," I tease.

"I don't think we're friends, Indiana."

"We're not friends? I wasn't sure." I play dumb. Teasing him is fun.

He leans closer to me, his mouth coming right next to my ear before whispering. "Friends don't want to do what I want to do with you, Honey."

His words send heat racing into my veins.

"Is that a promise?"

"You can bet on it." I laugh, feeling free and light and bright and shiny. It's new and exciting, and looking at him, like this, is something I didn't know I wanted. How can you know you want something when you've never felt it before?

"Alright, let's see it, Colt!" Rhett yells at Colt as he hops onto the back of the metal saddle with horns. I won't deny that he looks good up there. There's a twinkle in his eye that tells me he loves the attention on him right now. I subconsciously glance at Marigold. Her boyfriend, Grant, is telling her he needs to leave again.

"You just got here," she says.

"I know, and I wish I could stay, but I can't help it that I'm on call. I'll make it up to you," he tells her, making her giggle before kissing her hair and heading toward the parking lot. I avert my eyes, not wanting to get caught eavesdropping. The buzzer sounds, and Colt hangs on for the full eight seconds before jumping off and taking a bow. There is a sea of women vying for his attention, but it seems to me that he only has eyes for one.

"Okay, Indie! You're up!" Colt yells. I nod.

"Here goes nothing," I mutter and make my way to the entrance. The man there tells me the basics, and then it's up to me. When I get to the machine, though, I'm finding it difficult to find a way on. That's when I feel strong arms lift me, helping swing my leg over the saddle. I giggle and look down to see Knox has come to help me. My hero.

"You look like a real cowgirl up there," he says, grinning.

"Is that what you're into, Knox? Cowgirls?"

"I'm into whatever you want me to be, Honey."

I'm dizzy—drunk on his openness. Probably not the best way to go into riding a mechanical bull—but here we are. Knox stands at the edge of the arena, leaning against the railing, a disgustingly sexy smirk on his face. Like he knows what he just said has knocked me so off-kilter I can barely think.

The buzzer blows, and I hang on for dear life, doing my best to mimic what I saw Colt doing up here. Unfortunately for me, that's not at all what's happening—I'm flailing. It's like when you think you sound like a pop star singing in your car, so you record it, then you find out the truth. Well, the truth here comes in the form of me flying off a hunk of metal and face-planting into a plastic-covered mat. I roll over, laughing.

"You did good," Knox tells me, grinning and holding out a hand to help me up.

I chuckle. "No, I didn't. But you're sweet to say so."

"Wanna get out of here?" The heat behind his words doesn't escape my notice.

"If it's with you, then yes," I tell him.

In a surprising display of public affection, he presses a quick kiss to my lips before hauling me over his shoulder like he did the other night at the bar. The crowd cheers, and I blush what must be scarlet.

"Well, I think this is going to start some rumors," I tease.

"They're not rumors if they're true," he tells me, smacking my ass, causing me to squeal. *I really want them to be true.*

"You're making a habit of leaving family events like this, Indie!" Rhett calls along with a few wolf whistles. I try to wave from my perch and see Winnie leaning into Mare laughing, clutching her stomach.

As I'm carried out to the dimly lit parking lot, my brain clings on to "family events," and the warmth inside me glows a bit brighter. I've missed these kinds of nights. Carefree and surrounded by people you care about.

At the edge of the parking lot, Knox slides me down the front of his body, cupping my ass as I wrap my arms around the back of his neck.

"Do you make a habit of carrying women off?" I ask, playing with the hair curling on the back of his neck.

"Woman," he corrects. "Just one." My heart feels like it may break out of my chest at his admission. His mouth ticks up on one side, and I kiss the corner.

Knox is forty-one. A man in full. *Boyfriend* probably feels so juvenile to him, and even though it hasn't been that long, I'm feeling desperate to lay claim to him.

Back on my feet, Knox kisses the hell and the heaven out of me against his truck. He kisses me until I can't breathe and my lungs burn, but I don't ever want to stop. I want to be kissed by this man for however long I'm allowed.

KNOX

"Careful, Hazey!" I call to my little threenager. She's trying to climb a rock by the lake's edge, but her little feet keep slipping off it.

"Want to hold my hand while you do that?" Indie asks her. She nods, reaching up to take the offered hand.

We picked Hazel up from my parents' this morning after getting breakfast in town. We were on the receiving end of a few prying looks, but it's calmed down a bit since the festival a couple of weeks ago. My parents are trying their best to rein in their excitement, but the way my mom hugged Indie after Hazel ran to her arms gave her away.

When we got back, Indie wanted to do something fun with her. So now we're hiking around the lake, gathering wildflowers to make bouquets for the kitchen table.

"I like this one!"

"Oh, I love that one. It's just the pop of color we need. We don't have that many red ones." Indie holds out the flower basket for Haze to put her flower in. "What do you think, should we get some more yellow or purple next?"

Hazel's expression is one of concentration before announcing, "Purple!"

"Excellent choice, Hazey."

Sally hangs back with me while they walk along the trail in front of me, Indie letting Hazel climb up small rocks and jump off them, not bothering to keep her on task. Where I like to have a plan, or a schedule, she tends to be more flexible. Sometimes she drives me crazy, like finding all my pots and pans in different places because she thought reorganizing them would be helpful. *It's not for someone like me.* But if her moving my kitchen utensils means she's in my home, then I'll take that over the alternative any day.

My phone buzzes in my pocket.

Dad.

"Hello," I answer.

"Hey, son. Do you have a minute?"

"Sure. What's going on?"

"Well, the fence in the west pasture is down again, and I don't usually like to bother you because you have Hazel, but Rhett is at the school today, and Alder's on a call—"

"You can always call me, Dad. What do you need?"

"The cows got loose, and I need someone to help me round them up."

"Okay, just let me get Hazel's bag, and I'll head that way."

"Thanks, son. I'll see you in a little bit."

I tap my screen, raising my head to see Indie looking at me.

"Is everything okay?"

"Yeah, I just need to go help my dad with some cows. I'll have to cut our afternoon short."

"Oh. Okay, that's alright. We can make the bouquets another day," she tells me smiling.

"I want Indie!" Hazel shouts.

"It's okay, Hazey. I'll be here when you get back, and I bet you'll have fun with Grammy." Her immediate response is to help Hazel feel better. She's so good with her. My worries about her not wanting to be with someone who has a kid already have slowly begun to dissipate over the time I've known her. The doubt of her outgrowing me, wanting more, hangs over me. Remembering my own life at twenty-seven, Indiana's maturity is already leaps and bounds what mine was, but still, I'm having a hard time shaking my uncertainty.

As we walk back to the house, Hazel's walking ahead of us. I snag Indie's hand in mine, needing the connection to her. She leans into me in response, pressing herself into my side. I'm not sure if it's because our relationship is still new, but no matter how much she touches me, kisses me, looks at me, it's never enough. I can't get close enough to her.

"You know, and there's absolutely no pressure here, but if Hazel wanted to, I could keep her here, and we could finish our afternoon," she hedges quietly, making sure not to let Hazel overhear. The thought of her hanging out with Hazel while I'm gone *doesn't* strike fear in my heart like it might've even a few months ago. It's just that I've never left her with anyone who isn't family, and it's not a concept I'm familiar with.

"I wouldn't want to put you out. I'm not sure how long I'll be gone," I tell her, still unsure if I can relinquish this little bit of control I have. Hazel is the most precious thing in my life. Everything that involves her is a direct line to my heart. It's only ever been us, and she's only ever been my responsibility—solely.

"You know it's not like that for me. I love spending time with Hazel, but I also understand if you're not there yet, Knox.

I can be patient. I've got time—a lot more than you, old man."
She bumps her hip against me, and it's in this moment I know I
want all my days to be like this. Her beside me, teasing me and
wanting to spend time with my daughter. Care for us like I'm
dying to care for her.

"Hey, Hazey. Do you want to stay here with Indie today
until I get back?"

"Yes! Yes, yes!" she chants, twirling in a circle as we make it
to the edge of the yard before yelling, "Fairy garden!" and
running to check on her little moss houses.

A hand at my chest stops me. Looking down into Indie's
warm, brown eyes, I note her smile. Her lips are stretched ear to
ear as she reaches up to remove my ball cap, putting it back on
my head backward. With one hand, she crooks her finger,
motioning me to come closer before sealing her mouth to mine
in a kiss. It's brief but still travels down to my toes, promising
me more later.

"Thank you, Knox."

I smile against her mouth. "Shouldn't I be thanking you?
You're the one babysitting." She shakes her head at me.

"That's not what I'm doing, and I don't want you to think of
it like that."

"Then I won't."

"That easy, huh?"

"Yeah, Indie Baby. You want it, you got it."

"Oh really? Well, in that case, should I make a list or...?" I
swat her on the ass, and she giggles as she runs toward Hazel
with me chasing after her. When she gets there, she picks
Hazel up, spinning her around once before facing me again.

"Alright you two, I'm heading to Grammy and Grandpa's.
I'll see you in a little bit. Hazel, make sure Indie doesn't do

anything too silly, will you?" I place a kiss to Hazel's cheeks and then a quick one to Indie's mouth.

"We both got kisses!" Hazel announces.

"Is that okay with you, dragonfly?" I ask, worried she may not like sharing my attention when she's never had to before.

"Yes!" she says, then grabs Indie's face, pulling her in for a kiss as well. Indie's smile is brilliant, shining a light on the reservations I may still be harboring. *She wants this now, but will she change her mind?*

"We'll be fine, Daddy. Won't we, Hazey?"

"Yes!" her little voice rings out, giggling.

With the vision of them both chasing butterflies in the yard, I make my way to my parents, already in a hurry to get back to my girls.

Heading back down the familiar driveway, my lights shine on the road in front of me. It took longer to get the cows back behind the broken fence, and even longer to mend that. I sent a text to Indie, and she only replied with a picture of her and Hazel both holding up their thumbs. That was almost two hours ago, and when I texted twenty minutes ago to say I was headed home, I didn't get a message back. I'm sure there's a good reason, but I'd be lying if I said I wasn't a little nervous about it.

Taking my key out of the ignition and hopping out, I look in the bed of my truck at the chair I brought home. I was going to set it out when I got here, but the urge to get inside and check on Indie and Hazel is too strong. Practically running up the stairs, I unlock the front door and slowly open it. It's dim, a few lamps and the glow of the TV are the only light. I hang my keys up on the hook and slip my boots off.

I take a step, wondering if maybe she's putting Hazel to bed, when a small, high-pitched whine has my eyes cutting to the floor in front of the couch. *Sally? What is she doing in the house?* My eyes adjust slightly, and I freeze. The sight before me alleviates the tension that's built in my shoulders. It's the most beautiful thing I've ever seen.

Indie is lying on her back, one hand hanging off the edge of the couch by Sally, her face is relaxed in sleep, but the ghost of a smile pulls at the corner of her lips. Her other arm is resting on Hazel's back, hand gently placed to the side of her tiny head in a comforting way, holding her close in her sleep like she can't help it. I step closer, then catch a whiff of myself. *Shit. I smell awful.*

I'm as quiet as I can be walking to the bathroom; the bouquets they made catch my attention as I strip off my dirty clothes, tossing them in the laundry before attempting to take the quickest shower I've ever taken in my life. Once I'm under the warm spray, my mind wanders. My thoughts drifting to the fact that if I had taken Hazel with me, I'd still be getting her settled in bed instead of showering off this offending smell. It's really fucking nice to have Indie here.

I've never had someone to depend on who wasn't my family. And while I'm grateful I have them, that Hazel has them, having something—someone—just for me, is a pleasure I'm just realizing I've been missing. I haven't thought about anything but Hazel in so long, I'd forgotten what it feels like to want something for myself.

Stepping out of the shower, I grab my towel off the bar and

dry my body, wrapping it around my waist. I step into the hall and find Indie backing out of Hazel's room, closing the door behind her. I lean against the doorframe to watch her try to move as quietly as she can.

"Hey," I whisper.

Her head whips to me before she smiles, pressing a hand to her throat like she may have been stifling a yelp. "Hey," she whispers back.

"Did I wake you up?" I ask.

She shakes her head at me, looking sleepy and beautiful and like I want her to be mine. "I needed to let Sally out. Sorry I didn't answer your last text. We fell asleep watching *The Little Mermaid*."

"That's okay. Did you guys have a fun evening?" Her sleepy smile gets bigger at my question.

"We had a blast. After making our bouquets, we painted some dancing dinosaurs. I made mac and cheese for dinner because that was her request and because I don't know how to make much else. I tried to make enchiladas once, and..." While she speaks her arms float around with her voice in the hall. I could watch her tell a story all day, which is about how long her stories tend to take.

"How did that go?" I ask.

"It's a long story." She sighs.

"Tell me anyway."

She blushes, ducking her head slightly. "I should probably get home. It's late." *No. I don't want her to leave.*

"Stay."

"The night? With Hazel here? Are you sure?"

"Come to bed with me, Indie Baby. I want you with me tonight." *I want you with me always.*

She nods, and I hold out my hand for her. With her hand in mine, I lead her down the hall and through my bedroom door. As we lay in the bed, gentle kisses, legs entwined with one another's, hands gliding over exposed skin, I hear Indie's breathing slow—feel her heartbeat sync with my own. Whatever this is, and I think I have a pretty good idea, I need to make sure we're on the same page. Indie may be young, and I have no doubt she could find someone her own age, but I'll make her happy as long as she'll let me.

I just need her to want me back.

INDIANA

Sunlight streams in from the window, and I watch the dust motes dance in the beams. My lips stretch wide, remembering that I'm once again waking up in Knox's house, only this time it's not the guest room I wake up in, it's in his bed. Working to school my expression, I turn over to find the bed empty. *Huh. Well, that seemed like it was going to be a lot more romantic in my head.*

Standing from the bed, I slip into my shorts that Knox slid off me last night, blushing at the memory. We did little more than kiss while our hands explored each other, but if kissing Knox feels like *that,* then sex with him might very well kill me. My cheeks grow hotter at the thought. *I'm going to have to tell him I'm a twenty-seven-year-old virgin.* It's not like I haven't had the opportunity, I've just never wanted more with anyone. *Before him.* Now I can't imagine not wanting everything he'll give me.

I open the bedroom door as quietly as possible and walk down the hallway, peeking in on Hazel to find her still sleeping soundly. *Where is Knox?* Tiptoeing through the house, I finally make it to the living room where I come to a halt. The view from out the window starts to swim in my eyes, a choked sound making its way up my throat and out of my mouth.

Two chairs. There's two chairs sitting at the end of the dock where there used to be one.

He's walking back this way, looking every bit of devastatingly handsome he is. His teeth shine in the sun, flashing me a smile I'm coming to find is reserved for Hazel—but he's giving it to *me* now. Letting me in this secret club that's just been *them* for so long. I'm honored, and I'm moving before my brain registers it. I fling open the front door, skipping most of the steps, and don't stop until I leap, hitting Knox in the chest. A grunt leaves him at the force, but he catches me like I knew he would.

I spend no time saying good morning; my mouth is too busy for that. I kiss him with my whole being. I want—*I need*—him to know that I see him. I know him and what this gesture means.

"I never thought I would be figuring out my favorite way to wake up this late in life, but here we are," he says, and I choke again.

"You-you bought me a chair," I stumble over the words.

"Who said that was for you?"

I smack his chest and roll my eyes.

"I bought you a chair," he confirms.

"I—" *I love him.* Instead of letting that slip out, I tease him. "Are you trying to flirt with me, Knox?"

"I'm trying to do a hell of a lot more than that, Indie Baby."

"Oh? Tell me more."

"How about I tell you tomorrow night? Have dinner with me?"

"I have dinner with you most nights." I laugh. "Yes, I'll have dinner with you."

"Good. It's a date," he says, kissing my lips and carrying me back to the house.

"I can walk," I offer.

"I like you where you are."

"I like where I am too." The words I stuffed down a few moments ago echo again. *I love him.* Is that crazy? I've only known him for a few months, but it feels longer. My heart already has his and Hazel's names written all over it. Last night we made some decorations for Knox's birthday next week. A Happy Birthday banner and some painting on a tablecloth for the bar. I've already asked Winnie what Knox's favorite dessert is and to walk me through the baking process of making one. I'm not domestic, but I want to try for him—for them.

We haven't talked about it, but my continued presence in Knox's life automatically translates to being in Hazel's. She's quickly become this little light in my life that shines bright enough to reach the darkest parts of me I keep hidden. Unbidden to me, memories flow past the dam I've built, and I stiffen.

Yelling, arguing, ringing in my ears.

"Indie, you okay?" Knox's voice pulls me back.

"F-fine. I'm going to run home and shower. I need to work on a couple of things for Winnie and then schedule something with Ivy."

"Hey, what just happened here?" he asks, setting me down on the ground.

"Huh? Nothing. I-I'm really happy about the chair. Thank you," I tell him, lifting up onto my toes to press a kiss to the corner of his mouth. *I'll have to tell him eventually, but now's not the time to get into this.* "I'm going to go for a run later. Can I stop by after?"

He scratches the back of his head. *I can't keep things from him anymore. He's not an idiot.* "You can come over anytime you want, Honey."

I smile. It's a little wobbly, but it's the best I can do for now.

"If that's true, I'll probably be over so much you'll get sick of me," I tease, but it comes out more insecure than I wanted. *I'm going to screw this up, and I'll have no one to blame but myself.*

"That's not going to happen, Indie. I want you here, and Hazel wants you here and—"

"And Hazel gets what she wants," I finish, smiling. "Then be prepared for me to be over. A lot. I'll see you later. Tell Hazel for me?" He nods in acknowledgment before gripping the sides of my head and kissing me breathless.

"In case you needed reminding of how sick I am of you." I melt. *I love him.*

Knox Holloway is a man of action. A quality that, if I had one, would be at the top of a list for a potential husband. Han will have a field day psycho-analyzing that thought. *Potential husband? Who are you, and what have you done with my sister?*

I'm smiling when I speak again. "The feeling is mutual, Mr. Holloway."

He grins. "Well, thank God for that."

"Bye, Knox. Thanks for asking me to stay."

"Open invitation, Indie."

"Yeah? Next time, I want to wake up with you still in the bed with me."

"Oh? Why?"

"I'll tell you tomorrow night at dinner," I call, walking the path to my house. My smile begins to fade, already feeling the weight that disappears when I'm with Knox and Hazel settle back onto my shoulders.

If I want this to work, *and fuck I really want this to work,* I'm going to have to be honest. Not only with Knox but with myself.

KNOX

"I'm sorry your truck is acting up. I kinda love that old thing," Indie says from behind the steering wheel of her car.

"I know. It's a real shame," I tell her, knowing full well that my truck is fine.

"So why did we need to come all the way out here? I'm always down for a hike, but it's getting late, and I would have been perfectly happy with you making me dinner, rubbing my feet," she says, flashing me a smile before continuing, "and just staying in with Hazey tonight."

I believe her, but I also want to show her that life with me, though much slower paced than she may be used to, doesn't have to be boring.

"As much as I love a quiet night in, this is also an apology of sorts, if you remember," I tell her.

"Yes, I remember. You also mentioned dinner, but where are we possibly going to be getting dinner out here?" she asks, taking one hand off the steering wheel and gesturing out her window.

Last night I told her that I didn't like going to the movies. She was shocked and hurt to hear that even after I explained that I don't care for large crowds, but more than that, I don't like watching movies with other people because I don't like gauging my own reactions against others. She didn't like my explanation at all. I made it even worse when I said that going to the movies is silly.

I'm not exactly a glass-half-full guy, but I never want any cranky thoughts I have to dull her shine. So when she arrived at her home this afternoon, she found a note attached to her door.

I'm sorry I was an ass.
Have dinner with me?
-Knox

What she doesn't know is it took me most of the day to set our date up.

"The turnoff is just around the corner up here," I instruct, as we drive up the side of the mountain.

"Okay? I'm still missing where the restaurant is going to be. I'm fairly easygoing, Knox, but you don't want to see me hangry," she threatens.

I chuckle. "I wouldn't dream of it, Honey."

She turns onto the dirt road, following it a little further until the lights come into view.

"What's this?" she asks me, eyes wide, looking between me and my truck that's parked in the middle of a wildflower field. The bed is filled with pillows and blankets, and I have Christmas lights strung up around it. Behind it is a white sheet attached to two wooden posts that we'll watch our movie on.

Alder dropped off our food about five minutes ago in the cab of the truck.

"*That* is where we're having dinner tonight," I tell her.

"You're kidding. You did all this for me?"

"I did."

"I don't know what to say. No one's ever done anything like this for me," she says, her voice full of wonder.

"Happy to be the first, Honey," I tell her.

She parks the car and climbs over the middle console to sit in my lap, kissing me until I'm desperate for more before opening my door and sliding out.

"This is so beautiful, Knox," she tells me as she climbs into the back of my truck. "Thank you."

I open the door and reach in to get the food and the wooden slab to lay across the truck bed that will act as a table for us.

"You don't have to thank me, Indie. This is partly my apology, remember?"

"In that case. You're forgiven."

I look up at her, my pulse stuttering at the sight of her standing in the back of my truck, smiling at me like I'm some kind of hero for stringing some lights together and borrowing a projector from the hotel. I never want her to stop looking at me like this.

"You're so beautiful, Indie." My words cause her smile to widen.

"God, you're so gone for me, Holloway...aren't you?" The question is laced with uncertainty. *Does she not know?*

I hop up into the back of the truck, gripping the sides of her neck, her hands coming up to grip my forearms. "Yeah, Indie Baby. I am," I tell her, leaning down to brush her lips with my own, kissing her like she's the oxygen I need to breathe.

Once settled into our pile of blankets and pillows, I set the projector up on top of the truck behind us.

"What are we watching?" Indie asks excitedly, dipping her chips into the guacamole.

"One of my favorites. I think you're gonna like it."

"Ohh, now I'm even more excited. Another glimpse into Fort Knox." She's said this before, told me it was hard to get to know me. I don't want to make it hard for her.

"Not to you, Honey. You can see whatever you want." She smiles, leaning forward to kiss my lips.

"Thank you. This is so special to me. *You're* really special to me," she confides.

"Good to know. I think you're alright too," I bait.

She giggles. "Just alright?"

I don't know if I have the words right now to tell her how I feel. Instead, I lean over her, sliding my hand under her torso and tugging her down the back of the truck so she's lying flat against it beneath me. She reaches up and cups my jaw, pulling my mouth to hers. I don't want to keep my hands off her, keep my mouth off hers.

Kissing her like this has a drugging effect on me. I know it must be her because if kissing felt like this for everyone, I'm not sure how anyone stops doing it. The outside world fades, just her lips and her little moans remain in focus. She licks inside my mouth, tasting me, teasing me.

I slide my hand down her neck to her chest, groaning when I find her braless. I swipe my thumb over her nipple until it pebbles, then give it a pinch. Her mouth opens on a gasp and lets me slide my tongue in and swallow it, smiling at her reaction to me.

We kiss for a while longer, our hands exploring each other

—teasing. When Indie's stomach starts growling, I sit back to look at her. Kiss her lips once more, and then I set our food out on the wooden slab in front of us.

"Let's get you fed, Honey. I don't want you suffering," I say.

"If that's suffering, I think I want to spend the rest of my life doing it," she mutters quietly, curling into my side and resting her head against my shoulder. My whole body heats with the sentiment. I kiss the top of her head, wrapping my arm around her.

I know it's just an off handed comment. Meant to be funny, but doing anything with Indie forever is exactly what I want to be doing.

I hit play on the projector, and the movie starts. Indie lets out a delighted squeal.

"Are you joking?" She laughs, facing me.

"I wouldn't joke about this," I tell her.

"Is this really one of your favorite movies?"

"Cross my heart," I say, making an X over my chest.

She kisses me again. Hard. I never want to stop kissing her. I could live a thousand years, and nothing would come close to the feel of her lips on mine.

"This is the best surprise date I've ever been on," she muses, leaning back into me. I reach to my side into the bag I stashed here earlier and pull out the candy, laying it out in front of her.

"Cherry candies?"

"You said it was your favorite flavor."

"It was, but I think I have a new one." *Oh, well, now the candy seems silly.*

She opens a box of candies, popping one into her mouth. Turning her head, she looks up at me. "Come here," she whispers, and I lean down, letting her press her sour-cherry lips to mine.

"*That's* my favorite flavor," she whispers, her words hitting me directly in the chest.

Being her favorite anything makes me feel like I'm ten feet tall. Indie choosing to spend her nights with me, quietly reading or playing with Hazel in the wildflowers instead of going out or having wild nights like a twenty-something should be able to, tugs at me, leaving me with the nagging question I seem to always come back to. Will I be able to give her the life she should have? Am I enough for her?

INDIANA

Soft music plays from the speaker in the corner of the living room. I'm listening to it from the kitchen while setting up what I hope is a romantic dinner for Knox. His mom has Hazel tonight, so I thought it would be fun to make him dinner since he usually cooks, and after our date the other night, I just want to show him how much he means to me.

It's very unlike me to do something like this. I've never cooked a full meal that didn't involve a microwave, but Knox is a caretaker, and I just want to show him that I'll take care of him too. I blush. There are a lot of ways I plan to take care of him tonight. The past few weeks with him have been some of the most special of my life. I can see a future here, one I want badly. He and Hazel are at the center of it.

I check Winnie's written instructions again and make sure I'm properly cooking the pasta. Fresh pasta. That I made. Me. I giggle alone in Knox's open kitchen. I have a pot of boiling water on the stove with a heavy amount of salt in it. There's an Alfredo cooking in the saucepan beside it, and I have the seasoned chicken baking in the oven. My timing should come out perfectly.

I start wiping down the flour and egg mess off the counters. When they're clean, I grab two plates from the cabinet and utensils from the drawer. I take the sauce off the heat and drop the pasta into the pot. Winnie told me fresh pasta cooks quickly, so I've saved it for last. When I pull the chicken out of the oven, I hear his truck pull up outside. I quickly set it on the cutting board and reach for the bottle of wine I bought for us.

I open it as I walk to the island, setting it down next to the two glasses I have sitting out. A door slamming gets my attention, and I almost knock the bottle off the counter. I laugh a little at my nervousness. I test a piece of the pasta, and it's perfect. I drain it quickly, adding the butter and seasonings to the noodles before stirring. Okay, everything is ready.

The front door opens, and Knox tentatively sticks his head in the door. I grin. "Hi. Um, surprise." His answering smile is dazzling. Blue eyes crinkle at the corners, and his straight white teeth are on full display. He shuts the front door behind him before sweeping me into his arms, wrapping his big hand around the back of my head, scratching my neck with his beard as he nuzzles into it.

"What's all this for?" he asks into my hair, kissing my temple and then my cheek while he still holds me to him.

"I just wanted to do something for you. You're always doing things for me," I say quietly.

He pulls my head back so he can look at me before he responds. "Honey, you being here is doing something for me." I melt into him. I've never felt more safe than when I'm in Knox's arms.

"Well, that I can do. I really like being here with you. With Hazel."

"We really like having you with us. Hazel never wants you to leave," he tells me. My throat tightens with emotion, hearing that Hazel may care for me as much as I already care for her.

"You both may be in luck." I kiss along Knox's jaw. "I think I'm falling for Silverthorne," I tell him quietly, like it's a secret I only want to tell him.

"Is that so?" he asks. I nod, our noses just brushing. He smiles into our kiss. It's not full of heat like it was the last time he was holding me like this. Tonight, it's something else entirely.

What I feel for Knox isn't something I can name. It isn't something I've ever felt before, but it feels like...*devotion*. Like I could fall in step beside him and walk into a future I'm not sure about because I'm sure about *him*. He's kissing me like I'm the most true thing in his life. Maybe that's me projecting since he's the most true thing in mine.

He carries me to the kitchen table, propping me on the edge of it without breaking our kiss. I wrap my legs around his hips tighter. I don't want any space between us. He cradles both sides of my face and tips it up toward him, delving his tongue into my mouth. Claiming me. I reach up to fist his hair in my hands, tugging at the roots. I'm rewarded with a deep groan that embeds itself under my skin.

"Knox," I pant when he pulls his mouth back from mine. It's a question, but I'm not even sure what I'm asking. I'm out on a ledge somewhere, and it won't take much to tip me over. He starts placing open-mouthed kisses to my neck, pulling my dress down to expose my collarbone, my shoulders. "I..." I am delirious. I'm in a lust-filled haze. A state that exists between reality and all the fantasies I've ever had, and he hasn't even touched me yet. This is what he does to me.

"I don't think you understand how bad I want you, Honey," he rasps, slipping my sundress over my head. My legs loosen around him, and he leans back to look at me in my white lace bra and panties. "You're so beautiful," he tells me, pressing kisses down my chest before pulling the cup of my bra away and taking my hardened nipple into his mouth. His scruff against the sensitive skin and his hot mouth sucking has me gasping. He bares his teeth and nips, and *oh my god,* my vision goes blurry.

"Oh god," I moan, my eyes falling shut briefly, my grip in his hair tightening. His hum of approval vibrating against me. I want this man. He may want me, but he can't possibly know how insane with need I am for him. His touch, his laugh, his wit, his cock. "I want you. Please, I want you." I whisper these words over and over, not caring if I sound desperate because that's exactly what I am. I am filled with need and desire for this man like I've never known.

"I wouldn't want the dinner you worked so hard on to get cold, Indie. I want you to feel appreciated," he teases.

"Knox, I can think of seventeen ways you can appreciate me off the top of my head. Only four involve food and none include chicken fettuccine," I mutter. He laughs at that, breath caressing my skin.

"Okay, Indie Baby, let's get you taken care of then." *Thank God.* He lifts me again like I weigh nothing, walking us down the hall to his bedroom. It's dark here now, the afternoon sun has fallen behind the mountains. He unhooks my bra before laying me on the center of the bed and drags it down my arms, taking it with him when he sits back on the bed to look at me.

His blue eyes look navy in the dim light, and they're brimming with promises.

"I could stare at you forever, Indie." His voice is a deep rumble that settles right where the throbbing is between my legs. "Arms up." I whimper and do what he says. "Keep them there, or I'll stop. Do you understand?" I nod and try to whisper out a yes. He smiles, then leans forward, grabbing me by the chin to plant a firm kiss to my mouth. My arms reflexively go to touch him. When my hands get to his hair, he sits back again.

"You said you understood. Arms stay over your head, or I stop taking care of you," he tells me casually, like my chest isn't heaving up and down and I'm not gasping for air while soaking through my panties onto his bed.

"Please," I whine.

"Fuck, you look so pretty when you beg. Do you see what just the sight of you does to me? What your begging does to me?" He palms himself through his shorts, and I bite my lip.

"Show me. I want to see you." I don't say please, but everything I say right now implies it. He stands, taking his shorts and briefs off before coming to kneel in front of me again. My mouth hangs open. The thought of him inside me has my pussy clenching.

"I want you, Knox." Saying it now, I know how true it is. I want to give myself to him fully.

"You have me, honey. You've had me for a while." The way he says the sweetest thing I may have ever heard in my life while he's slipping his fingers beneath the band of my panties, pulling them down my legs, makes my head swim, and my heart gives a funny kick against my ribs. "Keep those arms up, Indie Baby, and I want to hear you" he murmers. My insides turn molten.

He takes an ankle in each hand, moving my feet up the bed to place them flat against it. I instinctively want to close my legs, but Knox stops me. "Don't hide from me, Indie. I want to see all of you." I let my knees fall open, and he groans. "Look at you, Indie. So perfect and wet for me." He runs his finger through my slick slit. "Can I taste you?"

"You don't have to ask for what's yours, Knox." At my words he leans forward and flattens his tongue against my clit. I nearly scream, fighting to keep my arms over my head.

"That's right, Indie Baby. Let go. I want you loud for me," he says before quite literally devouring me. I can't think, I can barely breathe. I can only feel, and fuck, the things I'm feeling. I never want to stop feeling this.

"Knox, I-I'm..."

"When you come on my tongue, I want my name on yours, Indie. You can scream as loud as you want; no one's out here but us." At that, I shatter. I'm a million tiny, fragmented pieces, each one screaming his name.

I'm boneless and feel like I'm floating when consciousness comes back to me. Knox is peppering my skin with kisses. "You're so fucking stunning when you come apart for me," he whispers over the scar on my shoulder before kissing it and covering my hands with his. He rubs up and down my forearms, massaging. "Flip over, honey." I smile.

"You know, you keep ordering me around, and I'm going to think I have a daddy kink." The startled laugh that comes out of Knox delights me. "Or maybe it's just you," I whisper.

"It better be just me," he growls playfully, turning me over to my stomach. I giggle, and he smacks my ass before kneading it. I moan as he walks his hands up my back to my shoulders, then runs his fingers the lengths of my arms and back up, giving me shivers.

"Knox?"

"Hmm...?"

"How are you so good at this?"

He chuckles, continuing his exploration of my body. "I wasn't aware that I was."

"If you could see my face right now, you would see the eye roll. I doubt I'm the first woman to tell you that."

"Indie, you're the first woman I've been with in over three years, and if I'm honest, there isn't a trail of women before that." That surprises me.

"You mean to tell me that you have *that* face and body, combined with your charm and wit, and you weren't a heart-breaker? I think that makes you more unbelievable."

He laughs again, kissing my shoulder. I turn over under-neath him, wanting to look at him. To see his face. I reach up and push his hair from his face. "You're special, Knox. You and Hazel. You're really special to me." My orgasm may have lowered my inhibitions, but it's exactly how I feel.

"You're rare, Indie. I feel like I've waited my whole life to feel what I do for you. I don't remember the last time I wanted anything. I've never *wanted* anyone. Not like this. Not like I want you," he tells me tenderly, leaning into my palm.

Air catches in my throat. The realization that I'm about to have sex for the first time, and it's with *him*. My body tenses, not because I don't want this. This is *all* I want. Him with me. *Inside* me. I want him to know, but I don't know what his reaction will be to a twenty-seven-year-old virgin. What sort of expectations he might think I have. My vision blurs. *Shit, shit, shit.*

"Hey, Indie, are you alright? We don't have to—"

"No, no. I'm sorry. I want to. Holy fucking shit, Knox. I really want to, I'm just-it's-I—" *I cannot form a complete sentence.* My mind is racing when all I want is to be here in this moment with him.

"Slow down, Indie," he whispers. Running his hands up the sides of my arms, squeezing them in his hands as he goes. He leans forward, kissing my temple where a tear has escaped. Then my cheek, my neck, my nose. All while squeezing my arms. "Tell me what you need, Honey."

"This. You. Touching me like this. Keep me here." My words come out rushed, but he hears me. Listens. He kisses a path across my chest, sucking one nipple into his mouth, then the other. His fingertips run up and down the inside of my thighs, making me buck against him. I'm half delirious at the feel of his hands on me; I can't imagine what he'll feel like inside.

"Knox," I rasp.

"Indie," he murmurs against the skin above my navel.

"I want you. Badly." I manage to get out.

"Do you want me like this?" he asks, hand slipping between us and circling my swollen clit.

"Yes!" I hiss.

"Do you want me like this?" he asks again, sliding those same fingers to my entrance and nudging one inside. It takes no effort. I'm so fucking soaked for this man. He curls his finger inside me, and I moan his name at the sensation.

"Fuck, Honey. You're so fucking soft. Gripping my fingers so tightly. Do you like when I touch you like this, Indie Baby?" he asks against my neck. I'm in a sex-crazed haze now. Fully under this man's spell. My hips are rocking into him on instinct, begging on my behalf. I want this man wholly, fully. Locked down by him. There's never been anyone else, and I don't ever want there to be. I find my voice.

"You should know I've never done this before," I say. My heart beats wildly when he bends to kiss me.

"Done this? Had a man on his knees for you, desperate to make you come?" *God, this man's mouth.*

"I've never uhm," I stutter again. *I'm not ashamed of it, so why can't I say it?* His eyes flash with what I think is understanding.

"You've never had sex before." It isn't a question, but his words are filled with wonder. I shake my head in confirmation.

"I haven't. I hope that doesn't change anything. It doesn't have to be this thing, I mean, I'm on birth control—I've just never wanted to *be* with anyone, like that—like this. And now. Well, now, I do," I ramble.

"With me."

I sigh. "Yes, Knox. With you." His answering smile is brilliant and my favorite. Bright white and on full display in the darkness, letting me see the slightly pointed tips of his canine teeth. I'm caught up in him. In so deep I can't see a way out, I don't want one.

"Are you sure this is what you want?" he asks tenderly.

I nod at first, but he presses me for more.

"Indie?" he asks, his voice deep and gentle and making me ache for him all over.

"I can't think of anything I've ever wanted more than *this,* Knox," I confess. Pathetically gone for him.

He nods, sapphire-blue eyes boring into mine when he speaks again. "You should know it's only ever going to be me again." I widen my legs further to cradle his strong hips, ready to have him, ready to take this next step with him, but he sits back to look at me. "Do you know how deliriously fucking sexy you are?" His words and the way he's looking at my body make me blush but also embolden me. "I've lost sleep thinking about this body, picturing what I would do if you let me have you like this," he admits. My whole body starts to hum.

When he leans his head down to my chest, he places a kiss between my breasts before taking one in his hand and sucking on the nipple, flicking his tongue across it as he does. The action draws a moan from me, and he releases me just long enough to give the same attention to my other breast.

"These tits. I've wanted to suck on these since you let me fuck your mouth, Honey." *The mouth on this man.* I've never in my life experienced something so fucking hot.

"Knox..." I whine.

"Let me take care of you, Indie Baby. We're gonna take this slow," he says softly, soothing me.

"I want you," I tell him.

"And you have me, but let's get you ready for me," he says, sliding his hand down to my pussy and pushing a finger inside me. I whimper, wanting, needing more. He circles my entrance while rubbing my clit with his thumb until I'm mewling. "You're so close, aren't you?"

"Yes, I'm—fuck Knox, I—" His hand stops, and I'm left a wanting, panting mess.

"You're dripping, Honey. So wet and soft and ready for my dick to fill you up."

"Oh my god, Knox. Please." I'm begging, pleading.

"Shh, are you sure you want this, Indie?" he asks, rubbing his hands up and down my thighs.

I nod. "Yes. More than anything. I want this, I want you."

He grips my chin, navy eyes sparkling in the dim light. Those three words on the tip of my tongue again, but I swallow them. "If you change your mind at any time, at any point, you have to tell me," he says. *I won't.*

"I'll tell you." He nods, nudging his length against my entrance, and I tilt my hips in response, a silent request.

Knox grants it, sliding himself into me slowly to let me adjust.

"Breathe, Honey." I do, dragging in a lung full of air.

"More," I urge. He sinks into me inch by miraculous inch. "How much more of you is there?" I ask, and his chuckling shakes me and the bed with it.

"We're almost there," he whispers. "How you doing?"

"Good. Really good. I'm not fragile, Knox. Please keep going," I plead.

"I don't want to hurt you, Indie."

"Doesn't the first time always hurt?" I ask. He sits back to look into my eyes. The care I see there dissolves any of the nerves that have still been clinging to me.

Tucking my hair behind my ear, he caresses me. "No, Honey. This is only going to feel good." He moves then, slowly. Letting me get used to the feel of him.

"Does that feel good, Indie?"

"Yes, oh god, yes." I moan. He pulls himself out a little then, gently rocking forward into me. I lift my hips to meet him, and the sound of our bodies together makes my eyes roll back into my head.

His hand trails down the center of my body, stopping at where our hips meet. "I'm gonna rub your little clit while your pussy gets used to my cock, okay Honey?" I almost come on the spot. Those filthy words out of his mouth have me teetering on the edge.

The noises I make when he starts to circle and thrust at the same time are unlike anything that's ever come out of my mouth in my life. I would be embarrassed if I had time to be. He pulls out of me slowly before filling me again.

"That's right, honey. Those noises you're making are driving me insane."

"Knox, I-oh god, that's good. Don't stop, please. I'm—" I suck in a breath, and Knox brings his mouth to mine, stealing it from me. He picks up the pace a little, but it's not enough anymore. I need more.

"More. Please," I beg.

"Does this feel good, Indie Baby. Having my cock buried so deep inside your tight cunt," he murmurs into my ear. I'm so close. The tension in my body is like a tight coil ready to release. "Do you like the way I take care of you, Indie Baby? How I take care of what's mine?" I'm floating, weightless.

"Yes," I pant out.

"Let me feel you squeeze me. Come for Daddy." *Fuck, that's the hottest thing I've ever heard.* I'm lost to the sea of pleasure that's been calling my name. Hearing *Daddy* this close to the edge while he's taking such good care of me. I'm tumbling, free-falling. I'm sensation and sound and Knox. I hear him call my name right before the weight of him collapses on top of me. Our breathing is the only sound in the room, heavy and erratic. We just lie together, a tangle of limbs.

I play with Knox's soft waves, feeling his heart slow and sync with mine.

"Is it always this good?" I ask into the dark room.

"It's never this good, Honey."

I huff a laugh, the action shaking us both. Tears blur my

view of the evening sky out Knox's bedroom window. I can't remember ever being this happy.

"Something amusing you, Indie Baby?"

"Just the afterglow, *Daddy*," I tease.

He chuckles, lifting his head to look at me. "You like that, don't you?" I blush because *yes, Daddy, I do*.

"Yes, Knox. I do. That's the hottest fucking thing I've ever experienced in my life."

"Damn straight," he half growls, tickling my sides and making me giggle. "Wait here, I'll be right back."

"Where are you going?" I call as he walks into the adjoining bathroom. I hear a drawer open and then the sink running. A few seconds later, he comes back into the bedroom with a washcloth, kneeling on the bed and gently parting my thighs again before running the damp cloth over me, cleaning up our mess. My face flames, the action so filled with intimacy I'm not used to, but I'm also oddly turned on by it.

"You really are the ultimate caretaker, aren't you?" I ask, my voice coming out breathy and quiet.

"I like taking care of you, and I want to any chance you'll let me," he says, tossing the rag in the basket by the wall and laying his head on my chest again.

"I want to take care of you too, Knox."

"You do," he tells me, sounding sleepy. I hum.

Here in the dim light of his bedroom, I feel words bubble up inside me, threatening to spill over. I bite my tongue and close my eyes against the sudden need to share. This moment is enough; I will live in it. I look out the window at the moon over the lake, and while listening to Knox's soft snore, I drift to sleep.

KNOX

I wake to the feel of a cool sheet instead of a warm body beside me. It's still dark in the room, and there's mumbling coming from somewhere in the house. I pull my briefs back on and walk out the door and down the hallway, stopping when I hear Indie's voice more clearly.

"It's really good here, Han. You would love it. You would make fun of me in my hiking boots and the way I look like a baby deer standing up on a paddleboard." she sniffs. *Is she crying?* "I'm doing it though. I'm living. And even though it's only been a couple of months, I think I'm falling for Silverthorne—for *him*." My chest warms, and realizing I'm listening to a private conversation, my ears do too. "Anyway, I love you. I miss you. Bye, dragonfly." *Dragonfly?*

I hear a couple more sniffs and round the corner. Indie's standing by the front window, wrapped in one of the soft blankets from the couch. She looks sad but hauntingly beautiful. I step out of the hall, the floorboards creaking beneath my feet. Her head snaps to me at the sound, a small gasp filling the space between us.

I raise my hands. "Sorry. I didn't mean to scare you," I say, my voice thick with sleep.

"No, *I'm* sorry. I didn't mean to wake you so early." She smiles at me, but it's not her normal smile—her real one. It doesn't reach her eyes. I've never seen Indie sad before.

"What's wrong? Who were you on the phone with?" I ask.

She holds up her phone. "Oh. Um, I was just calling my sister. Time difference and so I had to leave a voicemail. You can go back to bed." The way her voice wavers has me walking across the room, tucking her to me so she's in my arms again.

"I'm awake now," I tell her, kissing the top of her head and tucking the short strands of dark hair behind her ears. She smiles into my touch, leaning up on her tiptoes, presumably to kiss me, but I have to bend down so she can reach my lips. "Do you want to talk about it? Is she still mad at you?"

She averts her eyes, the ghost of her real smile slipping a bit. "I-I'm not sure anymore. I told you I said some things to her I can't take back, but that's only the tip of the iceberg there."

"Why don't you come sit with me and get it off your chest?" I know from experience that not talking about things can cause them to fester and grow.

She answers by wrapping her arms around my neck and letting the blanket that was covering her drop to the floor. Her, naked in my living room, staring up at me like she might be feeling what I'm feeling, is nothing I've ever experienced, and I know without a doubt that I'm fortunate to be sharing this with Indie.

"I have a better idea." Her voice is low and raspy from lack of sleep. She's kissing me slowly, slipping her tongue into my mouth, stroking mine with it. The thought of her tongue in other places on my body, doing other things is enough to have my cock digging into her through my briefs. "Take me back to bed, Knox," she murmurs against my lips. "Please."

She doesn't need to say please. I don't know when it happened, but I now have another woman in my life who I can't say no to—not that I would. I have this nagging feeling that anything Indie wants to do with, or to, me is something I'm going to crave.

Three hours later, we're both fully awake in my kitchen. After taking a quick shower, I came out to find Indie sitting at the kitchen table with one of her knees propped up, her chin resting on it. Bare feet, in one of my old, threadbare T-shirts with half her hair pulled back on top of her head, she looks like I want to see her there, in my usual chair, for breakfast every day.

"Good morning...again." She smiles up at me as I lean over the back of her chair, water droplets from my hair falling onto her. "You're dripping." She giggles.

"Isn't that supposed to be my line?" I ask, shaking my head so more droplets fall, causing her to blush. I kiss her warm cheeks and the tip of her nose before planting one on her mouth.

"What are your plans for the day?" she asks.

"I'm looking at her."

"Yeah?" She turns in her chair, still looking up at me. "What would you say to going on a run with me?"

"How long of a run are we talkin'?"

"Just the loop I usually do. The one that breaks off from the main drive here."

"I'm in, breakfast first?"

"Yes, food first always," she agrees.

Opening and closing more than a few cabinets, I scratch the back of my neck, looking at Indie. "I'm having a little trouble finding all my pots and pans this morning. You wouldn't know anything about that, would you?" I ask.

"Oh yeah, uhm so I read this article about how it could make cooking easier if you have all your tools and gadgets in designated places. For optimal use. I looked up the diagram and tried my best to get it right." I don't love that my kitchen has been reorganized. I like where I keep everything in here.

"I'm sure it's great, but *I* may need the diagram to find anything." I say.

"I'm sorry. I should have asked you first," she says quietly, looking uncomfortable.

"I'll figure it out, Indie. Let me make us some food, and then we'll go on your run." I wink, and she nods, smiling.

I make us scrambled eggs, sausage, and toast. A simple but high protein breakfast, and after the dishes are done, I change into shorts and a T-shirt. Indie goes back to her place to change, and I'm already missing her and the peace that her constant chatter brings me. I look in the mirror and find a smile on my face. Just a few months ago, I would have been thrilled with a few hours of quiet and alone time. Now, I want all my alone time to include her.

I look through the window toward her house and see her jogging back this way. I smile seeing she's wearing my hat again. I put two filled water bottles in one of my smaller backpacks and slip it on before walking out to meet Indiana on the porch. As she gets closer, I try to make out the words on her oversized T-shirt. D.I.L.F.? I feel my eyebrows shoot up to my hairline.

Upon further inspection, I notice it's covered in...frogs? Then I read the words underneath: Damn I Love Frogs. I laugh.

"I think this one is my favorite," I tell her as she stops in front of me.

"Your favorite what?" she asks, smiling up at me from beneath the bill of my old ball cap.

"Shirt. All your shirts say something on them. Usually something funny, the other day it was a little obscene."

"Obscene? I do not have a shirt that's *obscene*, Mr. Holloway." She presses her hand to her chest in mock shock before adding, "I think your age may be showing." It's her singsong tone that may be giving hers away at the moment.

"A few days ago, your sweatshirt had a crossword puzzle on it that, if you solved it, read Looking To Get Laid," I tell her.

"While I'm flattered that you stared at my boobs that long, I wouldn't call that obscene." She smirks.

"No? And what would you call it?"

"The truth, and it looks like it reached its target audience," she teases.

"Is that so?" I ask, pulling her to me.

Her smile is sweet and a little shy when she answers. "If last night is any indication, then I would say yes. Absolutely." I kiss her once on the mouth, then both sides of her neck. Her laugh has me smiling into her skin. "Are you ready to go for our run?"

"You know, if this is just about exercise, I can think of another way to get a workout in," I tell her, and she giggles.

"Running isn't just about the motion for me. That's a big part of it, but usually when I run, it's a way for me to clear my mind. Although today, I'm not sure I'll be able to think about anything but more of last night."

"Are you sure you want me to come with you?"

"Are you sure you can keep up, old man?"

I huff a laugh and give her cheek a kiss before stepping back to stretch. "Give me everything you've got, Indie. I want your legs shaking."

"You asked for it," she taunts, grinning at me before taking off down the driveway. I follow after like there's an invisible tether pulling me toward her. I would chase Indiana across the state just to be near her, to be close to the golden light she radiates. "Just do your best, Knox. Don't push yourself too hard. We don't want an injury at your age," she calls over her shoulder. I laugh, hoping she never stops giving me shit about my age.

When we started, three miles didn't sound like a lot, but I would be lying if I said that *my* legs weren't the ones feeling a little shaky.

"You did good, Knox," Indie tells me from her spot in the middle of the wildflower field between our houses. She's sitting down, reaching for one of her feet, stretching out her muscles.

"High praise," I mutter, and she laughs.

"Maybe next time, we'll bump it up to five miles?"

"Maybe," I say. *As long as there's a next time.* She leans back, lying in the tall grass.

"God, it's beautiful out here. How do you do anything but just be here?"

"Mostly I would say it's the three-year-old." I grin.

She chuckles. "I bet Hazel loves being outside."

"She does, but she's also been very into being a ballerina lately," I muse, dropping to the ground beside her.

"I've noticed that. All the twirling we did last week almost made me nauseous."

"Just watching you both was making me dizzy—and I know, that makes me sound ancient." I try to beat her to the punchline this time.

She snorts. "Have you given any more thought to dance classes? My sister and I both did dance when we were younger, and I looked up an article about dance and the brain, it can really be beneficial," she rambles.

"You looked up an article, huh?"

"Yeah, it wasn't a big deal; she just seems so interested."

"I haven't decided anything, but you don't need to concern yourself with things like that. I'll take care of it," I tell her. I take care of everything when it comes to Hazel.

"Okay, well, just let me know if you want any help then." Her tone is more subdued now. *Was I being rude?* I just get so defensive about anything having to do with Hazel, about anything that challenges my own way of doing things. But wouldn't it be nice to share some of that?

"I will," I say.

She just hums. I turn my neck to look at her. Eyes closed, the sun shining on her face, causing that hoop in her delicate nose to shine and the freckles across her cheeks to be more visible.

Her features are relaxed, a smile still curves her pink, plump lips. My ball cap is discarded beside her, and soft chestnut waves form a circle around her head like a halo. "You're so beautiful, Indiana," I say softly. Not silently, but not quite out loud. The curve of her lips stretches further, becoming a more prominent smile.

She tilts her head toward my voice, eyes opening slowly. "Look who's talking," she whispers.

"You think I'm beautiful?"

"You're the most beautiful man I've ever seen. And it's not just your face or your body, Knox. Your heart is stunning. It's a magnet for women like me."

"Women like you?"

"Yeah. You know the ones. They're quirky, kind of loud, on the younger side." She pauses to shoot me a wink. "They're hopelessly attracted to a beard and a deep voice. Throw in a few grunts and growls, and yeah—magnet." She paints me a picture, making broad strokes up toward the clouds floating by. She's beautiful in all the obvious ways—but it's the way her hands are flying around in the air right now that has me wanting her.

I reach across the small space between us, placing my hand on the side of her head to turn her back to me. "Indie Baby, there aren't any other women like you."

Her lips turn up into a goofy smile. "You shouldn't say things like that to me, Knox."

"Why not?"

"Because when you do, I-I'm not sure you understand what it does to me." She lets out a long breath.

"What does it do to you?" I ask, leaning over to kiss her lips, her eyelids, her cheeks, then just below her ear.

"It's a long story." She sighs in contentment while I explore which places I kiss elicit the most noises.

"Tell me everything."

KNOX

azel and I get home just before sunset. Getting out of the truck, I see a note taped to my door. Smiling, because I already know who it's from, I unbuckle Hazel and help her out. Then we run up the front steps. It's been two weeks since I made sure everyone in town knew that Indie was mine, and we've spent every day together since—except today. She's staying up at The Edgemont tonight and taking some photographs with Ivy for the website.

I pry the note off the door and study it for a moment.

Do you think about the future?

After I get Hazel settled with her new unicorn coloring book and stickers at the table, I start on our dinner. She has requested macaroni and cheese, no doubt Indie's influence. I told her we could do that, but she has to have some broccoli too. She accepted my terms.

"Oh, that's so pretty, Hazey. I love the different colors of the mane."

"I used pink and blue and green and purple."

"A great combination."

"Is Indie coming soon?"

"Indie isn't going to have dinner with us tonight, baby." I try to keep the disappointment out of my tone for her.

"I love it when she's here," she says, coloring.

"Yeah? I do too."

"She can live here. She could sleep in my room." I grin. If Indie lived here, it wouldn't be Hazel's room she slept in, but I'm still surprised by her generous offer.

"You would share your princess bed?"

"Mm-hmm and my stuffies and my pillows."

"That's pretty special."

"Yes. Indie is special."

"She thinks the same about you." She looks up at me, smiling widely at that.

After we eat our dinner and get changed for bed, we lie on the couch, watching a movie. Hazel curls into me, wearing the nightgown Indiana got her for her birthday yet again. When I feel my daughter's tiny body go slack, I wait for a few minutes before moving her to bed. I stroke her hair and soak in the moment. She will always be the center of my world, and I'll always do what's best for her.

I must be getting sentimental in my old age. Turning forty-two at the end of the week has really been weighing on me. Not because of my age, but it makes me think about Indiana's. She's still so young. She seems happy to be with me here now, but what about in ten years? Does she want more kids? Do I want more kids? Kids with Indie, a sibling for Hazel? Yeah, I think I would like that.

Scrubbing a hand down my face, I lift Hazel up and carry her to bed. I switch her salt lamp on and give her a kiss on the head, then step into the hallway. The house is quiet now, and the calm that I typically crave is replaced by wishing there was a five foot nothing brunette here, telling me about a podcast episode or the book she's reading. It's been one day, and I'm wishing Indie was here to help me put Hazey to bed and then have a drink out by the fire with me.

I grab my phone. Would it be pathetic to call her? Maybe send her a text? I decide I don't care.

I press the little phone by the picture of her and Hazel on the dock. It rings for half a second before I hang up. *It's been one day, Knox. Fuck, why did I do that?*

I scrub a hand down my face when it starts vibrating in my hand. *Indie.*

"Hello?"

"Hi. Did you just call me?" *So it went through.*

"Uh, I don't think so." *Why am I nervous, and why am I lying?*

"Oh. Okay. It says I have a missed call from you, but it didn't even ring. Anyway, sorry for bothering you." I scratch at my neck. Now she thinks she's bothering *me.*

"Actually. I did call you," I blurt.

"You did?"

"Yes."

"Well, I'm glad you did," she tells me and I can almost hear the smile in her voice.

"Yeah?"

"Yeah. I...I missed you and Hazel today. Can I tell you that without sounding needy?" She laughs at herself.

"I like you needy, Honey," I tell her honestly.

She huffs a laugh. "Are you flirting with me again?"

"If I am?"

She sighs. "If you are...it's working." My chest warms, and my lips stretch into a smile. I've never been good at flirting; for most of my life, I just didn't do it. But it's as easy as breathing with Indie. It's my natural reaction to her.

"Good to know."

"Are you smiling right now?" she asks.

"I am."

"Good. Me too. So what did you two get up to today?"

I tell her about our day, and then she tells me how things went with her at The Edgemont. Sharing our days with one another feels so normal, like we've been doing this for years, and at the same time, it's exciting, venturing into new territory like I never have before.

"I'll see you tomorrow, Knox."

"Goodnight, Indie."

"Goodnight."

Setting my phone down on the table, I pick up her note from earlier, reading it again.

Do you think about the future?

I grab a sticky note and write a response before walking over to her house to put it on her door for her to find tomorrow.

When I look back from the porch and see our two chairs side by side out by the lake, I think about the feeling Indie was telling me about.

I didn't know this was what I wanted until I felt it for the first time.

INDIANA

My stay at The Edgemont was amazing. Ivy set me up in the most adorable chalet, and I got to ride the gondola up and take some photos in the mountains. I picked up a few of the postcards I had made from the pictures I've taken in my time here, and they came out perfectly. I wrote a quick note to Han on the one I made from the lake view.

You should see it here, Dragonfly.
You wouldn't believe how granola I am now.
I love you. I miss you.
Love, Indiana

I come down the now familiar drive and notice Knox's truck is gone. He must have gone to work today. Is it insane that it's only been a day and I miss him? I park in front of the little white house that I've grown to love and see a note. My heart starts to gallop in my chest, and I fling open my door, dashing onto the porch before ripping it off the door to read it.

One line. Four words, and my heart leaps out of my chest.

I think about you.

I look around to make sure I'm still alone out here and hug the paper close to my heart, spinning in a circle. Walking inside, I rush to my desk, opening the top drawer to grab a sticky note. In my hurry, I pull it too hard, causing all my papers to fall out. Bending to pick them up, I see the one on top. Clutching it in my hand, I read the lines over and over.

I have to tell him. Tonight.

I'll leave him a note and ask him to come over before he goes to get Hazel. I'll tell him everything and hope he understands. Swiping a pen from the cup on my desk, I write a few short sentences before running over to stick it on his door. Sally stays with me the whole time, coming to lie on the porch when I'm back. It's like she knows I'm needing the comfort.

We sit on the porch for a while, listening to the world around us, staring out over the lake. My gaze is pulled to the big green house where I've spent so much time the past few months. I never imagined falling for them, but now that I have, it's impossible to think of a life that they aren't in.

I wait until I see his truck before I stand to get myself a glass of water, hoping to calm my nerves. He cares about me. I'm fine. I can do this.

Only when he races up the steps and sweeps me into his arms, I back out. I let myself get lost in him and what he brings me. Peace, when I haven't felt that way in so long. I let him make love to me and make me feel things I didn't even know to hope for. *I love him.* I've never been in love before, but I'm certain that this is what it is.

"Come to dinner with me tonight," Knox says from beneath me. I'm lying across him, sprawled across his wide chest, running my fingers through the hair there.

"Don't you have to pick up Hazel?" I ask, yawning.

"Yes. I want you to come with me."

"To your parents' house?" I prop my head up to look at him.

"Yes. I want you to come to my parents' for dinner."

"They aren't expecting me," I say, sitting up.

"I wouldn't say you would be completely *unexpected*," he teases. I think for a moment. This isn't exactly how I planned for the evening to go, but I'm selfish. I want this time with him.

"Okay, just let me change."

"You mean you don't want to show up naked?"

"You're full of jokes, aren't you, Mr. Holloway?"

"I've never been accused of that before." At that, I do laugh because I believe it.

"Maybe you just haven't been with the right person," I joke.

"If it wasn't you, it wasn't the right person," he says.

I melt into a puddle, emotion getting stuck in my throat. When he says things like that to me, it makes me happier than I've ever been in my life. But then I get this sinking feeling in my stomach, like letting Knox say things like that to me when he doesn't know everything is wrong.

I have to tell him. If I don't, I might end up losing him.

My first dinner at the Holloway house is now one of my favorite memories. It's full of laughter and even a little bit of roughhousing between the brothers. I sip a glass of wine with Winnie and Florence on the deck; Hazel is lying across my lap while I absently play with her hair. Watching all the siblings interact with each other is fun but also fills me with longing.

"Ugh boys! Stop before you hurt yourselves! Aren't you getting a little old for this?" Mary yells from the open window.

"Sorry, Mom!" Comes a trio of voices. We all laugh as they make their way up the deck.

"Do you have any siblings, Indie?"

"Just a sister," I answer.

"Yeah? Is she as annoying as any of my brothers?"

I force a laugh. "She's a handful, that's for sure."

"I've met her before. Remember?" Knox asks from the wooden railing.

"Mm-hmm. At the bar."

"She was pretending to be twenty-one."

"She was trying to get you to buy her a drink," I say, and he laughs.

"Is she still so forward?"

"She's always been that way. No is not an answer she's ever been willing to hear," I muse, then turn to Florence. "Were you still wanting me to work on the hotel website?"

"Please. Could you come by next week?" she asks me.

"Yes! With Anna wanting to take over the management side of things, I'm only at the bakery on Wednesday. How about I come that evening? Will you still be there?"

"I will be there."

"Are you sure you aren't upset with me cutting your hours at the bakery?" Winnie asks.

"Of course not. I understand, and I'm loving running the website. I think I have enough work to keep me busy between everyone y'all have put me in touch with."

"Okay, I just feel bad because you moved here for this job, and now..."

"And now I'm staying for—other reasons," I say, looking down at the sleeping girl on my lap.

"You about ready to head out, Honey?"

"Yeah, I think Hazel is too." I look up at Knox. God he's just so fucking handsome.

"I'll get her," he says, taking her off my lap, laying her against him.

"I'll see you guys later."

"Bye, Indie."

I walk into the kitchen and find Mary and Tom laughing together.

"I just wanted to say thank you for having me," I call from the doorway.

"Oh, of course. You're welcome anytime, sweetheart."

"Dinner was delicious, any chance I could get the recipe?"

"You're more than welcome to have it, but come over again, and I'll teach you." My chest expands at Mary's offer.

"Thank you. That would be great."

"Bye, Mom, Dad. Love you and thank you for dinner."

"Love you, son."

We walk from the big house to the truck, and as wonderful as the evening has been, seeing Knox's family and the love they have for one another, the overwhelm is starting to slither in. Grief is funny like that. No matter how long it's been. Pain is still pain.

"Thanks for coming with me tonight."

"Thank you for inviting me. Your family really is one in a million."

"I'm lucky."

"They're a little lucky to have you too."

"Just a little?"

I shrug. "Maybe a bit more than a little."

"High praise," he quips.

On the drive, I'm quieter than usual. Hazel is fast asleep in her car seat, and Knox is humming along to the radio. My lips curl at the sound. As I watch the shadowy trees pass by, my thoughts turn darker the closer we get to home. Once there, I get out of the truck, watching Knox head for the big house, but I stay rooted on the path to the guesthouse.

"Aren't you coming in?" he asks from the steps.

"Not tonight. I'm not feeling the best. Just a little headache, but I think I'll take a shower and call it a night."

"Stay here. I'll rub your feet and make you some tea." I melt a little more. He's exactly the kind of man I want, and I desperately want to let him hold me in those strong arms, take care of me—but I can't, not tonight. Tonight, I have some demons to face, and I think I may have to do it alone.

"As amazing as that sounds, I think I just want to get home and to bed. Rain check?"

"Open invitation," he reminds me.

"Goodnight, Knox."

"Goodnight, Honey." His use of my nickname has me almost ready to run up the steps and jump into his arms with Hazel. But I don't—I walk home alone.

After my shower, I change into my favorite pajamas and sit on the floor of my bedroom. A deep sense of dread fills me, settling into my bones. I haven't completely been living in reality for a while now, and this box in front of me is proof. I reach in, pulling out the stack of stiff papers. Then another, and another. I untie the twine, sifting through them.

My shoes got stolen from my gym locker again.
They were the purple ones I love.
I love you. I miss you.
Love, Indiana

No one gets the "write this down" bit.
I can't bear talking to anyone else.
I love you. I miss you.
Love, Indiana

I got my tattoo today.
The artist thought the needle
was causing me pain. I didn't
tell him why I was really crying.
I love you. I miss you.
Love, Indiana

Mom and Dad bought a condo.
In Cincinnati.
What the hell is in Cincinnati?
I love you. I miss you.
Love, Indiana

I'm drowning here, Han.
I think I'm scared to live more than
I'm scared to die.
I love you. I miss you.
Love, Indiana

Sorry, the last one was dark.
I didn't mean it.
I just needed to write it down.
I love you. I miss you.
Love Indiana

I have to stop reading when I can't see. The tears gathering in my eyes force me to blink. *It's me who shouldn't be here.* It's me who should be wasting away six feet under. Not my baby sister. Not Han. She wasn't meant to die. It might sound silly, but Han Holmes was only meant to *live.*

Moving here was supposed to be the beginning of me living, like I promised her I would. I reach for my shoulder where my dragonfly tattoo is inked over the old wound. We never should have been out that late at night. I knew better, but because I had made her come to me, I let her talk me into it. Then I was so *awful.* I swipe at my cheeks angrily.

I'm angry, and I'm still devastated. I've had it explained to me by multiple professionals in plenty of different rooms. They were all wrong though. My pain didn't come in waves like they said it would. My pain is the sea, and every memory is an undertow. I was constantly being pulled under by reminders, and everything reminds me of her.

I climb into the bed, cocooning myself inside the blankets. I need to start being honest with the people whom I've come to care about so deeply. They deserve that. And maybe if I can be honest with them, I can start being honest with myself. Closing my eyes, I think the words that I still haven't been able to say out loud. Words that were said to me almost a year ago that, now that I've started to feel things again, bubble up to the surface.

My sister is dead.

KNOX

"You had every opportunity. I *gave* you every opportunity." My hand grips my cell phone so tightly, I think I could crush it with one squeeze.

"That's not good enough, and now it will be up to me if I think it's in Hazel's best interest." As calmly as I can, I set the device down on my desk.

I stare at my phone screen, as if doing so will grant me some clarity. I've already started to run through the conversation in my head over again, and it's still not helping me make sense of it. After all these years—why now? When Emily passed, I went to them. I swallowed my pride and gave them a chance after they weren't there for their daughter. My first instinct is to go on the defensive. Let my lawyer brain take over and handle this like I would any other case. But ultimately, I know that's not what I should do. *I have to think of my daughter.*

I gather my things from my office in a daze; my mind turning over information. They weren't there. They have no idea how awful it was to watch. How hard it was to make a way forward after. The more I marinate in my thoughts, the angrier

I become. They don't get to decide it's worth it now. It should never have been a decision.

My heart rate has picked up, and I'm sure my blood pressure is spiking. I need to get home. I need to see Hazel.

If, for some reason, a judge has to get involved, I won't be representing myself. Very few times does that work out, so I start drafting an email to an old lawyer friend of mine, but my laptop dies in the middle of typing it. Leaning onto the desk, I press my palms into my eyes, trying to contain my frustration. I couldn't find my charger this morning because Indie was using it last and left it somewhere I'm sure it doesn't belong. These little quirks of hers are really inconvenient today.

"Knox?" a voice calls from the hallway. Cora. Sometimes I forget she's here.

I blow out a breath. "Hey, Cora. Did you need something?"

"Just checking in. You've been quiet in here today. Trouble with the girlfriend?" The side of her mouth quirks up like she's hopeful.

"I'm always quiet, and no trouble. Thanks for your concern." After our run-in at the bar, I've tried to keep my distance even more than usual.

She leans against the door jamb, crossing her arms over her chest. "You can talk to me, you know. You used to talk to me." She sulks. I'm not sure what she's remembering exactly, but we never really talked—unless it was about work. Cora was someone who seemed to understand that I didn't want a relationship, or maybe that was just something I had hoped she understood. I'm feeling the need to clarify, but I don't want any hurt feelings, especially since we work together.

"I appreciate the offer, Cora, and that you've always been

such a good *friend,* but I need to get going. Have a good evening."

"Sure." She gives me a soft, slightly sad smile as she slips from the room. I grab my things and head for the door.

"Oh, and Happy Birthday!" she yells from her office.

"Thank you." *What a birthday it's turned out to be.*

Glad to be out of the office and taking in some fresh air after the afternoon I've had, I'm almost to my truck when I hear my name being called again. It takes everything in me not to groan aloud. I'm barely hanging on.

"Hey, Knox!" I see Jeanie running toward me from her dance studio. Running isn't really necessary, seeing as I stopped walking as soon as she yelled my name, but she continues to do so.

"Jeanie. What can I do for you?"

"Oh, it's nothing. I just wanted to see if you could sign this form for me."

"What kind of form?" I ask, confused about why she would need one from me.

"For Hazel. We got her application a couple of days ago, but there were a few things missing, and one was the parent signature," she tells me, smiling. *What? I guess this is just the day of blindsides.*

"I'm sorry, Jeanie. I think there must be a mistake. I didn't sign her up for dance."

"You didn't? One of my new interns said a young woman dropped off the papers last week. Well, we have a spot open for her." I grit my teeth. *She said she would drop it.*

"Could I get back to you? I need to be somewhere, but I'll stop by sometime next week."

"Sure. That will be just fine. I'm excited to have her in class. She's such a bright little girl."

"She is. Thank you," I say and nod once before opening my truck door and heading home. *Did she really go behind my back and do this?* After I specifically told her I would decide and take care of it. It feels like she's constantly pushing my boundaries. Sometimes it's not so bad, a bathroom drawer reorganized or my entire kitchen rearranged. Other times, it's not listening and going behind my back. I could probably even get over that if it didn't have to do with Hazel.

I have a schedule, and we have a routine, and she can't just come in and change everything. Not without asking, not without communicating. I can't be with someone who doesn't understand that.

I *tried* to reach out to Emily's parents after the funeral. I offered them a spot in Hazel's life. When they didn't immediately accept, I wrote them off because fuck anyone who didn't jump at the chance to be in my daughter's life. And now, they what? Want to see her? Want to spend time with her? I'm not sure how to process all this. I need to talk to someone. I want to talk to Indie, but now I'm pissed at her too. I dial my dad, and it goes to voicemail. I try my mom, and the same thing happens. *Fuck, my head feels all scrambled.*

On the drive home it starts to rain, like even nature can sense my mood. Maybe I should take the night to cool off before confronting Indiana. I need to talk to my parents about Emily's family reaching out to me, and I need to take a minute. Only to my surprise, Indie is on my porch wearing a bright-yellow sundress and a matching bandanna in her hair when I pull up. Looking like pure sunshine in the middle of the rainstorm that's picked up.

Jogging over, I note she's filled the flowerpots on the porch with plants. Another thing she didn't ask me if she could do. I've had enough of things being sprung on me today. She can't come in and take over; I don't need her to do that. I can take care of everything myself.

"Well, hello, handsome. How was work?" she asks, her tone in contrast with my mood. For a second, I want to pull her into me, kiss her sweet lips, and get lost in her, but I can't keep acting like all these little things aren't completely throwing me off.

"Indie. I see you went ahead and planted the flowers." She tilts her head to the side.

"Yeah, I wanted to surprise you with them."

"Mmm, well, my day has definitely been full of surprises. I'm actually a little tired of all these surprises, Indiana."

"Indiana? The use of my full name doesn't sound too good for me. Am I in trouble, Mr. Holloway?"

She's being funny when this situation doesn't feel that way to me. "Not really. Especially since I had to learn that you signed Hazel up for dance class today. What makes you think that you can do that? Because we've been spending time together?" I'm downplaying what this is between us, and I know it. Hurt flashes in her eyes as I walk up the steps, causing my stomach to twist, but the pressure is too built up, and the release feels too good to pull back from. I fight for control but lose.

I erupt, possessed momentarily by my fear and insecurities. The storm inside me brews like the one overhead, and the haunting suspicion that I will destroy the one thing that's been bringing me more happiness than I ever expected is pushed to the side when deep down, all I want to do is cling to her.

INDIANA

There are things in my life that I'm not proud of, some I'm downright ashamed of. If I think about them too long, I start to get this creeping feeling. It's overwhelming and inescapable, like a blanket that weighs more than I can bear, crushing me slowly, inch by merciless inch.

It doesn't happen as often anymore, but right now I can feel the overwhelm starting to set in. *I will not pass out on Knox's porch with all of his family waiting to yell surprise just inside. Don't you fucking dare, Indiana.* I swallow the hot lump in my throat that's working its way behind my eyes. I've been in pain plenty of times to recognize its sharp razor's sting, slicing at the edges of my resolve.

Knox looks so angry. With *me.* I've never seen him so angry before. Frustrated, yes. Annoyed, frequently. But this? This is anger—and it's all directed at me. *Surely this is just a mistake.* My fingers are starting to tingle, and my ears are burning. I need to retreat; I don't have it in me to explain right now. His frustration is coming off him in waves, and it's doing its best to settle into me too.

"That's not fair, Knox. I-I d-didn't—"

The wind picks up, as if in anticipation of the storm Knox has brewing beneath his calm exterior. I'm helpless to stop this. My body paralyzed by the look of contempt I'm on the receiving end of. When the silence between us breaks, it's worse than I imagined.

"You didn't think about how this would affect anyone but you, Indie. You're always doing things that no one's asked you to do or taking things that don't belong to you. You've been doing it since day one, so I don't know why I'm surprised. You meddle and you push, and you don't fucking listen. I told you I would see about the dance class fitting into the schedule, but that wasn't an invitation for you to take it upon yourself." He stops, and I think the worst is over; I can apologize, I'll explain that it wasn't me. I can tell him that I'll work on it. I'm always working on it, and it's exhausting, but for him, I will. I'll do better. But he's not done.

"You know, it's no wonder your sister never calls you back. You're constantly inserting yourself in places you shouldn't be." I feel like I've been slapped. The pain has crossed from mental to physical. I'm squeezing my hands so tightly into fists that my nails are cutting into the skin of my palm.

I would like to argue with him. Explain that I didn't do this thing he's so upset over. Only it's not just this one thing, is it? I can't tell him that I'm a different person. I've tried to be someone else, and it's not possible for me.

His face has gone blurry, the unshed tears gathering and distorting his shape. My body is filled with dread and exhaustion and sadness that can only be described as devastation. I open my mouth, praying that the words will come to me so I can say anything that would make him look at me like he had last night, but nothing comes out. I'm frozen again, like I had been *that* night.

He rubs the back of his neck. "I'm not sure this is going to work. Our age difference is feeling less like a small roadblock and more like a problem." Another blow. This time to my ego. I've never thought him mean before, and maybe it's not that he's being mean, it's just that he's being honest, and the truth is painful. I nod. In agreement? I don't agree. In understanding? I don't understand. Maybe I nod to end this before it becomes too much, and I find myself waking up on the porch.

Darkness is setting in, and it's not just the clouds gathering overhead. There's rushing in my ears, drowning out my embarrassment.

Oh god. His family is just mere feet away, getting a front row seat to this. *Hazel.* Her name slices through me. It will kill me to lose my connection to her.

"I'm s-sorry," I rasp out and then walk past him as steadily as I can, down the stairs, into the rain.

I don't look at Indiana as she runs from my porch. I already know that I went too far, and I also know that it's not all her fault that I'm feeling so off-kilter. *Fuck.* I may not be very well-versed in having a relationship with someone, but I know damn well that speaking to her like that was so far out of line that I can't even see it anymore. Running a hand through my damp hair, I'm already contemplating going after her, to beg her to listen to my apology, when my front door bursts open, my mother, standing in the doorway.

"Mom? What are you doing here? Is Hazel okay?"

"Hazel is fine," she says in a subdued tone. I'm confused, and honestly, I don't think I can try to figure out one more thing today. I need for things to stop popping up. I need Hazel. I need Indiana. *Fuck.*

"Okay, then why are you here? Did you need to bring Hazel home early?" She doesn't answer my questions. Instead, she opens the front door all the way, standing to the side, giving me a view of my whole family. Each member stares back at me with expressions ranging from surprise to pissed off. "Why?" is the only word I can say.

"Indie," my mom says from beside me. I look into the kitchen where Alder holds Hazel on his hip. There's a banner above them that reads Happy Birthday that looks like the teamwork of Indiana and my daughter. In front of them on the island is a cake, next to the cake is another dessert that I would bet money on being a blackberry cobbler. *Fuck.*

I swallow against the guilt I'm being filled with. "I see."

"For someone who doesn't talk much, you sure said a lot just then," Ivy calls from beside Alder and Hazel, staring daggers at me.

"Daddy was mean," Hazel says quietly, making me feel even smaller than I did a second ago.

Florence steps forward, out of the group, looking like she's about to rip me a new one. "*I* signed Hazel up for dance class," she announces. My eyebrows shoot to the ceiling.

"*You* signed her up? Why would you do that?"

"Because she's been telling me, and anybody who will listen, for months that she loves dancing and wants to be a ballerina." That's true. She's been twirling around everywhere she goes. "I also told Jeanie to run it by you before I brought it up to Hazel, but if you want to be an ass to anyone it should be me, I guess." She looks at my daughter. "Sorry, Hazey. It definitely shouldn't be the woman who devoted the last month to planning a surprise party for you. Making sure the beer you like is available and who spent hours practicing baking blackberry cobbler with Winnie. Not to mention asking your family to clear the whole night so we could celebrate you." She pauses, taking a breath and looking around the room before landing back on me. "You're my brother, Knox, and I love you, *and* you were incredibly awful to someone who really cares about you just now. Someone who really cares about Hazel."

Being reprimanded by my baby sister on my forty-second birthday is not at all how I imagined my night going when I left my office. I deserve it though. I can't believe how awful I was to Indie just now. After she's gone to all this trouble. For me. Had I really said she had been *inserting* herself into my life? As if her wanting to be a part of my life isn't exactly what I want from her. Indie does things for people she cares about. I'm lucky enough to be one of those people, and I've just taken what she gave and used it as a weapon against her.

I need to see her. "Thank you all for being here, but if you'll excuse me I—"

"Need to apologize to Indiana before she decides not to give your ass a chance? Yeah, we'll excuse you," Winnie says from my other side, her eyes are threatening.

Rhett stands behind her as backup; he gives me a shake of his head. "Good luck, brother." I nod at him. Needing the luck that he's offering.

I look at the faces of all the people I love, only there's one missing. One I want to see mixed in with the rest for as long as I live.

"We'll take Hazey home with us, son. Come by tomorrow for lunch," my dad tells me as he walks toward the back of the house. It's not a request, and his words cause shame to boil over inside me. What he just witnessed is not a good representation of who he raised me to be.

I can see all the cars parked out back now as everyone makes their way to the back door until it's just me and the mess that I've made. Not only did I just make a horrible mistake, but my whole family got a surround sound performance of it. And Indie. *Fuck.* She just stood there while I railed at her, letting all my frustrations and insecurities get the best of me and push them onto her.

Stepping forward to Hazel, I take her little hand in mine. "I'll see you tomorrow, dragonfly. I love you babygirl." I drop a kiss onto her sweet head before Alder gives her to my mom.

"I love you, Daddy. You need say sorry."

"You're right, lovebug. And I'm going to."

"You deserve to be happy, Knox. You know as well as I do that things can change in a heartbeat. Don't let it get away from you." It's Ivy's words that seem to hit me the hardest. Having lived through all she has, including her accident up on the mountain this past winter, her words hold a lot of weight. I dip my chin in acknowledgment.

I'm down the front steps and running for her house in the next minute, praying she'll forgive me. I've made mistakes in my life, but I refuse to make letting Indie go be one of them. I'm almost halfway when a flash of color catches my eye. The yellow bandanna she had tied in her hair is now on the side of the main road, next to the path down to the dock. I stop to pick it up when Sally runs by me, down toward the water.

"Sally!" I call. *Come on, girl. I don't have time for this.* I follow her, wiping the rain from my eyes when I notice the small figure out at the end of the dock.

"Indie?" I yell to her. She turns, the look on her face in stark contrast to the woman I've come to know, come to love.

"Indie Baby, you're shaking."

"D-don't. You don't n-need to check on m-me. I-I'll be fine, Knox. I can handle myself. I'll stay out of your business and y-you can stay out of m-mine." Her words are stuttered. I'm not sure if it's from the cold rain soaking through her dress or because she's been crying. Whatever the cause, it doesn't change the effect it has on me. My chest feels cracked open; her pain is my pain.

"I'm so sorry, Honey. More sorry than I can even say. That wasn't fair of me, and it wasn't really about you," I say pathetically. My words falling flat in contrast with how appalling they were earlier.

"It s-sounded like it was about me. I c-can't—I can't be someone else, Knox. This is how I am—*who* I am. I do have trouble with boundaries b-but I d-didn't, I wouldn't do something like that with Hazel without your p-p-permission." She's so beautiful, but my heart breaks at her wounded expression.

"I know. I should never have said that. I should never have said any of that, and I promise you, I didn't mean it. I can't believe I—Oh, baby, I'm so sorry. I just want you, exactly as you are." My words do nothing to change the haunting expression she stares back at me with. "Can we go inside? You're gonna get sick out here, and I'll take care of you if you do, but I don't want you to be in any pain."

"I *am* in pain though, Knox." The crack in her voice splits me in two.

"I never wanted to hurt you like this. I—I'm so sorry," I try again.

She shakes her head. It's stiff and stilted but adamant.

"That's not—I've been lying to you. I've been lying to everyone." She throws her arms wide, and then the sobs come. Racking her body. "I'm broken, Knox. I'm so deeply broken." I need to touch her. I want to hold her to me, protect her from whatever this is.

"What do you mean, Indie? Let's go inside and talk about it. Get you some dry clothes, okay?"

She nods and walks past me; I follow her up to the guesthouse.

"It's going to be alright, Honey."

INDIANA

"It's going to be alright, Honey."

I want to believe him. It's just so hard when I've let myself believe I could do this on my own for so long. Opening the door, we drip all over the floors as we make our way to the bathroom. I grab us a couple of towels and throw one to him, and we slip our shoes off going to sit in the living room. He grabs a few logs and sets them in the fireplace, starting us a fire. Looking over his shoulder, our eyes lock, his squinting slightly, trying to figure me out. He deserves the truth. *Here goes nothing.*

"I haven't been completely honest about why I'm here," I say quietly.

"Okay," he says cautiously. "Then tell me."

"I didn't just have a fight with my sister, we were in an accident about ten months ago," I say softly.

His brows furrow. "What kind of accident?"

"A robbery—gone wrong. There was a shooting." I close my eyes tightly, fighting memories, trying to compose myself. I tap my fingers over my thumbs.

"You were shot?!" he asks, sounding outraged. I take a deep, steadying breath and slowly open my eyes.

I nod. "My sister and I were walking home after a night out. She'd just turned twenty-one, so I took her out. I knew she would be out anyway, so I figured she would be safer with me than without." I pause because that's not the whole truth, and if I'm going to do this, I need to do it right. "Actually, I *insisted* she come out with me. I forced her to abandon her plans, move the party to Atlanta, and let me watch over her."

"Sounds like you were being a good sister," Knox comments. He thinks so much of me. It kills me to lose this curated person I've shown him, but he should know who I really am.

"I wasn't. I was truly awful the whole night." My voice breaks, and I have to stop for a second. "I said some really *really* t-terrible th-things, Knox. Things I'll never be able to take back. Things no one—" I cover my mouth with my hand. I hadn't realized until this moment what a good job I'd done at keeping the truth buried deep. My words ring in my ears.

Just because I've always let you get your way doesn't mean the whole world revolves around you, Hana. I'm done. Just fucking grow up. You're such a spoiled brat! My heart feels like it's shriveling in my chest.

How could I have said that to her? Let her think I felt that way when she was the brightest light in my life.

Knox makes no move to get closer, but I can tell he wants to by the way he has his hands clutched tightly in front of him, knuckles white where the skin strains over them. "We were almost to our street when we passed by the corner bodega. There was yelling inside, and then I saw a man holding a gun, pointing it at the cashier. We stopped walking—*I* stopped walking. *I froze.* Just staring at the scene playing out, like it wasn't real. The man went to leave, but the cashier jumped over the counter to stop him. She wouldn't leave me. Han *screamed* at me to run, but I-I couldn't m-move."

Anger pulses inside me now, at myself, at Han for not leaving me.

"She was standing in front of me, shaking my shoulders, *begging* me to wake up, to move, to do *anything.* I can still hear the gun go off. See the look on her face, feel the sting in my shoulder. The bullet went through the right side of her chest and into me." I break then, covering my head with my hands. Knox moves to my side, cradling me into his arms.

"She's dead," I whisper. "She's dead, and it's my fault."

"No, Indie, no. It is not your fault. You didn't do anything wrong."

"I was supposed to keep her safe. I'm the big sister." I shake against him.

"Shh. I'm so sorry this happened to you, Honey."

"I lied. To you, to everyone. I didn't mean to, I just couldn't—"

"It's okay, Indie. I don't care about that right now. I just want you to be okay." His hands rub my shoulders, stroke my face.

"I don't know how to do that. You make me so happy, Knox. You and Hazel and your family. I want to be happy, but I don't know how to do that when I'm also so unbelievably sad, and I don't know when I won't be."

"I don't need you to never be sad, Indie. I just need you to let me be here for you—with you." I sit back to look at him.

"You still want me?"

"Indie Baby, that was never in question."

"I know you need things a certain way, and I can work on it, but I'm never going to get it all right, Knox, and I can't be scared you'll leave if I mess up," I tell him. It's the truth because the fear of losing him makes me sick.

"I just need *you*, Indie. *I'll* work on it. I won't ever treat you that way again. *That* I can promise you. My fear won earlier, it won't again," he vows, and I smile. This is the man I've come to know. Knox really is a good man. "I've never done this before, and this could be the worst time to do it, but you have to know I love you. I'm *in* love with you."

"You're in love with me?"

"Completely."

"Why?" I question. *Why am I questioning it?*

He laughs, taking my face in his hands. "Where do you want me to start?" he asks, kissing my forehead. "Your heart that's bigger than you?" *Kiss.* "Your smile that lights up brighter than the sun?" *Kiss.* "The way you care for Hazel?" *Kiss.* "The way you tell a story like it's a full-length novel?" *Kiss.* "How you demand attention without even trying?" *Kiss.* "Your charm? Your wit? Your sweatshirts?" *Kiss. Kiss. Kiss.*

Another sob breaks loose from my throat. "I'm so in love with you, Knox. I was so scared you wouldn't feel the same," I whisper. "Not after hearing all the baggage I come with."

"You are worth the wanting, Indiana. I started falling for you the day you kicked me off the end of the dock." He kisses me again. Hard. I kiss him back with all I have until he pulls back to look at me, and I remember something he said before.

"Can I ask you a question?"

"Anything."

"Um, earlier, you said that what happened on the porch—"

"Have I told you how incredibly awful I feel about that or how I'll make it up to you?" Knox cuts in.

"You did…but you said it wasn't about me. What was it about?"

He takes a long breath in before letting it go. "I had a phone call this afternoon, one I wasn't expecting, and it completely threw me off. To be honest it really pissed me off, but more than that, it scared me. Emily's parents are asking to be in Hazel's life, now after everything, and I—well, it's kind of a long story." I almost smile hearing him say the words I say to him so often.

"Tell me," I encourage, and he does. We bare our souls to one another all night, exorcising our own demons but not doing it alone, and when the morning comes, my cheek pressed into Knox's warm, bare chest; my pain isn't gone but it's not mine alone to carry anymore.

I make two phone calls, starting with one I've put off for too long.

"Hello? Indiana?"

"Mom?"

INDIANA

B *eep.*
"I love you."
"I know."

"I think it's time," I say into my phone. "You'll be happy to know that I won't be doing it alone from now on." I breathe out a sigh. "I called Mom and Dad. They're coming to visit me next month, *annnnd* you won't believe this, but Knox—the man from the bar who stood me up. And before you start, he had a good reason. Actually, he had the only reason that I could forgive. He has a daughter. She's beautiful and funny and she likes me. She likes playing with me. She's curious and—"

I choke a little but manage to swallow it down. "She reminds me of you. Knox even calls her dragonfly. He has a tattoo on his thigh of one that looks like the one I got for you. So hot, right?" I choke a little on my laugh.

I pause. Knowing this next part will be the hardest. It's

another goodbye. One I've been prolonging, but one that feels inevitable.

"I don't know if you hear the things I say, Han. I guess I just hope that you do. Believing that somewhere out there, my words make it to you helps me. I hope you're at peace, or I hope you're giving someone hell, whatever it is that you want. I miss you. I miss having you *here*. There isn't and there won't be a day that goes by that I don't wonder what you would do or say or tell me. I've been telling Hazel stories about us as kids, and one day, when I have more kids, I'll tell them all about you. God, you would have been the best aunt." I break a little, allowing the sob that's built in my chest out. "All this to say, I'm going to be okay. This place is good for me. The people here are good for me. I love you. I miss you. Bye, Dragonfly."

KNOX

Indie is humming softly from the bathtub while Hazel is coloring in the doorway, after insisting it was fine for her to be there, and asking her questions. I'm sitting in the corner of the room looking through postcards. After my birthday two weeks ago, I wasn't sure if she would want me to read them, but she doesn't want any secrets between us. Some of her words make me laugh, and some of them make me want to scream.

I look at the woman in my bathtub. She's so lovely, just looking at her, how she treats the people around her, you wouldn't think she'd been through something so horrific. I love that part of her—every part of her.

"Is this blue or purple?" I look over to the crayon Hazel is holding up.

"I think it's blue," I say.

"I was asking Indie."

Indie coughs to hide her laugh. It doesn't work.

"I think it's a dark purple," she answers thoughtfully.

"Dark purple," Hazel repeats, then starts coloring again. I

want to roll my eyes. It seems she's less interested in my opinion these days and more concerned with Indie's. I read another postcard.

> I went on a run today.
> My lungs were screaming and
> I won't be able to walk tomorrow.
> But I did it. I'm trying.
> I love you. I miss you.
> Love, Indiana

Pride swells in my chest thinking about how far she's come. She's been through hell and come back even stronger.

"Okay, I think it's time for me to get out. I'm starting to prune. Thank you for letting me use your tub. I couldn't get the stopper on mine to work."

"You can have or use anything of mine, Honey." I drop a kiss to her head. "Hazel and I will go outside and wait for you."

"I'll be out in just a few minutes. I'm so excited to gather flowers with you today, Hazey."

"Me too!"

I help Hazel carry all her art supplies to the kitchen and set them up at the table for her.

"Remember what we talked about?"

"Yes."

"Remember not to tell Indie until later, right?"

"Yes. It's a surprise!"

"That's my girl." I kiss her head as Indie walks into the room, stealing my breath in just her cotton T-shirt and shorts.

"I'm just going to grab our basket and book, and we can head out, Hazey."

"Okay, Indie." She hops out of her chair and over to the door where her blue rubber boots are.

"Are you going to be joining us, *Daddy*?" She does this every so often. Calls me Daddy in a way that's just suggestive enough to make me want to hear her say it in other situations.

"I think I'll leave it to you girls today if that's alright. I have a couple of things I need to get done around here."

"Of course. We'll be fine, won't we, dragonfly?" Her use of Hazel's nickname hits me in the chest. I know she misses her sister, and she always will, but if Hazel and I can be here for her—can help mend that sadness with our love, then that's what we'll do.

"Yes!" Hazel yells, grabbing Indie's hand and walking out the door with her.

Once they leave, I book it down the hall and open the closet. I grab the drawings that Hazey colored, and the banner we worked on. Winnie made me a dozen chocolate croissants, and then we have the big surprise for the living room wall that I've been working on since our first hike without even realizing. When Indie gets back from her dinner with Florence tonight, Hazel and I are asking her to move in with us.

For the next few hours, I watch the girls walk around the lake, picking flowers while I stash all the please-move-in-with-us supplies under the counters in the kitchen. My phone vibrates with a message from the group chat.

ALDER

> Family dinner next week. Doing one of those sweet reveals with pink or blue smoke. I'm thinking of jumping out of the helicopter with a special parachute, yeah?

IVY

You're not doing that, Action Hero.

WINNIE

OMG can I make a cake?!

WINNIE

Wait. Then I would know. Can I know?!

RHETT

If Winnie gets to know, I get to know.

BABY LO

Finally! I can start shopping for my new baby
niece or nephew!

ME

ALDER

No one gets to know yet.

WINNIE

Smiling, I set my phone down and see Indie and Hazel walking back toward the house. The clock says two fifteen, and she's working at the bakery with Winnie before dinner. Making sure to keep all the decorations hidden, I stand in front of the counter doing my best to look nonchalant.

"Hi, Daddy! Look!" Hazel yells excitedly, running into the house, holding a book.

"What do you have there?" I ask, picking her up and setting her on my lap.

"Indie's book!" she says, opening the book to flowers pressed between pages.

"We'll add some of our descriptions about them later when

I get back," Indie tells her. She comes to stand next to me, wrapping an arm around my shoulder. She kisses my temple softly and runs a hand through Hazel's hair. "I have to go to work. Let me know if I can come by later. It shouldn't be too late I don't think."

"Yes." Hazel and I say at the same time.

Indie giggles. "Well then, I'll be back. I love you."

"I love you!" Hazel tells her, still flipping through the book on her lap. Indie's smile splits her face in two before leaning down to kiss her head.

"I love you," I tell her, pulling her to me for a quick kiss on the lips.

"Okay, I have to go, or I'm gonna be late."

"Then you better get going," I say, but I pull her to me again, kissing her, feeling her smile into it.

"Bye, Knox. Bye, Hazey. See you later."

She walks out the front door, and I watch her all the way to her car. Then I track her car until it disappears down the road.

"Okay, Hazey. Want to help me get this place ready?"

"Yes!" she agrees.

I start measuring the spaces on the wall while Hazel sets her drawings out. With any luck, Indiana Holmes will be sleeping here tonight and all the rest of them too.

INDIANA

I've been at the bakery for three hours, and Winnie and I have consumed two chocolate croissants and almost a whole loaf of strawberry bread. After picking flowers for us to press into these little books I ordered for me and Hazel, I left feeling lighter and more grounded than I have in almost a year. Hearing Hazel say she loves me has had me on cloud nine all afternoon.

I'll be having dinner with Florence tonight to go over the designs I made for the hotel website and take some moody shots of the interior. I'll save the rooms and lobby photos for during the day so I have better natural light.

"So he just painted the house for you without you even having to ask?"

"He did. Rhett is big on grand gestures. He kind of had to be. I made it difficult to get close to me for a while. I just couldn't admit to myself that things might work out for the best. I'm a work in progress."

"Understandable. I went almost a whole year without

admitting that my sister wasn't here anymore." I freeze. "Sorry, that was dark."

Winnie reaches across the counter and grabs my hand. "I hate that she isn't here. I hate that you have to miss her." I love that she doesn't say she's sorry. It's not that someone saying it makes me upset or uncomfortable; it's more that Winnie is thoughtful in talking about loss. Having been through it at such a young age, I'm sure she's heard it all.

"Thanks, Win."

"Knox isn't the only one who loves you, you know?"

I nod. "I love you too. You've welcomed me in with such grace in a time when I needed it so badly. Thank you."

"Oh my god, don't make me cry."

"Sorry. I just want you to know what taking a chance on me has really meant for my life. For the first time in a very long time, I'm starting to see more light in the world than darkness." Her smile is sweet—just a little watery.

"Yeah, that seems about right. Silverthorne may just be a small town, on a map in Colorado, but it's helped to heal more than one wandering soul."

"I'm happy to have landed here, and right now, I'm really happy to be in this bakery with the most amazing pastries I've ever had."

She huffs out a laugh. "Aw, shucks. You really think so?"

I spend another hour here, talking over some events that we could host. Having a few baking workshops and possibly offering the space for classes would be a really fun way to give back to the community. Winnie agreed and is already blocking out some time in the schedule.

"Alright, I'm off to my next job," I tell her.

"You're an angel. I know Lo really appreciates you helping

her out. Between you and me, I think she's working on something but hasn't told anyone yet. That's why she's so excited for you to revamp the website."

"Consider me intrigued. I may needle her for information," I say, grabbing my running bag and swinging the strap over my head.

"Bye, Indie. Tell Baby Lo hi for me—and maybe don't tell her I just called her Baby Lo," she says, and I laugh.

"I'll try not to let it slip out. Bye, Win."

I'm thinking about hosting a photography course as I walk over to the hotel. If more people start being interested in my service, that is. My stomach growls, reminding me I'm starving, so I'm looking forward to my dinner with Lo. The town is quiet besides the music coming from AJ's. The hotel is all lit up with warm amber light spilling out from the windows. I push open the glass door and hear the clinking of glasses from the restaurant, smell the wood furniture polish mixed with leather.

"Hi, welcome to The Holloway Hotel. I'm Marilyn. How can I help you?" a pleasant voice calls from behind the check-in counter.

"Hi, Marilyn. I'm Indiana. I'm supposed to meet Florence here for dinner. Do you know where I can find her?"

"She was in her office, but she was worried someone had thrown out some papers she needed. If you follow the hallway, you'll either come across her in the office there, or you can open the back door and see if she's there."

"Perfect. Thanks, Marilyn." I walk down the hall and look at some of the photos on the wall. They're so cool. There are some vintage landscapes and a few photos of the original owners of the hotel. I grin, loving the vibes. I peek my head into the office and find it vacant. Lo must still be out back. I debate whether I should just wait here, but there's a nagging feeling in my stomach.

It's most likely nothing, but I'm compelled to open the back door.

Move, Indiana!

I look back from where I came and see nothing that should cause the hair on the back of my neck to stand up. I'm probably overreacting, but the pull I feel is undeniable. Slowly, I make my way to the back door when I hear a crash. I flinch back away from the door.

Please, Indie! You have to run!

The feeling washing over me is not something I can ignore though. Not something I can brush off. Taking a deep breath, I fling open the heavy wooden door as hard as I can. The sound of it swinging back into the building reverberates off the bricks.

Stepping out of the hotel, I look down the small alleyway. What I see turns my veins to ice, but this time, I don't freeze.

Run, Indiana! We have to run! And I do.

Without another thought, I reach inside my bag, leaping down the concrete steps. I run faster than I ever have in my life, launching onto the man's back, screaming as loud as I possibly can. He struggles but won't let go of her. He throws an elbow at me, catching my brow, but I refuse to let up, hitting his head as hard as I can with one hand.

"Help! Call 911! Help!!" I scream over and over, praying someone hears me. Then I flip the safety switch on the taser in my hand, pressing it into him until he falls over, twitching and rolling away from us.

My eyes snap back to Lo. "Florence! Oh my god, Florence! Help! Someone help!" Leaning over her, my hands hover over her neck, her body. Her eyes are open, but she isn't moving, isn't saying anything. I'm afraid to move her. I don't know how badly she's injured. I don't know what he did to her. Bile crawls up from my stomach.

No. Focus on Florence. Help Florence. She cannot die. I won't let someone else die.

"Florence, can you hear me? Don't move, you're hurt. Please blink if you can't talk."

She blinks, and I sob.

"You're going to be fine, Lo." I reach into my bag, searching for my phone, when I hear a voice call from behind me. Whipping around with my taser in hand, I see that it's Marilyn. When I look back, the man is gone. Scanning the trees, I see a figure disappear into them. *Shit.*

"Florence! Oh my god, what happened? Is she okay?" she asks, hand coming up to cover her mouth.

"Call 911! She's been attacked." She pulls her cell phone out and holds it to her ear. I relay everything I know to the paramedic on the phone. Florence still hasn't spoken. Marilyn is sitting on her other side now. I find my phone and dial Knox's number, not knowing who else to call. I turn slightly, and Florence's hand shoots out, grabbing my arm tightly.

"I'm not going anywhere, Lo. I'm staying right here, okay?"

"Hey, honey. I didn't think you would be done so soon."

"Knox?" my voice breaks saying his name. Just hearing his name brings me some tiny piece of comfort right now.

"What's wrong? Where are you?"

"I'm at the hotel. I'm fine but—" An ambulance siren sounds close by.

"But what, Indie? I'm losing my mind here."

"Florence was attacked. At the back of the hotel. I got him off her, but he *hurt her.*"

"You got him off her? Is she okay?"

"Not completely, but she's alive. I'm so sorry. They're taking her to the hospital now. I'm riding with her."

"I'll be there soon," he says before hanging up. I look at Florence, she has tears streaming down her cheeks when the paramedics ask me to stay back. She clutches my arm tighter.

"I can't leave her. Just tell me where to move," I tell them.

I sit there while they evaluate her, then I walk into the ambulance, staying beside her on the metal bench, letting her squeeze my hand while tears make a line from the corner of her eye to her ear. Reaching out, I swipe them away with my sleeve.

"I'm here, Baby Lo. I'm here." She blinks in response.

When we get to the emergency entrance, I hold her hand until they take her through the doors that I'm not allowed through. I pass her hand to Marigold and then sit in the waiting room.

The police arrive soon after, and I'm asked multiple questions, answering them as best I can. They ask for my taser, and I hand it over to them.

"We have search teams out looking for a man who fits the description of the clothes that you gave us. If you remember anything else about him, please call us at the number on the card we gave you. Is the number you gave us the best one to reach you on if we have any more questions?"

I nod. "Yes, that's my only phone number."

"What you did tonight was very brave, Ms. Holmes. You may have saved that young woman's life." Both officers nod before leaving through the glass doors. It's about this time that the whole Holloway clan shows up. Winnie and Rhett are here first. Winnie holds my hand, and Rhett gets me a hot tea.

"Have they checked you out yet?"

"I'm fine, guys, really. I'm just worried about Florence, and I think the adrenaline is wearing off. I'll be fine soon."

"How is she?" Knox asks, coming to a stop in front of me, holding Hazel in his arms.

"She was responding to everything in the ambulance; she just wasn't speaking. There haven't been any updates since," I repeat the same thing to them that I said to Rhett and Winnie earlier.

"Christ. She was attacked? By who?"

"I don't know. I didn't recognize him, and I didn't get a good look at him. I'm sorry, I should have—"

"No, baby. None of this is on you. You—I can't believe you just..."

Tom and Mary arrive after that, and I repeat all that I know. It's only a few minutes after that Marigold comes out with an update for us.

"Florence is physically okay. There is bruising to her neck and chin. No concussion," she says. *Thank God.* "She'll have a sore throat, and it may be painful for her to speak for a few days, but she's going to make a full recovery."

"Can we see her?" Mary asks.

"Yes. She's awake and alert. I'm going to prescribe her something to sleep, and she shouldn't be alone tonight."

"She'll stay with us," Tom says.

"Alright, follow me." I stand but reach for Hazel.

"I'll stay out here with Hazel. You all can go ahead." Knox hands her over to me, and I sit back into my chair with her, letting her cuddle into me with her blanket. He leans down and kisses me. It's quick but firm and very welcome.

"I love you."

"I love you," I reply.

I hold Hazel's head to my shoulder with one hand and pat her back softly with the other.

When Ivy and Alder walk in, I tell them which room Florence is in. Ivy hugs me and Hazel tightly after I repeat the events of the evening. As awful as it is to relive the fear and the panic, if it helps them to hear it, I'll keep telling them what happened.

"Indie, you could have been injured as well," Ivy says.

"I could have been," I repeat.

"I'm so glad you're okay. Has someone checked on you yet?" Alder asks.

"I don't think I need to be seen; I'm fine." It's true for the most part. The headache that's coming on is a small price to pay to make sure Florence was okay.

Hazel is dozing when Knox comes back out.

"How is she?" I whisper.

"She's okay. Shaken and sore, but she's going to be alright." The relief at hearing that makes my shoulders relax. When they do, I start to feel a little soreness in my muscles. I must have been tensing them since the hotel.

"She's okay," I repeat.

"Thanks to you. She still isn't talking. Her throat hurts too badly, but she was able to write down what happened. I guess the fucker surprised her, yanked her to the ground, and then started choking her." His jaw is clenched so tight, I'm worried he'll break his teeth. I shudder. "She said she fought for a minute but then her vision started going fuzzy. She remembers you leaning over her and talking to her. She said she's able to remember everything," he tells me quietly.

"She must have been so scared. I should have gone out

there sooner. I had this awful feeling, but I didn't listen to my instincts quickly enough," I admit. *Could I have prevented this?*

"She's alive because of how you reacted, Indie. I don't know how to thank you for that."

"I don't want a thank you, not for something like this. I just want her to be okay."

"She will be."

I nod. "Okay."

"Mom and Dad are taking her home with them, and I need to get Hazel home. Come home with us? Please?"

I nod. "Yes, please."

I keep hold of Hazel until I buckle her into her car seat, covering her with her blanket. Knox holds open my door for me, stopping me before I get in.

"Are you sure you're alright, Honey?"

"I'm alright. I'm with you, so I'm alright," I tell him.

He kisses my lips softly—it's so painfully gentle—before helping me into the truck. Before we start the drive home, he pulls me into the middle seat and keeps his hand on the inside of my knee when he isn't using the gearshift. Like he knows I need his touch right now.

I lean the side of my head that wasn't hit onto his shoulder and let my tears fall silently. Feeling safe enough to let myself feel the effects of tonight.

Knox Holloway is my safe place.

Indiana

The truck is mostly quiet, my hand is warm, fingers laced with Knox's on the seat between us. My tears have dried, and I'm trying my best to keep my focus on the fact that Florence is okay. It's hard knowing whoever did this is still out there though. We've seen multiple police cruisers on the way home, patrolling the area. There's less activity when we get out of town and further into the mountains.

When we get back to the house, it's dark. The moon is full, reflected on the lake, and illuminating the guesthouse down the road. As much as I've come to love it, the thought of staying there tonight has my stomach in knots. I don't want to be alone. I want to hold Hazel on my lap and let Knox rub my feet. *Now I'm being needy.* I'm emotional, my head is hurting a little more than I let on before, and my body is working through memories that claw at me.

I'm so relieved that Lo is going to be okay—at least physically—but my worry is for her mind. My situation was different, but I know what it's like to have your peace destroyed. I want to be there for her in whatever way I can if she wants me to be.

"Hey," Knox's deep voice cuts through my worried thoughts.

"Hi."

"Are you sure you're okay, Honey?" he asks, reaching across the cab to cradle my cheek in his big hand.

"I'm okay. I'm just worried about Florence."

"I know. I am too."

"I-I don't want to be alone tonight, Knox." My voice comes out quieter than I intended. It's weak, raspy from screaming earlier.

"That wasn't an option, Indie."

Smiling, I place my hand over the one he still has on my face. "Thank you."

I'm not sure if I'll ever understand life. The worst and best things that have ever happened to me happened to me in the span of less than a year. I'll never not feel the loss of my sister, and nothing in this life will ever replace her. I can only live a life that she would be proud of, that she would laugh with me over. That starts with loving Knox and Hazel with everything I've got. Opening the truck door and stepping onto the dirt road, I watch them make it to the top of the stairs, turning to wait for me.

When I meet them, Knox pulls me to him by the back of my head, kissing me hard at first, then softening. "I love you, Indie. I don't know what I would do without you."

"I feel the same way."

"Also, please keep in mind when you walk inside that I never thought this is how the night would have ended up," he tells me, confusing me before opening the door and switching on the light. When I walk in, tears fill my eyes again, this time for the most romantic thing I've ever seen in my life.

Cuckoo clocks, dozens of them, fill the wall. They're all different sizes and styles. All incredibly beautiful and take me back to a home that was overflowing with love.

"When did you—" I cut myself off, taking a breath.

"Hazel and I set it up this afternoon. I started collecting the clocks when you mentioned them."

"That was-that was months ago," I say, locking my eyes with his.

"It was. And I knew then that you were going to be in my life, Indie. I wanted you then. I want you now. And I—we—would like for you to live here with us." Hazey stirs in his arms, opening her eyes.

"Will you live with us, Indie?" I look around the room, taking in the finger paintings and a banner hanging in the kitchen.

"I've never wanted anything more than to live with you, Hazey."

She holds her arms out, and I walk into them. Who knew two tiny arms could bring me so much joy. I kiss her cheek, smelling her baby-scented shampoo. "I love you, Hazey. So much."

"I love you," she says back to me, still sleepy. My heart explodes. Then Knox squeezes us together, and my ovaries do the same. *Where had that come from?*

"Do you want more kids?" *Are you fucking kidding me?* I slap a hand over my mouth. His eyebrows are up to his hairline. I move my hand from my mouth to his. "Wait. No. Don't answer that. I'm so sorry. I'm tired, *really* tired, and my filter is nonexistent when that happens." He smiles under my fingers.

"You look so pretty when you blush for me, Indie Baby."

"Alright, let's get you to bed, Hazey." I grip under her arms and carry her down the hall to bed. I lie beside her for a while after reading her *Where The Wild Things Are*.

"I'll eat you up, I love you so, Hazel Emilia Holloway," I whisper.

No, I'll never not miss my sister, but I will let myself feel this love that's being offered. Let people love me when I need it. I'll let Knox wrap his arms around me and feel Hazel's small hand in mine and remind myself that *this* is the whole point. I'm not sure how it happened or why, if it's fate or happenstance, but something brought me to Silverthorne.

I'd like to believe it was Han, and it's just like her to know it before I did, that the man from the bar all those years ago was meant to be mine.

The time between Florence's attack and summer has flown by. She's speaking normally again, the rasp almost completely gone. Her recovery is going well, considering. If she and Indie had a bond before, they've become family in recent weeks. Indie has visited Lo every day since the attack, and Lo stayed the night with us a lot in the first week following it. She's been back at her place and at work for a full month now. Security cameras have been installed, and the hotel has hired a night guard. The man who did this is still out there, but the police have been unable to identify any new leads.

As upsetting and frustrating as that is, they believe it was random; he was spooked and moved on. I don't know if I can believe that, and I'm not the only one. The community has been shaken over it. Silverthorne isn't a perfect town, but nothing like this has ever happened in all the years I've lived here. They've set up a town watch list, all taking turns keeping an eye on things. Lo doesn't like the attention, but she's grateful for the concern and really seems to be doing okay, which makes her declaration a surprise.

"I'm leaving Silverthorne," Florence announces at my parents' house during family dinner.

"That sounds like a good idea, dear. Where are you going? And how long will you be gone?" my mother asks, setting the bread rolls on the table. I look at Indie who just stares at Lo before she gives her an encouraging nod. *So she knew.*

"I don't mean I'm taking a vacation. I'm *moving away* from Silverethorne," Lo says.

"What? Why? Where will you go?" Alder asks a series of questions.

"Are you sure you've thought this through? I mean after what happened." Winnie hedges.

Lo smiles at us all, just a hint of sadness in her eyes. "I love you all. More than I'll ever be able to say. I truly hit the lottery when I was born into this family. You've taken care of me and also let me grow into who I am every step of my life so far. I've relied on you for guidance and support. With that being said, I'm sure. This was already the plan before—before everything happened. I purchased a bed and breakfast in Northern California about six months ago. The plan is to renovate, and then it will be The Holloway Inn," she explains.

My mom's eyes look shiny, and my dad places a steadying hand on her shoulder. "We knew one day you might have to chase a dream, Florence. You've always been so adventurous, even as a child," she says.

"When? When were you going to tell us?" Rhett asks.

"Well, I was going to after I talked to Indie that night. I had a business opportunity for her, and she's only just accepted it this week." Everyone in the room looks to Indie.

She clears her throat. "Um, I'm going to be running the hotel."

"So this is a done deal?" my father asks. He doesn't sound upset, more resigned.

"Yes. This is what I want. It's what I need to do. I refuse to put my life on hold because of the actions of some psycho."

"As you should," Ivy chimes in. "Don't let that animal take anything from you, Lo. We'll support you. We will *all* support you."

"Absolutely," I agree. "Whatever you need."

"Be prepared for your family to be there on opening day of The Holloway Inn," my mom says, tears shining in her eyes. "I'm so proud of you, baby girl."

My dad stands, walking over to where she stands in the dining room, bringing her into his arms. "You've always been a fighter, Lo. You're made of such tough stuff. But you're still my baby girl."

"Always, Daddy. I love you all. I hope you know that the reason I feel like I can do this is because of all of you," she tells us.

I look over at Indiana. She turns her head to meet my eyes, hers filled with unshed tears. I smile at her, wanting to reassure her. I mouth I love you, and she mouths it back. What an amazing time in my life. To find the love of my life and have my whole family in the same town—if only for a little while.

"I'm sorry I didn't tell you. When I said no more secrets, I meant it, Knox," Indie blurts out, breaking the silence when we get home. Hazel has been asleep in the back, and I've been quietly thanking God and the universe that I get to keep her. She must have mistaken my being quiet for being upset. I'm not though.

"I'm not mad, Indie. In fact, I'm—happy. I didn't know I would ever feel like *this*. Then you happened."

"Yeah? I must have missed the air horn and clapping," she drawls.

"You didn't see the fireworks that spelled your name?"

"Was that before or after you made the speech?"

"After, obviously," I quip, and she laughs, a sound that I would recognize anywhere now, sliding over the bench seat in the truck to climb onto my lap.

"Have I mentioned I love you?" she asks.

"Yes, but not nearly enough."

"I love you," she says, leaning in to kiss me.

"I love you, Indiana. I love you"—*kiss*—"and I love you"—kiss—"and I love you," I tell her before pulling her out of the truck with me. Hazel wakes up from her nap, still sleepy but happy. Always my happy girl. Indie picks her up, snuggling her close while we walk down to the end of the dock, sitting in our chairs. Two chairs. It wasn't that long ago that I thought having two chairs would be nice. It turns out it's not nice. It's *everything*.

We watch the sunset, turning from a soft yellow to a brilliant orange. Well, Indie watches the sunset. I watch her, cradling Hazel in her arms, playing with her hair, and kissing her head. The love they have for one another is more than I could have hoped for. It's the most precious sight I've ever seen. Indie catches me staring.

"What?" she asks.

"Nothing. You're just so beautiful."

"I'm glad you think so, Mr. Holloway. I think you're stuck with me." She grins at me, nose scrunching.

"Lucky me," I tell her. Because I don't know how it gets better than this.

"Lucky you," Indie agrees.

"How did I ever get to be this lucky?"

She sighs, making a show, like she always does. Like she has so much to say, and I'm on the edge of my seat to hear every last word.

"It's a long story."

"Don't leave anything out."

The leaves are changing colors outside now, telling me that summer is over—the best summer of my life. Life with my girls has been so good to me. I used to be a little skeptical of people falling in love. I understood the concept but never the emotion behind it. The chemical reaction that I would hear explained never really made sense to me. Until Indiana.

She came into my life and completely turned it on its head. Not realizing that I had given up hope of finding someone to go through life with. If it hadn't happened by then, I just assumed it wouldn't, and I made peace with that. Watching my brothers find love, seeing it change them into the men they are. Now, I know that's what real love does. It transforms.

For the last three years, I've felt like my heart was full. I had my family. I had Hazel. When Indie showed up out of the blue, it's like it expanded.

I look in on Indiana getting Hazel ready for the wedding. I've spent the last four months watching these moments between them. Hazel adoring Indie, and Indie indulging her every request. They've started their own collections and a whole fairy village in the backyard. The cuckoo clock wall has expanded. We now have a table full of rocks and a cabinet full of dinosaur figurines. There are shelves upon shelves of flower books, and then there's the gallery wall of postcards. Indie will explain them all to Hazel one day when she asks why her aunt Han isn't here.

"Okay, braid is all done and pinned perfectly. I'm just going to put these flowers in. You have the most lovely hair, baby."

"Thank you. I love yours."

"I love *you*," Indie says offhandedly while putting little yellow flowers in Hazey's hair.

"I love you too, mommy." Indiana's hands freeze momentarily before she continues with her flower placement. I see her left hand come up, swiping her face quickly. She leans forward and presses a long kiss to the braided crown on Hazel's head before squeezing my daughter's shoulders lightly.

"All done, baby. You look perfect."

"Thank you!" she says, turning around to hug her neck before running toward me. "Look at my hair, Daddy!"

"Oh, it's so beautiful, Hazey. You're the most beautiful little girl I've ever seen!"

"Thank you," she says shyly. "I'm going to show Sally!" Then she's off.

"Hi," Indiana says.

"Hi, Honey."

"How long have you been here?"

I walk over to her, pulling her into my arms. "Long enough to hear the new title," I say, grinning.

She pulls back to look up at me. "Is that okay?" Her voice is tentative but deeply hopeful, melting me.

"More than okay. She deserves to have a mother, and you more than deserve the title."

Smiling, she gets up on her tiptoes to kiss me slowly at first, then with more force. I lean back, needing to tell her something.

"Do you remember that question you asked me a few months ago?"

"I ask you a lot of questions. You're going to have to be more specific."

I smile, looking at this woman who's brought me back to life, made me feel young again, and showed me how to believe in love.

"I want more kids, Indie. If they're with you, I want them." A brilliant smile breaks across her face

"I love you, Knox."

"I love you, Indiana."

Being with Indiana is wanting in all forms and all definitions. I want her wholly—mind, body, soul. In every lifetime, in every timeline; she is worth the want.

THE END

ACKNOWLEDGMENTS

Another love story that came from my brain is out in the world and I'm thrilled to have made it this far. My heart is so full. I may have imagined these characters and come up with their story but it wasn't a solo endeavor. I have so many people to thank.

Firstly, if you gave this book a chance and read it all the way through, thank you. It means so much to me.

To Joe, your love is a gift that fuels me and lets me express myself without fear of rejection or judgement and that's something I'll treasure always. You are my safe place and my caretaker when I've been taking care of others all day. Thank you, I love you.

To Ginsa, the collaboration and brainstorming sessions and countless hours of help that you have given me with this book are all reflected on its pages. This book would not be here without you, and I can't begin to tell you how instrumental you are not just in my writing process but also in my life. Soul Ties.

To Bailey and all my lovely indie bookstore owners, THANK YOU, you are a driving force in this community and we love you for it. Thank you for giving our books a chance and a platform. You mean so much to us and I'm eternally grateful for you.

And last but certainly not least, my ARC readers. Thank you so much for taking a chance on this story and taking the time to read and review it. My heart is full. Ya'll are rockstars!

XO, Bea

About This Author

Bea Borges is a romance author living out her small town love story in the Ozark Mountains with her husband and two magical children.

She enjoys trash TV, baking treats, and hosting friends. Most days you'll find her reading, writing, or watching a romance, but if not, she's probably hiking.

She writes love stories with flawed characters that are still so deserving of love.

Follow her on Instagram or TikTok to keep up with new books she's writing, and the parts of her life she's sharing.

@beaborges.author